BLACK CROW CABIN

BOOKS BY PEGGY WEBB

THRILLERS

Snow Brides

Savage Beauty

The Ally

All the Lies

Just One Look

COZY MYSTERIES

A CHARMED CAT MYSTERY SERIES

Magnolia Wild Vanishes

SOUTHERN COUSINS MYSTERY SERIES

Jack Loves Callie Tender

Elvis and the Dearly Departed

Elvis and the Grateful Dead

Elvis and the Memphis Mambo Murders

Elvis and the Tropical Double Trouble

Elvis and the Blue Christmas Corpse

Elvis and the Bridegroom Stiffs

Elvis and the Buried Brides

Elvis and the Rock a Hula Baby Capers

Elvis and the Pink Cadillac Corpse

Elvis and the Blue Suede Bones

Elvis and the Devil in Disguise

Elvis and the Heartbreak Hotel Murders

PEGGY WEBB
BLACK CROW CABIN

bookouture

Published by Bookouture in 2024

An imprint of Storyfire Ltd.
Carmelite House
50 Victoria Embankment
London EC4Y 0DZ

www.bookouture.com

Copyright © Peggy Webb, 2024

Peggy Webb has asserted her right to be identified as the author of this work.

All rights reserved. No part of this publication may be reproduced, stored in any retrieval system, or transmitted, in any form or by any means, electronic, mechanical, photocopying, recording or otherwise, without the prior written permission of the publishers.

ISBN: 978-1-83525-293-2
eBook ISBN: 978-1-83525-292-5

This book is a work of fiction. Names, characters, businesses, organizations, places and events other than those clearly in the public domain, are either the product of the author's imagination or are used fictitiously. Any resemblance to actual persons, living or dead, events or locales is entirely coincidental.

PROLOGUE

SODA SPRINGS PARK | MANITOU SPRINGS, COLORADO

Six weeks earlier

He strolled through the park unnoticed, a short, middle-aged man with thinning blond hair and no distinguishing features, his manner so mild and unassuming he could join any crowd and leave no impression whatsoever.

He'd lived his entire life neglected and overlooked. The resulting ball of rage inside him had been his undoing many times.

Not this time. He'd learned to channel his anger, to see his shortcomings as an advantage. He was Everyman. Your helpful next-door neighbor. The quiet man you always spoke to on the street. Your dependable shopkeeper, or grocer, or delivery man. The man who always sat on the middle pew of the church, his dedication on full display.

He was the one you never saw coming.

He sucked on a lollipop and carried a small paper bag that held others in a variety of flavors. He knew his target favored grape, but you could never tell when a five-year-old would change his mind. He stationed himself on a park bench underneath a covering of trees and waited.

The wait was no more than five minutes.

There he was, like clockwork. Little Eddie Greene, his freckles shining in the sun, his gap-toothed smile wide as he broke free of his mother's hand and set off, kicking his soccer ball.

"Eddie, don't go far." His mother, Marsha Greene, spread a blanket on the ground near the swing sets then plopped down and whipped out her cell phone. As usual, she was distracted, a rail-thin, harried-looking young woman with wispy blond hair escaping its ponytail. Coordinator of the youth group at her church, she was always on her phone.

"See how far I can kick the ball!" Eddie yelled.

She glanced up. "I see you," she called back, but she didn't. Not at all. She was already talking on her phone again.

She didn't deserve Eddie. No, she did not.

As he moved closer to the boy, watching the direction Eddie kicked the soccer ball, he congratulated himself on making the right choice this time. He was brilliant. Yes, he was. He'd studied his target for months. He knew everything about Eddie Greene and his family—their routine, their habits, and most of all, their vulnerabilities.

Eddie drew back a sturdy leg and kicked the ball into the trees.

Perfect. He didn't have to count on Marsha Greene's lack of attention.

The ball rolled to a stop two feet from where he was standing, grape lollipop in hand, warm and welcoming smile on his face.

"Great kick, Eddie." He bent to the boy's level. "Would you like a grape lollipop?"

The boy nodded, his cowlick bobbing.

He unwrapped the sweet treat then smiled. "I'll play ball with you, and I have a whole bag of lollipops."

"Okay."

He took the boy's hand and led him away.

That's how easy it was to take the things other people treated carelessly.

They vanished quickly into the thick trees. Within minutes, he was on the way home with his prize. Undetected by anyone, particularly Marsha Greene.

He glanced at Eddie, so innocent and gullible. So trusting. It would be a pity if the boy wasn't the right choice.

He'd had to bury his last two mistakes.

ONE

LOGAN RANCH | OUTSKIRTS OF MANITOU SPRINGS, COLORADO

Present day

Early morning came softly to the small ranch tucked in the foothills of the Rockies and surrounded by forests so old they carried the secrets of Rachel Logan Maxey's ancestors going back for generations. The pink and gold glow turned the weathered barn, the tilting gazebo, and even the ranch house, that appeared to have grown out of the rocks and trees surrounding it, into a watercolor painting worthy of the great Western artist Bruce Wyler.

But inside the bedroom where Rachel suddenly awoke among the covers, tangled from a night of worry, morning stormed in with the power of an avalanche. The scent of magnolias was everywhere, though there wasn't a tree or a blossom in sight. It wafted from her curtains, swirled around her bed, drifted under the windowsills, over the doorsills, and through the vents. The fragrance was so strong she wanted to pull the sheet over her head.

Unnatural disturbances in nature and unexplained scents in the air are omens of bad things to come...

Rachel tried to ignore her mother's warning, reaching out from beyond the grave. But Delilah Broussard Logan had never been a woman anyone could ignore. She was the star-kissed singer of sultry blues, born to a mystic on a full moon in New Orleans when the magnolias were so pervasive the fragrance got caught in her dark hair and dusky skin. No matter how hard she tried, she could never wash the sweet scent away.

How such an artistic woman, with the Creole blood of her African and French ancestors, fell in love with a brash Irish rancher named Patrick Logan and moved to Colorado was one of the legends in Rachel's family. In spite of the harsh climate and the expectations of Delilah's in-laws, she never lost the romantic and mystical nature of a creative soul born under the sign of Aquarius and labeled "the Bohemian" by a mother-in-law who never understood her. Rachel's own beloved grandmother, Victoria Logan.

Pushing thoughts of her mother aside, Rachel climbed out of bed. When she picked up her sensible robe and equally sensible slippers, she felt the first prickle of fear. Both smelled faintly of magnolias.

The two other times she had smelled that flower—so closely associated with her mother and the Deep South from which she hailed—the scent had been a warning of news that shredded Rachel's soul. *We regret to inform you...* First, *your parents are dead.* She had been only eighteen when they had died instantly in a horrible car crash on the way to a cattle convention in Denver. And then three years ago, *your husband is dead.* Rachel couldn't even bear to think of the way he had died, on a battlefield so far away from home in the service of his country.

"I will not give in to this," she muttered.

She marched out of her bedroom, through her front door, and down the long, secluded driveway to the mailbox, reveling in the crisp autumn air and the privacy of the ranch that allowed her the freedom of enjoying simple tasks like getting the Sunday edition of the paper in her robe and slippers. She retrieved *The Gazette,* a daily newspaper from nearby Colorado Springs, and tucked it under her arm.

As she headed back to the house, she froze. The thicket of bushes on her right stirred, as if an unseen hand had set them asway.

"Who's there?" The sudden fragrance of magnolias paralyzed her, pulling her backward to a childhood where she never knew which mother she would encounter on any given day—the Delilah whose lavish love turned her small world into a place of fairy tale magic and endless wonder, or the Delilah whose dire predictions and mystical connection to nature turned Rachel's world into a dark and forbidding labyrinth with no map to guide her out.

The bushes moved again, ratcheting up her fear. She had a watcher.

Run! Run! Her mother's voice rang through the air, as clearly as if she were standing beside Rachel.

But she was rooted to the ground, frozen by the warning of magnolias and fear that the madman known locally as the Collector had materialized on her ranch.

This unknown man had been terrorizing Manitou Springs and the surrounding area for more than a year, sneaking around snatching small, inexpensive items from other people's property. Like a phantom, a puff of wind, a dream no one could recall, he always came and went without a trace.

But when he escalated from stealing ornaments from gardens and small appliances from kitchens to walking into a park in broad daylight and snatching little Eddie Greene when no one was looking, sheer panic gripped the town.

Suddenly, Rachel's heart constricted with terror. Had the Collector come for her son?

She tore up the driveway, her heart racing. Bursting into her house, she bounded up the stairs and flung open the door to her son's room. The family's aging dog, Sam, lifted his head from his doggie bed as if to say, *What's all the fuss about?*

Joey was curled in his own bed, still sleeping, his curly red hair tousled, his face dewy with the innocence of a four-year-old. Relief made Rachel weak-kneed. She closed her son's door then peered into her daughter Susan's bedroom to assure herself that both her children were safe.

Standing in the doorway, watching her oldest child breathe —dark-haired and as secretive as her grandmother Delilah— Rachel collected herself. She went downstairs to the kitchen to put on the coffee and pop some frozen blueberry muffins into the oven, practical moves that reflected her no-nonsense approach to life. Her grandmother, the most sensible woman Rachel knew, would approve.

But the world has a way of showing you that you are not in charge, no matter how much you try. And it will use any means to teach you the lesson.

As she sat down with her first cup of coffee to read the newspaper, the headline leaped out at her:

MISSING BOY FOUND IN DENVER LANDFILL

Her first thought was *they have found Eddie Greene.* She was devastated. No parent deserved this.

Rachel's anxiety climbed higher with every word:

The skeletal remains of four-year-old Whit Langley, who had been missing for seven years, were discovered yesterday by a forklift driver at the Westside Landfill in Denver, Colorado.

She remembered the exhaustive search for the Langley boy —similar to that for Eddie Greene—and the extensive television coverage, the heartbreaking pleas of both sets of parents for any information leading to the discovery of their missing sons.

And now this unspeakable horror was right on her doorstep. She continued reading.

So far, the police have no leads. But multiple similarities between the disappearances of the Langley and the Greene boys are being investigated.

Stunned, her coffee forgotten, Rachel stared at the newspaper as if she could take murder off the table and force the shocking headline to transform into something positive, news of an engagement or the upcoming fall festival. The steam rising from the coffee pot suddenly took a turn from chicory to the fragrance of magnolia blossoms. She flew to the pantry for air freshener. She chose one that smelled like cinnamon, hoping the spice would be strong enough to wipe out the fear and the overpowering scent that had come uninvited into her home and set up housekeeping like a pesky guest who wouldn't go away.

In spite of her mother's dazzling, larger-than-life presence, Rachel had been born practical and had remained that way all her life. Being a sensible woman, she was going to let nothing ruin her Sunday off with her children and her grandmother. They deserved a life—and certainly one day—free of the unholy terror that had been unleashed by the vanishing of Eddie Greene in Soda Springs Park. And now, the grisly discovery of the bones of another child in a city too close to home for comfort...

As if thinking had conjured her up, Victoria Logan marched into the kitchen, already spruced up in blue jeans, Western shirt, and cowboy boots. Her short gray hair framed a lined face still bright with intelligence and curiosity, while her spry movements and her Western garb belied her seventy-five years.

"Coffee smells good," Rachel's grandmother said, as she poured herself a cup then studied Rachel with blue eyes that never seemed to fade. "Are you wearing your mother's perfume?"

"No." Alarm skittered through her. Did her grandmother smell the mysterious scent of magnolias? In all the years Rachel had struggled against the pull of things she didn't understand, her grandmother had appeared oblivious. Even worse... was her grandmother's mind failing? "I don't wear perfume. Remember?"

"Of course I do. I was just checking, that's all. You always hated the Bohemian's perfume. Smelled like gardenias or magnolias or some such New Orleans nonsense." Her grandmother sank into a kitchen chair and leafed through the paper to the classified ads. "Your ad looks great, Rachel."

Relieved for the change of subject, Rachel cradled her own coffee cup as she read over her grandmother's shoulder.

For Rent: Apartment in the Rockies. 1 bedroom w/bath and kitchenette. Private entrance. Peaceful setting on ten acres in the countryside on the outskirts of Manitou Springs, right under the slopes of Pikes Peak!

The remnants of their ranch—the acreage she hadn't sold in an attempt to survive—was a fifteen-minute drive out of the quaint box-canyon town of Manitou Springs. And it *was* beautiful, even without the care her grandparents then later her husband had lavished on it. The photos she'd posted of the rock gardens she and her grandmother loved, the massive birch trees lining the driveway, and the picnic area they'd carved at the edge of the forest showed her home to its best.

Peaceful was an accurate description of the place when Joey was in preschool and Susan was in second grade. When the children were at home, that description might be stretching the truth.

The ad had been running for six weeks with no takers.

Once Rachel left a crack open for worry, it grew teeth and claws then rampaged through her and took over, no matter how she struggled to remain positive.

"If I don't get a renter soon, I don't know how much longer I can keep the ranch on my salary, Gran." Rachel was a schoolteacher, and proud of her profession, but her salary was modest, at best.

"Look at this, hon." Victoria had turned to the entertainment section and tapped the paper with a blue-veined, weatherbeaten hand that told its own story of a woman accustomed to hard work and not too proud to let it show. The article was about her favorite television show designed to give aspiring writers a shot at fame. "Augusta Harper says you just need to put yourself out there, and good things will follow. Talk the apartment up with your schoolteacher friends, and I'll bet people will be flocking to rent it."

"Unlike Augusta, I'm not a famous novelist, and I certainly don't have my own TV show."

How was an ordinary woman with no accomplishments the world would notice going to attract the attention of a potential renter?

Since her husband's death three years earlier, Rachel had managed to take care of her children and hang on to her home with no one to help except her grandmother. Both of them thought of it as a huge achievement, but who else cared? Certainly not Worry, still sitting on her chest like a beady-eyed monster, just waiting its chance to pounce again.

"Hon, maybe you ought to reconsider Jen's offer to lend you some money? Just till you can get back on your feet." Gran got up to refill her coffee cup then turned to give Rachel her famous, piercing blue-eyed stare that showed she meant business.

"I'm not taking my sister's money."

"You wouldn't be *taking* it. You'd pay it all back."

"No, Gran." Taking her older sister's money would feel like failure to Rachel. "If I don't get a renter soon, I'll find a weekend job." Though Rachel wasn't certain even the additional bit of income would be enough to counter the sky-rocketing cost of living. And she hated the idea of giving up Sunday afternoons in the park with the remnants of her small family.

Rachel turned the conversation to her most pressing concern. "They found the bones of that little boy who vanished in Denver seven years ago, and the police think the murderer might also be the one who took Eddie Greene. I'm scared to death for the children."

"I've never known a better or more vigilant mother." Gran came over to put an arm around her. "You're doing everything possible to keep them safe."

"But is it enough?"

"Hank Carson would come over here in a *heartbeat* if you asked." Gran cast her another knowing look. "Nobody would dare mess with the children with a decorated war hero on the premises."

Rachel pictured her husband's best friend and comrade in arms, a tall, handsome Texan whose easy-going nature was a perfect camouflage for the fierce warrior who would not hesitate to fight for those he loved. He had been the family's guardian angel since Max was killed in battle.

Warmth and a feeling of well-being flooded Rachel, as it always did with the mention of Hank's name. In the three years since he had moved nearby to watch over his fallen friend's family, Rachel had felt his love like a laser beam, aimed straight for her heart.

She knew he would jump at the chance to move in and protect her and her family from the current threat, even if it was only temporary. But she was too independent to bring in a man —any man, even one as amazing as Hank—to do a job she was perfectly capable of handling.

Or was she just too stubborn? Her conscience pricked her as her children's voices drifted down the stairs, the excitement of being alive, the innocence of youth, the laughter and the hope that floated around them like colored kites. How long could she keep them safe with only the help of her grandmother and an ancient dog?

Sam's barking and the children's chatter signaled this was just another typical Sunday morning.

Except it wasn't.

The faint fragrance of magnolias lingering around the coffee pot and wafting from the blueberry muffins she took from the oven told her so.

TWO

SODA SPRINGS PARK

Manitou Springs was as well-known for its city parks, that appeared to be as far removed from the town as it was from Pikes Peak, and the eight natural fountains believed to possess healing waters. Soda Springs Park at the north end of the shopping district was surrounded by mountains and trees, and featured a spring nearby, making it popular for family outings.

Rachel entered the park, keeping her two children and her grandmother close as she glanced around for signs of trouble. Even under her intense scrutiny, the park looked completely unthreatening, as if this were an ordinary Sunday afternoon.

Turned golden by the afternoon rays of an October sun filtering through trees showing the bright colors of fall, it appeared peaceful. Looking at the crowd who had flocked there to play on the swing sets, sun themselves on the park benches, and enjoy the fountain, you'd never guess that little Eddie Greene had vanished from this very place just weeks earlier.

Being at the scene of the crime brought back the memory of the candlelight vigil held for Eddie on the town square. The citizens had turned out in droves—Eddie's kindergarten teacher and classmates at the elementary school where Rachel taught, the entire staff and congregation of the church where his mother Marsha was director of youth, the owner and employees of the construction company where Eddie's father, Daryl, worked, the mayor and the city council, shopkeepers, grocers, delivery boys, and parents who feared their children would be next.

Victoria had stayed home with the children while Rachel stood sandwiched between Hank Carson and the quiet mailman who had delivered her mail for the last six years.

As Marsha and Daryl Greene pled for any information that would lead them to find their son, many in the crowd wiped their eyes, while some openly wept.

With his arm wrapped securely around his wife as if she, too, might vanish at any moment, Daryl added, "A week before my son was taken, the Collector sneaked into our house and took Marsha's waffle maker from the kitchen. Then he went into our son's room and left a teddy bear. He even left his calling card from that stupid Tarot deck. I *know* he took Eddie. You *know* he took Eddie. Find the monster." His voice cracked. "Bring our son home."

The mailman turned to Rachel and Hank, his face stricken by shock and the sense of loss everybody in the town shared.

"It's hard to believe something like this could happen in our safe little town," he murmured.

"It's truly terrifying," Rachel agreed, giving the mailman's arm a sympathetic pat, because that's what you do when tragedy strikes. You unite with other good people you've known for years who would do anything to drive out the crime that has somehow infected their private paradise.

Now, as Rachel made her way to the park benches, she tried to shake the sadness the memory evoked, as well as her anxiety. Discovery of the Langley boy's remains in Denver changed everything for her. Protecting her children from a kidnapper had been bad enough, but keeping them safe from a *murderer* was a nightmare.

Before they left home, she had suggested one of the other parks, but her children set up such a clamor, she dropped the subject. She couldn't bear the idea of making Susan and Joey fearful and curtailing the outdoor activities they needed to thrive. Growing up was hard enough without adding adult-sized anxieties to the mix. She'd just have to be more watchful, both at the ranch and in public.

As she ushered her small brood toward a park bench underneath a birch tree, she felt a shift within herself, as if the low-life who had snatched a child only a year older than her own four-year-old son was still lingering at the water fountains or behind the trees to kidnap another little boy.

The pervasive sense of fear almost sent her fleeing back to the safety of her modest ranch. And yet, hadn't she been at that very ranch when she heard the news of loved ones' deaths that turned her world upside down?

As she passed underneath the birch tree, the leaves began to dance, though not a single breeze was blowing. Her mother's words whispered through her, a remembrance, a heartbreak, a warning.

Nature is always true to itself unless evil is afoot...

Rachel forged ahead, trying to ignore the omen, as she had done through the years. She staked out the bench with their picnic supplies and instructed her children to stay within eyesight. But the leaves continued to whisper, *look, listen.* The warning was so strong it sent chills through her. If there was ever a time for her to pay attention to the lessons her mother taught her, wasn't it now?

The town, once renowned for its quaintness and low crime rate, no longer felt safe. Though some people said no one in their community could possibly have taken Eddie, that it had to be a stranger visiting Soda Springs Park that day, most believed it was the elusive criminal called the Collector.

An intensive search had turned up no clues. Speculation ran high, and fears even higher. People were buying new locks for their doors, installing security systems at an unprecedented rate, and keeping their children indoors, or close at hand. The mere whisper of the name, the Collector, made the townspeople apprehensive, especially parents who feared for the lives of their young children.

As Rachel watched her children play, she scanned the area for suspicious characters. There was nothing to see except some teenagers, skateboarding in the distance, and a little boy about the age of her own son Joey approaching from the direction of the parking lot, sucking on a lollipop.

Her daughter Susan, seven going on seventeen, was bossing her younger brother around at the swing sets. No surprise there. She'd taken the role of mothering on her thin shoulders after she realized her daddy was never going to come home again.

Even worse, she had insisted on wearing her red magician's cape. Rachel's younger sister, Annie, had sent it from Italy three years ago for Susan's birthday. It was now bedraggled and far too small, but Susan refused to part with it. She had even invented magical properties for the cape, probably because she had received it on the first birthday she ever celebrated without her daddy.

She claimed it gave her girl power and made her strong and protected her and her brother from ghosts and goblins and mean kids. But her most heartbreaking claim was *the cape makes me invisible when I need to be.*

Watching her daughter twirl, her dark hair and the red cape flying out behind her, Rachel wondered if Susan would ever learn to relax and just be a carefree little girl again.

Not for the first time since Rachel's husband died, she wondered if she was clinging too hard to the past, if she should take her older sister Jen's advice and move to her neighborhood in Florida, make a fresh start. Not only for the sake of her children but, also, for herself. After all, Jen was a much-sought-after psychologist who had built a thriving practice by helping people discover their own courage and desire to survive life's tribulations, both large and small.

Rachel didn't mean to project her anxiety, especially not to her grandmother sitting on the park bench beside her, serene and content to watch the children at play, her cropped gray hair ruffling in the wind, her eyes networked with laugh lines that spoke of age and humor. But Victoria was quick to pick up on her audible sigh.

"Everything's going to be all right." She patted Rachel's hand.

"I wish I believed that, Gran."

Her grandmother's prediction seemed as far-fetched as if she'd told Rachel her military hero husband hadn't really been blown to bits by a car bomb in Afghanistan, and the home she was struggling to keep on an elementary schoolteacher's salary in the midst of economic chaos would start sprouting money trees.

Suddenly, movement in a hedgerow on her left caught Rachel's attention. A man in black sweats and black face mask was skulking along, obviously trying to hide himself behind the hedges. As if that weren't enough to derail Rachel's thoughts of financial ruin and disaster, what she saw next set off alarm bells. The man crept along, keeping a parallel path to the little boy she had noticed earlier heading toward the swing sets.

Her mothering instincts kicked into high gear. A quick glance showed no harried mother in hot pursuit of her threatened child. No one nearby to intervene.

Suddenly, the scent of magnolias swirled around Rachel, so intense she felt slightly nauseated.

Danger. Danger.

The warning screamed through her, a clarion call to action. But what? What could she do?

The man hunkered down and began to close the gap between himself and the small child.

"Gran, call 911, and grab the children." Acting on instinct, Rachel raced toward the stranger with the only weapon she had, a soft-side hamper containing their picnic sandwiches and a metal thermos of lemonade.

"*Stop!*" she screamed, but the man continued to close in on the child. "Somebody help!" she yelled, but nobody came to her aid. Nobody was willing to get involved. Though life in general had taken much from her, she still ran most afternoons, more as a form of release than a bid for physical fitness. Her long legs and the speed that had won awards for her high school track team so many years ago gave Rachel the advantage.

She steadily gained ground, but she still wasn't close enough to rescue the child. Before she could reach them, the man grabbed the little boy's arm. The child gave a yelp, but the predator covered his mouth with a large hand.

Horror filled Rachel.

Not again.

A quick glance behind her told her nobody else was coming to the boy's rescue. It was all up to her. She sucked in air and doubled her effort. Before the would-be snatcher knew what was happening, she was close enough to swing the hamper by its shoulder straps.

"Hey, *you!*" she yelled.

He paused and she landed a glancing blow on his arm. Surprised by the unexpected attack, the man lost his grip on the child.

"Get away from me!" he yelled at Rachel.

"No, I'm a mother. You leave that boy alone!"

She drew back her weapon again and landed a solid wallop to his kneecap that rocked him backward. Momentarily stunned, the man stared at her as if she were an invading Martian before he raced toward a thicket of trees, limping.

The fracas and the sound of metal thermos connecting to bone finally got the attention of the crowd. In the ensuing chaos, mothers screamed for their children, dogs barked, joggers collided on the track as they stopped to watch, and teenagers filming with their cell phones abandoned skateboards to get a better view.

A large, misguided woman in bright yellow pants screamed, "You bully!" then huffed up and tried to wrestle the picnic hamper away from Rachel.

"Back off!" Rachel elbowed her out of the way to get to the little boy, who was hunkered down, sobbing.

She scooped him into the safety of her arms. "It's okay, sweetheart. Everything's going to be okay."

Wasn't that the mantra of mothers everywhere? Miraculously, it worked, and he collapsed against her, sniffing.

"That bad man made me drop my lollipop."

"We'll get you another one."

"Two?" He gave her the sly smile of kids everywhere who know how to outwit adults.

"At least two. Where's your mommy?"

He pointed to a young woman barreling out of a Honda, frantic, a lipstick clutched in her hand. Her bottom lip, painted a blazing red while her top lip was bare, told the story of a woman too vain to watch after her own child.

Rachel wanted to put her arm around the young mother and say, *Don't you know how fast the people you love can be taken from you?*

In the distance sirens wailed, the eerie sound that signifies disaster coming closer by the minute. Help was on the way. But, also, so was trouble.

Two hours later, a jogger's video of Rachel had gone viral on Twitter.

THREE

TELEVISION STATION KKTV | COLORADO SPRINGS, COLORADO

That evening, Rachel was sitting in the green room of KKTV-TV in Colorado Springs, a brief six-mile drive east from Manitou Springs, waiting for her interview on *Sunday Night Special with Dawn Williams* and remembering exactly how she'd ended up doing something so foreign to her nature.

When Dawn first called her after seeing the video from the park, Rachel had turned her down. "I don't do TV appearances."

"Oh, but you *must!*" Dawn told her. "You're today's biggest news story."

"I'm sorry," Rachel said. "The answer is still no."

Only a follow-up telephone plea from Marsha Greene had convinced Rachel to appear on *Sunday Night Special*. Not only did they attend the same church, but their sons had often played together.

"Daryl and I need your support," Marsha had said. "The discovery of that little boy's bones in Denver..." She choked up and then regained control. "We're hoping the other child's murder will revitalize the local investigation and help us find

Eddie... before it's too late." She broke down then, sobbing quietly.

Rachel gave her the space to grieve. Finally, she said, "I'm so sorry, Marsha. Of course I'll do anything I can to help."

There were snuffling sounds as Marsha blew her nose and regained her composure. "My husband and I know how fiercely protective you are of the children under your care at school. We want you to help us spread the word to all parents to be more aware of where their children are, especially in view of what happened in Soda Springs Park today—and with the Collector still on the loose."

How could Rachel say no? The mere mention of the Collector chilled her to the bone.

The notorious criminal had gone undetected for more than a year because he was only stealing inexpensive items from his victims' gardens—small garden ornaments, potted plants, lawn chairs, and small outdoor tables. At first, nobody reported these petty misdemeanors, thinking the neighbor's large and obnoxious dog might have carried off the plastic pot of petunias and left the chewed-up remains in the woods, or neighborhood children might have grabbed a chair or a little table to make a playhouse.

But by the fall of last year, the Collector had started going into houses. Most of the reports came from Manitou Springs, but eventually reports of breaking and entering began to filter in from Colorado Springs and several of the ranches in the surrounding area. He was still taking inexpensive items—a lamp, a dining room chair, a cheap vase anybody could find at the dollar store, a toaster-oven, a red blender. Still, people felt invaded, violated, especially when their framed family photographs started disappearing. Their reports poured in with such regularity an enterprising reporter at *The Gazette* dubbed the thief the Collector for the very domesticity of his stolen goods.

Then in May of this year the Collector had stepped up his game. Family pets started disappearing. Did they wander off? Were they picked up by random strangers passing by who decided on the spur of the moment they wanted a pet of their own and didn't much care who they hurt getting one?

Because of the sheer number of pets vanishing and the tight perimeter in which they disappeared, the random theory was quickly discarded in favor of laying blame for the diminished pet population at the feet of the Collector.

When the news broke, the Collector confirmed the suspicions by leaving a calling card from the Tarot deck at the scene of his crimes to taunt his victims. It was Justice, a card that foretells unkind people will be punished and reap the consequences of their actions. Conversely, this card also signifies that hard work and sacrifice will be rewarded. But why the Collector moved from taking pets to kidnapping children was still a mystery.

And now, the elusive Collector was linked to murder. Both the manhunt and the terror in the town were at an all-time high. And Rachel had put herself right in the middle of it.

She sat in the green room in front of a bank of mirrors that showed every flaw while the TV show's makeup artist and hair stylist both worked on her. Suddenly, she caught a whiff of magnolias. Despite the fact that Rachel had asked the couple from the neighboring ranch to come over and stay with Victoria and the children while she was gone, she had the sinking feeling she would regret coming on this show.

The scent of the iconic flower from her mother's childhood home in New Orleans became more pervasive, swirling around the green room in a fragrant fog. As much as she disliked having the gift of knowing, Rachel knew that nature never lied.

She whipped out her cell phone, punched in her gran's number, and breathed a sigh of relief when she heard Victoria's voice. "Is everybody okay at the ranch? Do you have the children close? Are the neighbors still with you?"

"Relax, hon. Everybody's here. We're all fine. We've got the TV on to watch you."

When Rachel pocketed her phone, the stylist patted her arm and said, "When we finish with you, people are going to think you're a movie star."

She lifted Rachel's wild mane of curls and proceeded to slick them back with a ton of hair product, and Rachel fought the urge to leave her chair and return to the cocoon of her ranch. Only her resolve to support Marsha and Daryl Greene kept her rooted to the spot.

The sleek style turned out not to be as bad as Rachel had imagined. It emphasized her high cheekbones and dark eyes. For a moment she saw a glimpse of Delilah peering back at her from the mirror. The sense of gazing back in time was heightened by the scent of magnolia blossoms lingering in the air.

As the tall, skinny makeup artist whipped out a mind-boggling array of cosmetics and set to work, Rachel's high natural color vanished under a layer of pancake makeup so thick it looked as if it had been slathered on with a trowel. She followed with mascara and products with names Rachel didn't even know. For the finishing touch, she painted Rachel's naturally full lips a garish pink that made her look as if Joey had given her one of his enthusiastic, strawberry-jelly laden kisses.

Both women applauded their own work, exclaiming, "Wow! Perfect."

Only if I wanted to be in disguise, she thought as they led her toward the studio. The idea weighed heavily on Rachel that her fifteen minutes of fame would call attention to her family. Only the conviction that she was lending support to Eddie's grief-stricken parents and raising awareness of child predators kept Rachel moving toward the studio.

. . .

The set of *Sunday Night Special with Dawn Williams* was lit to show Colorado Spring's popular television personality at her best, spotlights aimed to pick up the platinum highlights in her short bob and the cosmetically enhanced fullness of her glossy red lips and sculpted cheekbones. Males tuned in by the score just to see her. Being likable and approachable saved her from the jealousy of the females in her viewing audience.

Sitting opposite her on the set, Rachel felt like a toad.

After a brief recap to her television audience of the afternoon's events in the park, Dawn showed the teenager's iPhone footage then introduced Rachel.

"This evening's *Sunday Night Special* guest is an ordinary person just like you and me, a third-grade teacher at Manitou Springs Elementary whose quick thinking in Soda Springs Park this afternoon turned her into a hero. Rachel, tell us what was going through your mind."

"I saw a child in danger and instinctively ran to help. I only did what any mother would have done under the circumstances."

"But you *didn't*. You were *extraordinary!*"

"Thank you." The compliment sent a hot flush to Rachel's cheeks. Being in the limelight was harder than she'd imagined. She particularly disliked being portrayed as something she was not.

"You have no training in the martial arts or self-defense of any sort, and yet you saved another young child from being kidnapped with nothing more than a small picnic hamper filled with four bologna sandwiches and a thermos of lemonade!"

And there it was. Rachel's private shame aired for the whole world to see. She couldn't afford ham and cheese on rye, or even turkey with sliced dills, lettuce, tomatoes, and real mayonnaise. She'd packed lowly bologna sandwiches with nothing more than a smear of mustard for her children.

"My children like bologna." *Oh help*. At home she often

mimicked her children's habit of calling it *baloney san'wiches*. Had she said that on television? Plus, she'd sounded defensive. She could even feel herself jutting her jaw at a stubborn angle. She forced her chin down and made herself smile at Dawn. "The thermos bottle was metal."

"Indeed, it was. You could hear the second blow you landed on the video footage. Can you describe the man for our audience?"

The sketch done by the police artist earlier that afternoon flashed on the screen.

"As I told the police, I didn't get a good look at his face. There was nothing unusual about his size. He was medium height and build. He wore a black cloth face mask, and his baseball cap was pulled low over his eyes. I did notice the cap was a Colorado Rockies one. His hair was blond and kicked up in a slight curl around the cap, and I could see a hint of light-colored facial hair on the outer edges of his mask."

Dawn replayed video footage of the would-be kidnapper limping from his last blow with her voice-over. "The police are still looking for this man who allegedly attempted to abduct a young boy in Soda Springs Park this afternoon. Considering the blow to his kneecap, he might go to one of the area's medical clinics. If you have any information on him, please call."

The sketch flashed on the screen again while the call number scrolled across the bottom. Dawn continued her commentary.

"The man you see on the screen was foiled from snatching a child this afternoon by our brave guest, Rachel Maxey. She not only stopped the kidnapping but provided the first eye-witness account of the man who could possibly be responsible for kidnapping five-year-old Edward Greene from Soda Springs Park six weeks ago. If you have seen this man or this child, please call the number on your screen."

Rachel's heart broke when the little boy with a face full of freckles, a gap between his front teeth, and a wide smile filled with hope flashed on the split screen. The missing child could just as easily have been Joey.

While Dawn continued her spiel, Rachel ached for Eddie's parents, waiting in their own green room for their chance to plead for the return of their son. What fresh pain were they feeling? Were they still hopeful, especially in light of the discovery of the Langley child's remains? Were they searching for clues in everything they saw or heard?

"Further speculation is that the man Rachel Maxey effectively chased off in the park this afternoon could be the Collector, who has terrorized members of our viewing audience since April of last year."

Dawn's explanation to the audience matched everything Rachel knew about the Collector.

After she completed her litany of the Collector's criminal activities, she turned to Rachel. "Do you think it's possible the man you foiled in the park was the Collector?"

"I saw nothing to indicate he was or wasn't."

"But the Collector escalated from small garden decorations and household items to pets. He's elusive, he's smart. Though his signature calling card was found in the home, it was *not* found at the park where Eddie Greene was kidnapped, which leaves room for doubt. What's your opinion of the Collector? Did he ramp up his game to include snatching little children?"

Stunned, Rachel sat in her chair, too scared to speak. The Collector was terrifying. There was *no* doubt in her mind that he took Eddie. But if it had been him in the park this afternoon, she was the one person who could identify him.

She had two small children at home, watching *Sunday Night Special* with Victoria. In spite of the neighbors being there, all of them were exposed, vulnerable, helpless with no one to protect them except their aging border collie, Sam.

Anyone might waltz into her house and snatch Joey,

including the man she'd foiled with four bologna sandwiches and a thermos who might want to replace the little boy he didn't get today in the park.

And what if the Collector was listening to Dawn plant the seed that Rachel believed him to be the kidnapper and could identify him? What if the Collector decided to dispose of Eddie and snatch Joey as revenge against Rachel for the unflattering things said about him in this interview?

"Rachel, we're waiting for your answer. Do you believe the Collector is snatching little children? Yes or no?"

She felt trapped, sick to her stomach. She had fooled herself into believing she could have a positive impact on mothers, but she was merely a pawn in the ratings game Dawn Williams was playing.

"I don't know enough about the Collector to have an opinion on the matter. But I do know this." When Rachel leaned in close, Dawn let her perfect façade slip by showing irritation. "Since the kidnapping of Edward Greene, I am watching my children more closely, paying strict attention to where they are, who they are with, and what they are doing at all times. I urge every mother and father in the viewing audience to do the same thing."

Dawn went to a commercial break while Rachel's lapel microphone was removed and Eddie's parents were ushered onto the set. Both of them looked as if they had aged ten years since their son vanished. Marsha was even thinner, her blond hair hanging around her gaunt face like a limp dishcloth, while Daryl appeared to be a pale copy of the swarthy, hearty man who always greeted you with a huge grin and a big handshake.

"Rachel, thank you." Marsha enveloped her in a tight hug, then hung on, as if the very act of clinging to another mother could magically bring back her son.

"You're more than welcome, Marsha. I hope your interview brings in a clue that will help find Eddie. Please call me if there is anything else I can do to help." Eager to get home and see for herself that her children were safe, Rachel left the studio and made her way to her vehicle, grateful for the well-lit parking lot that made it hard for somebody to creep up behind you.

She had supported grieving parents and issued a challenge that could possibly save the life of another child.

But had her reluctant turn as a fly-by-night celebrity put her and her family in the crosshairs of a madman?

FOUR

THE HIDEAWAY | LOCATION UNKNOWN

He stared at the television screen, entranced. Once more, *Sunday Night Special* was portraying him as a star.

Dawn Williams was beautiful and so was her voice. He watched her show every Sunday night. His witch of a mother would have called it an obsession, maybe even an abomination because it featured a woman men lusted after.

He didn't care what the old biddy thought. She was gone, gone, gone, and he was famous. Yes, he was. And getting more famous by the day. Thanks in part to the ever-lovely, ever-sexy Dawn Williams.

As she recounted his stellar achievements, he danced a little jig around the room, pausing to view himself in the mirror. He looked two feet taller today. He *was* two feet taller, thanks to Dawn Williams and other reporters who didn't know who he was, but recognized his genius anyhow.

Dawn even told her guest, Rachel Maxey, and her millions of fans that she believed in his higher nature. She believed in *him!*

He was a legend. A living, breathing legend.

In a town that bragged about having a crime rate seventy-six percent lower than the national average, he had singlehandedly wiped the smirks off their faces and shown them what a criminal mastermind could do. During his long spree, he had left behind a trail of fear and discontent that would not be matched in his lifetime. If ever.

And he was just getting started. Oh yes, he was!

He would have imitators by the score, but none would ever match him. His name would be on the lips of people for years to come. They would write books about him, Broadway shows, songs. They would probably name buildings and streets after him.

But, oh, most importantly, his children would pass his bloodline, his legendary history, and his remarkable genes from generation to generation. He was planning to have a house full. A dynasty.

And he knew just the perfect mother.

There she was. Right in front of him.

He pressed his face so close to the television screen he could lick her luscious lips. She was cool and hot at the same time. Ready.

"There you are, my sweet. There you are."

No, not Dawn. She only served to spread his fame. If necessary, he could use her as his backup plan. Mother of his dynasty, Plan B. But that wouldn't be necessary. No, it would not.

This time he didn't plan to fail.

The object of his desire sat opposite Dawn. He reached out to trace the outline of her beautiful face.

"Perfect in every way."

He couldn't decide what was more mesmerizing, her dark eyes or the fact that she was a ripe vessel for his future children. She'd proved she could have children. They were both unworthy, snot-nosed brats, but *his* children with her would be perfect.

He could hardly wait to start his own family with her.

He twirled till he got dizzy. Then he sat down on the floor and laughed so long and so hard the blackbirds that of late had started gathering in the trees beyond his window at sunset lifted toward the sky, wings outspread, feathers beating the air until it turned so dark he forgot everything except his own evil intent.

He raced to shove open the window and scream at them. "Fly, my beauties. Fly!"

As if he had pulled them by a string, the entire flock turned their hard yellow eyes on him. He grew another two inches taller under two dozen spotlights of approval.

He had been singled out by a murder of crows. Oh yes he had!

They had all come to bless his mission. To crown him. To anoint him.

A burst of power surged through him. He turned his back toward the mirror to see if he was sprouting wings. Huge black wings that would cover everything he touched. Everything he wanted. The entire planet.

He was a creature of feathers and cunning. He was invincible.

FIVE
LOGAN RANCH

As Rachel drove home, it was hard not to rehash her TV interview.

It had her stomach tied in knots. If a criminal who was a mastermind at evading the law was responsible for Eddie Greene's disappearance, hopes of finding the child plummeted and the odds of more unsolved disappearances escalated.

Had the Collector been watching? Would her statement enrage him, make him believe Dawn and Rachel were spreading rumors that would paint him as a fiend? Even worse, would that little tidbit about him snatching children, so casually dropped into the interview, turn into a ticking bomb in the Collector's mind, an idea that would grow louder and more insistent until it propelled him into an explosion of pure evil?

The clear October night sky was dusted with stars and shot through with silver from a generous moon. Evil thoughts had no place in this spectacular display of nature. Rachel forced herself to concentrate on the beauty of her surroundings. Her spirits lifted when she came in sight of her home's wooden sign—VF RANCH—still hanging over the entrance, though it had long ago ceased to be a working ranch.

When Victoria and Finn Logan built the ranch more than fifty years ago, they made sure the house, the barn and every shed and fence blended with the mountains and forest. Years of harsh Rocky Mountain winters had weathered the house and the barn, the toolshed and the fences, so they appeared older than they were, wizened and welcoming, almost a living, breathing entity that reached out its arms to Rachel every time she navigated the winding, birch-lined driveway.

This was Logan land, with the Irish Logans' coat of arms hanging in the hall just inside the doorway, along with the family portraits.

Gran and their border collie, Sam, greeted Rachel at the door.

"You were great on the TV show." Victoria kissed her cheek. "I'm proud of you."

"Thanks, Gran." Rachel glanced down the hall. "Where are the neighbors?"

"I sent them home. They're getting up early tomorrow to repair their pasture fence."

"*Gran*! I wanted them here to protect you and the children. I'm scared to death of what the Collector will do next."

"They've only been gone five minutes."

"I don't want you and the children unprotected for even *one* minute."

"I'm perfectly capable of protecting this ranch and everybody on it. I fended off coyotes and mountain lions when you and your sisters were little, and I'd do it again. No two-legged coward is going to get the best of me."

Her grandmother was a fierce, strong-willed woman who fought her own battles. Rachel had the sinking feeling she could never make her grandmother understand the gravity of having the Collector on the prowl for children.

"Where are Susan and Joey?"

"I've already tucked them in. They wanted to wait up for you, but I wouldn't let them since tomorrow's a school day."

"Good call." Rachel tried not to show her anxiety by racing off to check on her children. She didn't want to make her grandmother feel as if she were no longer capable of taking care of them. Besides, the dog was quiet. If the Collector was anywhere on the premises, he would be in a barking frenzy. "Did they behave?"

"They were angels."

"I doubt it." Still, it felt good to have something to smile about.

Rachel dropped her car keys in a tray on the table underneath her favorite portrait. It was an oil painting of a young Victoria and Finn in jeans and well-worn cowboy hats, holding the reins of a beautiful horse, the distinctive, dappled white Appaloosa, where their only son, six-year-old Patrick, sat in the saddle.

With his signature Logan red hair blowing about in the wind and a wide smile that showed his crooked front teeth, Patrick Logan could have been mistaken for his grandson, Joey.

Seeing the direction of Rachel's gaze, Victoria said, "I still miss both of them." Her face was a map of love and loss, not only for the husband and son who were taken from her too soon, but also for the other children she would have had except for the ovarian cancer that invaded her shortly after Patrick was born.

"I know you do, Gran. So do I." She put her arm around her grandmother and kissed her cheek. "I know you're a warrior woman, but make sure you close your curtains and lock up tight before you go to bed. The Collector is very dangerous."

"You've got the Irish blood of the Logans running through your veins, Rachel. We don't run. We fight."

Rachel sighed as her grandmother headed toward her bedroom. The family coat of arms hanging beside the family portrait featured a red heart struck through with a stake and the motto *Hoc majoram vitus. This is the valor of my ancestors.*

That was all well and good, but Rachel didn't count on her ancestors to protect her from a man who murdered children. She raced upstairs to check on Joey.

He was in his cowboy bed, his tousled red curls, so like his grandfather's, butting up against the chuck wagon carving on the headboard, both arms flung over his head and all the covers kicked down to reveal his pajamas featuring the Big Bird character from his favorite TV show. Seeing him still always came as a sort of shock. During every waking moment, he was in perpetual motion—climbing trees, tossing stones into the creek that ran behind their house, racing with his dog, waging war in imaginary castles and forts, building toad houses, riding stick horses with fierce names such as Thunder and Lightning and Storm Boy.

She pulled the covers back over him, tucked them under a cherubic face that in time would likely take on the chiseled features of Clifton "Max" Maxey. Her heart hurt that Max would never see his son grow into a man.

She studied her husband's photo on the bedside stand, softly illuminated by Joey's night light, a big man with laughing blue eyes and a shock of wavy blond hair. "Max, I promise I'll make sure he remembers you." Their son had been a mere eleven months old when Max was killed. "I promise I'll raise him to be a good man."

To do that, she had to keep him safe. She smoothed back Joey's hair, kissed him on the cheek then checked the locks on the double bedroom windows. Though there had been no predictions from the weatherman regarding rain and fog, the hopeful star-studded sky had vanished behind an ominous gathering of clouds and threatening mist that floated close to the ground.

The nature of fog is always to hide things that can become our worst nightmare...

Was the Collector hiding out there? Rachel's worst nightmare was that Joey might be the little boy he took next. She closed the curtains so not even a glimpse of the beautiful boy sleeping in his bed could be seen from the outside.

With one last glance at her son, she went through the connecting bathroom into Susan's room. Her daughter's bedroom was typical of little girls her age, pink, ruffled, and frilly. She was sleeping curled into a ball, as if she were trying to keep her dreams as private as her waking moments.

Susan had been four when Max died, old enough to notice her mother's grief, to be confused by the way her small world suddenly shifted from laughter to tears, from joyful romps with her mother in the sun to a somber mood that left little room for the spontaneity she'd once enjoyed.

As Rachel watched her daughter, she wondered whether she had chosen the right path for her children, particularly Susan.

Last week when Hank Carson dropped by to check on them, he'd expressed concern about her living in such a remote location, especially with the Collector on the prowl. An echo of her sister Jen's sentiment, though Hank had not mentioned Florida as a perfect destination for them.

Jen thought it was her duty as the older sister to dish out advice, whether Rachel asked for it or not. In their last conversation she'd said, "I don't think it's safe for you to stay on that ranch with just Gran and the children. Move to Florida so we can take care of you."

"I'm not going to let anything or anybody defeat me."

"Change is not *defeat*, Rachel. You can't live the rest of your life in dreams of what you once had. And you certainly need to get away from that psychotic criminal out there. Move here. The kids will adapt."

Rachel had no doubt Joey would. But what about Susan and Victoria? Her daughter had already formed close friendships that would be very hard to leave behind. And her grandmother still proclaimed herself a cowgirl, born and bred in Colorado, fonder of the horses Rachel had been forced to sell than she was of most people. How could Rachel ever uproot either of them?

Jen had never understood their grandmother's attachment to Colorado. Neither did their younger sister, Annie, an artist who had moved to Italy as fast as she could after college graduation. Neither of Rachel's sisters even pretended to understand why Rachel couldn't leave the ranch.

Telling herself she might someday buy back the little Paint filly whose white markings on her chestnut coat had made her Victoria's favorite, Rachel had kept enough acreage to include the barn out back, sturdy and leak-free, still smelling faintly of hay.

It was also filled with memories, and she couldn't bear to part with it. Another sign of clinging to a life that had vanished along with Max, her sister Jen had said.

Pushing uncomfortable thoughts from her mind, Rachel leaned over the bed and kissed her daughter's cheek.

"Sweet dreams, sweet girl," she whispered then tiptoed back downstairs.

She was surprised to find Victoria in the kitchen making two mugs of hot chocolate. She passed a steaming mug to Rachel.

"I got to thinking about Daryl and Marsha's interview tonight, and I couldn't sleep. They were so torn up, they could barely speak."

"That's what I've been trying to say, Gran." If Rachel hadn't been so frightened for her children, she'd have stayed behind at the TV station to hear their interview and lend further support. "They are terrified the Collector will kill Eddie like he did that other little boy in Colorado. Jen wants us to move to Florida, you know, so we'll be close to her."

"I could still strut my stuff in a swimsuit." Victoria winked over the rim of her mug. "Or you might put a horse in that empty barn. The kids would love it, and I could still ride if somebody would help me into the saddle."

"First, I've got to get a renter, and it looks like that will take a miracle."

"You worry too much. Augusta says the meek run from life but the brave grab it by the horns and ride it wherever they want to go."

Not Augusta again. Was Victoria's obsession with the popular TV show a sign that she was drifting into her own world, or a simple pastime for the woman who no longer had straying cattle and killing cold winters to worry about?

Victoria rinsed out her cup and put it in the dishwasher. "This glamorous gal is headed to bed. Got to get up with the chickens tomorrow."

Alarm skittered through Rachel once more. Was her grandmother showing early signs of Alzheimer's, the same disease that had slowly stolen the lives of so many seniors?

"We no longer have chickens. Remember?"

They didn't have the chicken coop either, the nesting boxes, or the fenced-in yard where the chickens took dust baths and pecked at insects and even settled their differences with ruffled feathers and posturing.

"Of course I do. And good riddance, I say. I was so tired of that old rooster waking me up I was getting ready to wring his neck and put him in the stewpot." Victoria blew Rachel a kiss. "See you in the morning, sunshine."

She marched down the hall with her head high, going to the playroom that had been converted to a bedroom on the first floor to accommodate the arthritis that slowed her steps and was slowly reshaping her like one of the ancient wind-gnarled trees on the property.

It was all a grand act that broke another little piece off Rachel's heart. Her grandmother had loved everything about ranching and their small spread, every animal, large and small, the wide-open spaces, even the dirty and dangerous jobs such as mucking out stalls, helping livestock with a difficult birth, and braving storms to rescue a calf that had wandered off.

Sam, taking his cue from Victoria, watched until she was out of sight then trotted up the stairs where he would keep vigil over the children from his doggie bed inside Joey's bedroom. Now eleven years old, even he was slowing down, especially on the stairs. How much longer before he couldn't climb them by himself? And was he even capable of protecting the children, especially from the Collector?

Was she?

SIX

With her family safely tucked in for the night, Rachel went into the first-floor office to check her emails. More than any room in the house, it reminded her of her husband Max. He'd been a big man, and the massive oak desk that had belonged to Rachel's grandfather had suited him perfectly. He'd personally built the sturdy oak shelves on the wall behind the desk then filled them with books on ranching and history and aviation, all the things he'd loved, including family photos and the trophies both of them had won in high school track. The sport that brought them together.

Resisting a trip down memory lane that would only emphasize the turn her life had taken, she opened her laptop and went straight to her emails. Inquiries on her rental flooded in, all dated after *Sunday Night Special with Dawn Williams*. The first fifty emails filled her page, and they kept coming.

"Good grief. I don't even know where to start."

She started at the most recent and worked her way down. Many of them she deleted after one glance.

> I saw you on TV. I've always wanted to know a celebrity…

When I discovered I'd be living in the house of somebody famous...

After I watched Sunday Night Special, I googled you. I'm thirty-four and single and looking for somebody exactly like you...

I own my own spread in Wyoming and it needs a woman like you...

I'm a producer with WKWJ Entertainment and want to make you a star...

Do you come with the room...

Rachel was deleting emails so fast she almost missed the one from the famous artist Bruce Wyler, who lived in the trendy section of Locust Point in the Bronx. He was looking for a quiet place to paint.

I'm doing a study of life in the Colorado Rockies, past and present, and must finish these paintings in time for a gallery opening next spring. Your place sounds ideal. The private entrance, as well as the proximity to so much history, is especially appealing to me. You're only miles from the ranch owned by the original Marlboro Man and also the Pro-Rodeo Hall of Fame and Museum of the American Cowboy. The rich history of the railroads is represented right on your doorstep under the awesome beauty of Pikes Peak.

After your lovely interview with Dawn Williams, I know you'll be flooded with potential renters. I hope I'm not too late. I'm willing to pay you more than your asking price, within reason, of course, and I would love to move in immediately.

> I've attached letters of reference.
> Oh, I almost forgot. You can see my work here.

Rachel followed the links to stunning watercolors done by Bruce Wyler, the long list of galleries where he'd exhibited, and his official website. She already knew his work, and his letters of reference were glowing. There was nothing to fear by bringing him into her house with her family. She expelled a long breath she felt as if she'd been holding in forever then sent a quick reply and glanced at the clock. It was so late on the East Coast she doubted he'd be up reading and responding to emails.

Still, she had a renter. She could feel it in her bones.

Rachel closed her laptop then stood up. It had been a very long day, and tomorrow would prove a challenge. Getting her students settled after the weekend always made Mondays the hardest day. Additionally, they'd be revved up about seeing her on TV, and she knew they'd ask a million questions.

The noise—a slight rustling outside—caught her in mid-stretch. She froze, listening. There was nothing to hear except the ticking of the grandfather clock in the hallway and the scratching of Sam's toenails as he padded down the stairs.

Her dog had heard it, too. And there it was again, stealthy sounds right outside her window.

Sam gave a sharp bark as he pounded her way then skidded to a stop in the doorway.

"Good boy." If an intruder were outside, her dog would be the best chance of catching him. Still, her children came first. Always. Not hesitating for a second, Rachel grabbed the heavy military-grade flashlight out of the bottom drawer of the desk.

"Sam." Rachel pointed up the stairs. "Guard the children."

Reinvigorated by his purpose and the familiar command, the dog bounded back upstairs while she raced toward her front door.

A blast of chill night air and the black curtain of night met her, while fog curled around her ankles like something alive, something that would swallow her whole if she'd let it. Shaking off the image, Rachel trained her light around the front yard.

"Who's there?"

The night was still, reluctant to give up its secrets. Rachel waited in the doorway, searching the darkness with the high beam of her flashlight. It would serve as a weapon, too. Max had always told her that. A heavy club that could be used to knock an attacker cold.

Praying she didn't have to use her makeshift club, she took a step onto the front porch. Was that movement in the trees? She turned the intense beam toward the natural park and picnic area she and Victoria had created at the edge of her property after the shrinking ranch took the children's favorite pond along with the last forty acres she'd sold.

There was nothing to see except a few confetti-colored leaves blowing in the night wind. Still, Rachel sensed a faint aura of evil that sent prickles along her skin and a chill through her bones. Someone had been on her property. They might still be there.

Be brave.

She ventured toward the porch steps, gauging the distance back to her front door and calculating that even if someone suddenly ran out of the darkness toward her, she'd have plenty of time to make it back inside and secure the locks. She'd have Victoria and Sam to help her. An aging grandmother and an equally aging dog.

"Is anybody out there?"

The night swallowed up her question. Again, she swept the beam of her flashlight through a yard empty of everything except signs of the life Rachel had made for herself and her little family. Joey's tricycle and Susan's bike leaning against the picnic table, the stone frog the kids had named Ribbit perched near the latest frog house Joey had built, Victoria's gardening basket still sitting on the front porch swing where she'd left it before they went to their Sunday picnic in the park.

Had it only been this afternoon? Their outing seemed a lifetime ago.

Rachel was about to turn off her flashlight and go inside when she heard a wail that chilled her to the bone. Her heart pounding so hard she could barely breathe, she burst back into her house to see Victoria down the long hallway to the first-floor bedrooms, peering around her door frame.

"Gran, did you hear one of the children?"

"Yes, it was Susan. I was headed that way."

Victoria emerged holding a double-barreled shotgun in her hands. She knew how to use it, too. Or, she once had. Heaven only knew what she'd hit if she blasted away with it tonight.

"Stay here," Rachel told her.

"Don't worry. Nobody's getting past me. My gun is loaded and I know how to use it. Go on. Check on Susan."

Rachel took the stairs two at a time. Her daughter stood at the bay window overlooking the yard. She had draped the tattered red cape over her gown.

Oh, Susan. When a piece of a mother's heart breaks off it makes a tiny pop like a silver spoon striking the rim of a fine china cup.

"Somebody's out there, Mommy."

Susan always dropped the more grownup Mom when she was scared and resorted to her babyhood name for her mother. Rachel's blood ran cold as she hugged her close then peered out the window until her eyes adjusted to the darkness. There was not a sign of anyone, not a shadow. And yet, Rachel felt a lingering sense of unease as if someone had been there, leaving behind his bad intentions.

What had she missed on her cursory survey of the yard? The Collector was an unknown evil who moved through their lives like fog, leaving nothing to mark his passing but heartbreak and a terrifying chill.

Rachel's blood rushed through her body like a river gone wild. Or was it the voice of Delilah?

Bad intentions leave a palpable trail.

Rachel whirled from the window, turned her back on the past, and sought to reassure her daughter.

"There's no one outside, sweetie. I checked."

"You're sure?"

"Positive." Their dog came through the open door, wagging his tail. "Look at Sam. If anybody were outside his hackles would be up and he would be growling."

"He barked. I heard him."

"He was probably dreaming about herding cattle."

"But I *saw* somebody looking up at my window. A bad man."

"You saw a bad man in the park, and that's enough to make you imagine he came to your yard." Praying she was right, Rachel led her daughter back to bed and tucked the covers around her.

"But Mommy, the man in the yard had yellow hair."

A chill shivered through Rachel. Had the kidnapper she'd foiled come looking for her? She'd felt the presence, the same sense of danger she'd encountered in the park earlier that day. And the dog *had* barked. Briefly, she wondered if she should have let Sam into the yard instead of sending him back to the children.

"I promise no bad person can come into your house. You have Gran and Sam and me to take care of you."

"Will you sleep with me? Just in case?"

"Of course. I'll put on my pajamas and come right back upstairs."

"Promise?"

"Cross my heart." Rachel had stopped saying *and hope to*

die after Max was killed. She'd stopped a lot of things, then, including getting a peaceful night's sleep. Being protector for her family meant nights spent in the children's room fending off the ghosts and goblins of childhood, nights prowling the dark house trying to discover the source of phantom noises, sleepless nights worrying about bills and other problems that grew exponentially in the dark.

When Rachel returned downstairs, Victoria was still waiting with her shotgun. "Is Susan okay?"

"She's scared, and so am I. I'm going to sleep with her tonight. She thinks she saw someone in the yard, but I found nothing. I'm just so exhausted from the day and this constant vigilance that I hardly know what to think or do anymore."

"You're doing fine, hon. Go on upstairs to Susan and get some rest."

Rachel kissed Gran goodnight, then brushed her teeth, slid into pajamas, and went back upstairs, hoping her daughter was fast asleep.

Susan was sitting up in bed waiting for her, arms crossed on her narrow chest, still wearing that awful cape. She'd dragged her baseball bat out of the closet and propped it on her bedside table. Rachel wanted to cry.

"Oh, honey. You don't need the cape and the bat. I'll always take care of you."

"I thought you forgot."

While Rachel stowed the baseball bat in the closet, her daughter clutched the cape tighter. She couldn't bear to take the one thing that made Susan feel better, no matter what kind of advice Jen gave her about setting boundaries and being firm.

"I'll never forget you and Joey. And I certainly won't leave you without protection."

"Promise?"

"I promise." As she climbed under the covers, Rachel hoped it was a promise she could keep.

SEVEN

Sam's barking and the simultaneous ringing of the doorbell made Rachel shoot out of bed. Her feet tangled in Susan's bed skirt, bringing reality crashing down on her. Her robe was downstairs, she'd slept hardly a wink, and Monday mornings were far too busy for her to deal with an unexpected caller.

"Sam. Good boy." In the hallway she stooped to pat his head, and he quieted down. The doorbell rang again as the dog followed her toward her bedroom.

She grabbed her robe but gave up her search for slippers. A glance in the dressing table mirror showed her thick curls sticking out like a Brillo pad. She raked her hand through her hair and headed to the door. Whoever had the audacity to show up unannounced this early would just have to take what they got.

When she got to the door, a shiver went through her. She was expecting no one, and none of her friends ever dropped by without calling.

"Who's there?" she called.

"Bruce Wyler. I'm answering your ad."

Last night's intruder flashed through her mind, and she felt a trickle of uncertainty.

"Mrs. Maxey? Are you still there?" He gave a short laugh. "I'd really like to see the apartment."

She couldn't afford to lose a renter, and his references were stellar. She swung open the door then stood there, stunned. Was this a mirage? Backlit by the sun, Bruce Wyler seemed to shine. Fair skinned and golden eyed. Wearing a buckskin jacket with fringe, tinted the shade of melted butter by the morning sun.

"Hello," he said. A silver Land Rover was parked in her driveway. "I hope I didn't disturb you. I'm looking for Rachel Maxey."

"That would be me." She self-consciously belted her robe tighter. The famous artist looked exactly like all his photos on his website as well as the newspaper and TV coverage she had seen through the years. And he wanted to rent *her* room. "I thought you were in New York."

His laughter was as appealing as the rest of him. "I've been in the area for weeks—painting. As you can imagine, a hotel room was totally inadequate to meet my needs." He glanced around her property. "This place is everything you said and more. I hope you don't mind my showing up like this. I answered your email, but I guess you didn't get it."

"No, this is..." *Money in the bank. Security. Breathing room.* As if to confirm her judgment, she glanced at her dog. He'd settled on the floor at her feet, content. No alarms there. "Perfect." She hoped she didn't stare when she said that. "Come in, and we can discuss the rental. I'll get you some coffee."

She led Bruce to the kitchen, keeping up a stream of chatter, while Sam trotted back upstairs to be with the children. "I teach so I only have time for a very quick tour of the apartment. Have a seat." She waved toward the breakfast table in a nook with a sweeping view of the forest and distant mountain peaks. "Sugar, Mr. Wyler?"

"No, black. Call me Bruce." He sat nearest the window. "Amazing view. So peaceful."

As if they'd been waiting for their cue, the kids hit the floor upstairs, running, and immediately started a loud squabble over who got the bathroom first. Add Sam's excited barking into the mix, and Rachel worried her rent money was going to be flushed down the drain.

"I have two children. And a dog. Which, of course, you know." Suddenly there was the unmistakable sound of Victoria's cowboy boots on the hardwood floor, heading toward the kitchen. "And a grandmother. But the children are in school most of the day. And the dog is getting old, so he mostly sleeps."

"I'm old, too, but I don't sleep all day." Victoria stood in the doorway in red cowboy boots, well-worn blue jeans, and her favorite, much-faded turquoise cowboy shirt. "My name's Victoria Logan. Who are you?"

Bruce was enchanted. He pushed his chair back, strode toward Victoria, and took both her hands.

"I can hardly believe it. The authentic Old West standing right in front of me." He leaned over to kiss her hand. "I'm the man who is going to paint you and make you famous."

"I don't pose." Victoria pulled her hand back and marched over to busy herself at the coffee pot. "Fame is all a crock of nonsense."

Rachel quickly tried to make amends by introducing Bruce and adding that he was the new renter.

Victoria turned on the charm. "Well, young man. We're glad to have you on board, and we'll all do our best to stay out of your hair." She shooed Rachel toward the door. "Get dressed. I'll keep Bruce in coffee till you get back to show him the apartment. If he behaves himself, I might even offer him some pancakes."

"Just coffee."

Hoping for the best, Rachel hurried off for a quick change then tied back her hair into a low ponytail. When she got back to the kitchen, Gran was dishing up pancakes while the children, perched on barstools, were eyeing the stranger with the suspicion they'd display if he were green with horns and had just climbed up from a pond of scum.

Rachel gave her children a *behave-yourselves* look, and they turned their attention back to their pancakes. In time, they would get used to someone else being on the property.

While Gran took charge of the children, Rachel showed Bruce the basement apartment and was surprised at his enthusiasm, especially when she told him she'd pick up the towels and sheets from the laundry basket in his bathroom at four every Wednesday and Saturday and toss them in with her own laundry.

"Your personal things will be up to you," she told him. "There's a laundromat two miles east of here."

She was thrilled when he didn't balk at those arrangements. She'd briefly weighed giving him the option of coming into the main house through the basement door and using her laundry room, but that didn't feel like the right or the smart thing to do. Three years of being a single parent had taught her to be hyper-vigilant and extra cautious. She told him the door would remain locked to ensure privacy for him as well as the family.

"That's perfectly logical and agreeable," Bruce said. "I'll be out sketching most of the day, anyhow."

He signed the contract and paid the first month's rent in cash. She left him settling in while she went back upstairs to consult with Victoria.

"Are you going to be okay with Bruce Wyler as our renter? Since he has his own entrance and will be gone most of the day, it won't change things much around here."

"I'm onboard with anything that solves our financial problems. Don't worry, Rachel. We'll all going to be fine."

"I hope so."

"I *know* so. You have a good day at school. I'm going to be gone most of the day with my quilting club."

"Have a great day with your friends, Gran."

In spite of the morning's chaos, Rachel was only five minutes late loading the children in the car and heading off toward school. As she drove the familiar route, she glanced at them in the back seat.

"What did you think of our new renter?"

She saw Susan's shrug in the rearview mirror. But Joey was as excited as his sister was nonchalant.

"Can I have a cowboy jacket like his?"

"We'll talk about it later, Joey."

Susan leaned toward her brother. "That means *no*."

"*Mom-my!*"

Joey's high-pitched decibels and plaintive wail spelled trouble. Rachel couldn't handle any more today.

"Susan, it means just what I said. Joey and I will discuss the coat tonight."

Her daughter's blistering silence could mean anything from *I don't care* to *I don't believe you* to *I wonder if I can have a play date with Lulu and Wendy*. Susan maintained her stoic silence all the way to school, a welcome respite for Rachel.

With a renowned artist in her apartment and rent money ready to deposit in her account, she relaxed and enjoyed the drive. It was a sunny, gorgeous day, and the neighbors were outside taking advantage of the weather to repair their pasture fence. They waved when they saw her, and she waved back.

The mailman's car was stopped at a rural box one ranch

down. He honked his horn as she passed by, and she gave her horn an answering toot.

Life had been good in Manitou Springs before the advent of the Collector. Almost idyllic. For a brief interlude, Rachel saw that it might be that way again.

But a faint aroma crept into her car, and her optimism vanished as suddenly as it had come. Like snuffing out a light. The scent was faint, at first, and then it swirled about her in a thick fog...

The unmistakable warning of magnolias.

EIGHT

MANITOU SPRINGS ELEMENTARY SCHOOL

When Rachel pulled into the school parking lot, the horror predicted by the magnolias came true. Cops were everywhere, their cars circled around the campus perimeter like old Western Conestoga wagons fending off the enemy, their uniforms visible at every entrance.

Rachel's first thought was a school shooter. But the scene in front of her lacked the horrific upheaval of a school shooting. There were no clumps of terrified children and teachers outside, nor was anyone being ushered out. In fact, Jake Clement, the crossing guard, was on duty and children were entering the school, some of them accompanied to the door by parents who usually waited in their cars to see their children safely inside.

Still, Rachel's sense of imminent disaster persisted. The scent of magnolias followed her out of the car, and she felt the looming shadows of the mountains. What secrets did they hold?

Getting her two children out of the car was like trying to herd frisky calves into the corral. It didn't help that her mind was whirling with horrible possibilities. The incident in the park, the Collector, Susan harboring fears no child had any business carrying, and now *this*. Police everywhere. If Rachel could, she'd have raced to the top of Pikes Peak just for the release of screaming where no one would hear.

As she escorted Joey to his preschool room, the murmuring of teachers in the hall took on a life of its own. There was an undercurrent of eminent disaster as if a flood of terror had already been unleashed and was about to wash them all away.

She delivered Joey safely to his room and decided she wouldn't let Susan out of her sight until she was safely stowed in second grade. When they were within sight of the door, her daughter bolted and was swallowed up by her classmates. All of them were milling about the room, crying.

Their young teacher, a petite brunette named Tanya Beasley, had red-rimmed eyes. She looked as if she were barely holding herself together.

"Tanya, what's wrong?" Rachel whispered.

"Lulu Vargas was taken from her home last night. She's just... *vanished*." Tanya snuffled into a tissue, her face a mask of sorrow.

The news shattered Rachel's heart. Lulu and Susan were best friends. Except for a hitch in plans, her own daughter would have been there when Lulu was taken.

"I can't believe this..." Fresh terror for her own daughter and her students almost bent Rachel double. She wrapped her arms around Tanya to keep both of them from flying apart. "How are the parents?"

"Broken-hearted. Inconsolable."

Rachel's heart ached for the Vargas family. "How on earth did it happen?"

"You haven't heard about it already?" Tanya regained her composure and handed Rachel a fresh tissue from her pocket. "It was all over the news this morning."

"I didn't see the news this morning." Rachel wiped her own tears. "I can't believe the Collector has struck again."

Rachel thought about the dark-haired little girl who had just moved into a new house in Manitou Springs' newest subdivision. The younger of two daughters. Her dad Rafael, a carpenter; her mom Gracie, a nurse; her sister Juanita, a fifth-grader who had Type 1 diabetes. For weeks Lulu and Susan and Wendy had been planning to have an overnight party after Lulu moved so she could show off her new room.

Sheer luck was the only thing that had kept all three girls from being there last night. The paint Gracie special-ordered for Lulu's room had not arrived, and she didn't want her friends to come until her walls were the exact shade of purple she loved.

Rachel got weak-kneed thinking about the close call. "Do they have any clues?"

"The kidnapper left a Tarot card in her room, just like he did when he left that bear in Eddie Greene's room."

Horrified that the Collector was now snatching children right out of their beds, Rachel glanced at her daughter, now huddled beside her friend Wendy, both of them sobbing. It took every bit of her restraint to harness the mother who wanted to scoop up her child and run.

"My daughter and Wendy are devastated. They were a threesome with Lulu."

"I know." Tanya hugged her again. "But I've got this. Go. Your students need you."

Rachel found her students clustered in small groups, some of them crying, others whispering, all of them looking like a miserable lone calf that sometimes gets lost on the range in a storm.

If Max were here, he'd remind her to get through her day one moment at a time.

She closed her door and steeled herself for being her students' strength, their counselor, their protector, and their current source of comfort.

"Just let me be enough," she whispered.

And then she opened her arms and her heart.

NINE

THE HIDEAWAY

He was so clever. Yes, he was.

He had chosen a job that was flexible. As long as he did his work, he had a certain amount of freedom. He could hurry and get home early, or he could take enough time to do the small errands necessary to create the future he planned.

Never let it be said that he was less than brilliant at anything he set his hand to.

As he parked his car in the garage, anticipation sizzled through him. The girl was waiting for him.

He bounded up the stairs, two at a time. She was still sleeping. He'd given her enough pills to make sure of that. He pulled up a straight chair and sat beside her to watch. She was a beauty with abundant dark hair framing a heart-shaped face. She'd be an asset.

The minute she came to, she lunged at him. Had he taken the wrong child?

This one was a street fighter, kicking and screaming, "This is not what you said!"

"Stop that!" he ordered, but she lunged at him again, her

claws bared. Her strength was surprising considering she was so small, and that she had been drugged since the previous night.

She knew how to attack, too. One well-placed kick narrowly missed his groin, and her little hands raked his arm, bringing blood. Fortunately, the scratch was on his left bicep. He would be able to cover the mark with a long-sleeved shirt.

"If you don't stop that, Daddy's going to do something bad to you."

"You're not my *daddy*!" She spat at him, her contempt on full display. He had to admire her spunk, even as he briefly regretted choosing her instead of one of the other sweet little morsels so easy to pick. Such a plethora of young beauties, he could hardly believe his good fortune.

He wondered if his childhood would have been different if he had shown the same defiance to the witch who spawned him. Would his life have turned out better if he had dared spit in her face and call her the names she deserved? Would she have learned to respect him? To back off and leave him alone?

While his mind was wandering, the girl twisted so fast she almost got loose.

"Fighting won't do you any good. Even if you could get away from me, there's no place for you to run except thousands of acres of forest filled with cougars and all manner of wild things that would be only too happy to eat you alive."

The shock of hearing that brought tears to her big dark eyes. They were her best feature. Oh yes, they were.

With the right training and the proper guidance from a loving father, she would turn into a striking woman who could use those eyes to convince men to do anything she wanted.

Oh, he was brilliant. Yes, he was. He had not made the wrong choice at all. He knew how to pick them. Yes, he did.

"I want to go home," she whimpered.

"You *are* home."

With that, he left her in the bare room with nothing but the cats and turned the key in the deadbolt on the door. A day without food and water wouldn't hurt her. It might even teach her to appreciate the shiny new life that lay in front of her.

You had to be firm with children, firm but loving. You had to teach them respect in a way that wouldn't break them but would make them remember who was boss. You had to take discipline as seriously as providing food, shelter, and clothing. All the best parenting books said so.

Of course, he put his own spin on things, but didn't every good parent do that? Especially the ones as smart as he was.

He stood in the hallway a moment, listening until her whimpers began to subside.

There. She would come around. Just like Mikey.

He tiptoed across the hall and opened the door to his new son's room. He was curved into a sweet ball, still sleeping off the sedative that kept him out of trouble while his daddy had been so busy growing their family. Both little hands were tucked under his cheek, and his little face was turned toward the door.

Had he missed having supper with his daddy last night? Of course he had, but that couldn't be helped. It took time to find the right sister for him, and even more time to execute all his plans for their family. Their perfect family.

He kissed his son on the cheek, then tiptoed from the room. He couldn't contain himself from dancing down the hallway. He stopped his gleeful jig long enough to take out his keys and unlock all the deadbolts on the door.

Anyone watching his jaunty walk downstairs to his own apartment would have seen his dual nature, madness and genius, playing across his face in equal measure, supreme self-confidence and aching self-loathing spooling out behind him like a black carbon ribbon that stained everything it touched.

Soon, he'd be moving upstairs with them. Oh yes, he would. Happy, glorious moving day! He salivated just thinking about it. He was hungry for everything that was to come. Ravenous.

His feathered friends were waiting outside, a cloud of cunning perched in the treetop, begging to be the chosen ones.

"Eenie, meanie, minie, moe."

He was an expert marksman. Oh yes, he was. The crows fell, one by one, until there were four, the magical number, symbol of strength and family. His mantras. Oh yes, they were.

Thanks to the crows he was growing stronger every day. Soon he would rival the Biblical heroes Samson and Goliath. He would surpass the leviathans of the deep. He would fly higher than the eagles. He would own the sky and the earth, unrivaled in power and strength by man and beast, as strong and immovable as the very mountains that surrounded him. People would quake at the sight of him.

The murder of crows perched on high cawed their blessing as their four fallen feathered brothers offered their blood so that it filled the cup to the brim. Delicious red courage. Dark crimson evil. The nectar of legendary heroes.

He drank until the cup was empty. As the blood tide coursed through him, he smacked his lips with satisfaction.

Back inside, his backpack was waiting where he had left it. He pulled her photograph from it, and removed it from the silver frame. He spat on the frame and tossed it into the garbage can. If his hammer hadn't been upstairs, he'd have flattened it into an unrecognizable piece of junk.

But he didn't want to walk back up the stairs, undo all those locks, then trudge back down just for the satisfaction of obliterating the silver frame that represented another life for the beautiful woman in the photograph. Oh no, he did not.

"Hello, darling." He kissed her smiling face, leaving behind a smear of crimson, then carefully placed the photo into a frame worthy of the exalted being she would become. "There. See? Isn't that so much better?"

TEN

MANITOU SPRINGS ELEMENTARY SCHOOL

Rachel was glad when the chaotic morning was over, and she could join the other teachers not on Monday lunchtime duty who had gathered in the teacher's lounge.

There were three of them—Rachel, Lulu's teacher Tanya Beasley, and the oldest of the group, gray-haired, motherly Suzye Bishop, who taught Lulu's sister and was two years from retirement. The mood was somber as they grabbed their lunches from the refrigerator then turned on the small TV to hear Lulu's parents at the press conference outside the sheriff's department.

Sorrow had bleached both of them so that Gracie and Rafael, once so vibrant, looked as gray as putty. They were both short, but the angle of the camera and the large American flag behind them made them seem even smaller. Gracie leaned into her husband, her face a river of tears as she listened to him plead for Lulu.

"She's just a little girl. I'm begging you, whoever took her, please bring her home. That's all we want. Just bring her home safe."

"Please," Gracie whispered, and they both broke down in tears.

The camera cut away to the sheriff who said there were no new leads in the case. He ended the briefing with a short statement. "Finding both Lulu Vargas and Eddie Greene is our top priority."

He left without taking questions, and the regular reporter for the noon news came back on camera. He was a smooth-talking, dark-haired young man with matinee idol looks. "The Collector has struck again."

He stood on the set at the TV station, interviewing none other than Dawn Williams.

"Dawn, tell us about your personal encounter with the Collector."

"I had just returned from walking my dog. Though there was no sign of forced entry, I knew the minute I went into my house something was off."

"What did you do next?"

"At that time there was no reason to call the police, so I systematically searched my house. That's when I noticed it."

"What did you see?"

"My photograph in a small silver frame and my signature fragrance, *La Vie est Belle*, were both missing from my dressing room. The Collector left his calling card behind." Dawn smiled directly into the lens as the camera panned closer to her. "I want my loyal public to know that I am completely unharmed, and there is no damage to my property. As I've said before on my show, the Collector is something of a genius at taking small things that somehow appeal to him while leaving the scene undisturbed and remaining undetected."

"A *genius*?" Tanya Beasley scoffed. "He's the most dangerous criminal the city has ever seen. How does she get by with spouting such garbage on TV?"

"Don't they all?" Suzye said.

Though Rachel's sister Jen had often talked of the lasting psychological damage done to victims of breaking and entering, even if nothing major was stolen, she kept the information to herself. The hatred in the world was bad enough already without her adding fuel to the flames.

While talk swirled around her about the pros and cons of Dawn Williams and her show, she turned her attention to her tuna sandwich and another brief statement from the reporter, echoing the sheriff that there were no leads and no new developments in Lulu Vargas' disappearance.

"This is unbelievable!" Tanya said. "Everybody in this town is on edge, and Lulu's classmates are devastated. I wish we had one little thing that would make them feel better."

"Her sister Juanita told me something that might help." The fifth-grade teacher looked around the room as if somebody might report her and take away her pension.

"Well," Tanya said. "What is it, Suzye?"

"She said there was no sign of struggle or forced entry. Lulu's room looked like she just got out of bed, walked out the back door, and left it wide open."

"Didn't alarms go off?" Rachel thought of her own house, still lacking a security system, and how easy it was for a child to vanish. When she had saved enough money from her rental income, she was going to shore up her security.

"Juanita said they don't have one yet," Suzye said. "The house is still new."

"Lulu's a very responsible little girl." Tanya wadded her napkin and shot it into the garbage can. In high school she had played forward on a championship basketball team, and she never got over her love of shooting hoops. "I can't believe she would do that."

Suzye pushed her glasses up on her nose and closed her

lunch bag. "But maybe if she did, she's simply run away and is somewhere safe."

"That would be wonderful," Tanya said, "but I can't see a happy seven-year-old running away. Besides, I don't know if telling my students would help them or just raise false hopes."

"I agree with Tanya," Rachel said. "We don't know enough to tell our students anything without the risk of starting rumors."

The three teachers nodded their agreement, and Suzye headed back to her classroom.

"Rachel." Tanya reached to touch her arm. "Do you have a minute?"

"Yes." She glanced at her watch. "Four to be exact."

"I overheard Wendy and Susan talking in the girls' bathroom. They had no idea I was in the stall. I think they're keeping a secret."

Was her daughter capable of secrets? The answer was a definitive yes. Sometimes Rachel felt as if Susan was literally vanishing beneath that battered old cape, piece by piece, rushing headlong into forbidden territory that had no map, the labyrinth of her own complicated childhood.

"What did they say, Tanya?"

"The only thing I gleaned was that Lulu had a secret, and they had made a pact not to tell anyone."

Children kept secrets all the time. That they hated their parents for not getting them a dog, that they were planning to run away someday, but not tonight when there was roast beef in the oven. But one involving a little girl who had vanished was not only serious. It was dangerous.

"I'll see what I can find out."

"I knew you would. And since I don't know if it has any relevance to Lulu's disappearance, I'm not going to say anything to the detectives yet. I would hate to see two little girls put through the wringer for nothing."

How did you thank someone who has just handed you a ticking time bomb? Rachel found the grace to do it anyway. Then she went back to her classroom and waited for the endless school day to be over.

ELEVEN

After the bell finally rang, Rachel gathered her children into the car and studied her daughter. Her eyes were red-rimmed from crying, and she shrank into the back seat as if she wanted it to swallow her whole.

Rachel slung her tote bag into the passenger side of the front seat along with her briefcase of papers to grade. Then she turned to face her children.

"Susan, Joey. Today has been a really hard day for all of us. I want both of you to know it's okay to cry and feel upset about Lulu. If there's anything you want to talk to me about, we can talk while I drive or after I get home. You know you can tell me anything. Right?"

Susan nodded, morose, but Joey shouted, "Yes! Can I call Hank to build a tree house when I get home? He said he would."

"I don't think Hank is coming today, Joey. Maybe some other time."

"When?"

"I don't know."

"Call him and ask. I want a tree house! You *promised*!"

Had she? Probably. Didn't every mother occasionally agree to a child's request, no matter how outrageous or extravagant, just to buy five minutes of peace? Still, with her daughter in the back seat carrying the weight of the world on her shoulders and her son issuing demands like Hannibal driving elephants over the Alps, Rachel suddenly had this overwhelming sense of defeat, as if she were failing both her children on all fronts.

She was never going to get any mother-of-the-year award, but she was going to try and do better. Starting with the tree house and then moving on to Susan's secret and the hideous red cape.

"I'll tell you what, Joey. As soon as we get settled down at home and I have a cup of tea, I'll call Hank."

"Yay!" Joey bounced on his seat. "Hank's a good guy, right, Mommy?"

"Yes. Hank is a good man."

"Not like Jake."

Alarm skittered through Rachel. "The crossing guard?"

"Yes."

She could see her son in the rearview mirror, nodding so hard his cowlick bounced up and down.

"Why is Jake a bad man?"

"'Cause he gived me candy at recess. But I threw it away 'cause you said *Joey, don't talk to strangers and don't take gifts.*"

How could this have happened right under her nose? The crossing guard was from a prominent family in Manitou Springs, and he had been carefully vetted. No one had ever reported any deviant behavior from him, at least, not as far as she knew. Could a report have been made and then covered up?

Suddenly Jake Clement loomed large in Rachel's mind. Blond, baby-faced, pouty lipped, mid-thirties, the kind of man young women called cute and cuddly, the kind of man people immediately trusted because of his wide smile and his impeccable manners.

What was he doing working as a crossing guard anyhow? When he'd been hired four years earlier, there had been talk at school about having the most educated crossing guard in Colorado. Some said he had a law degree. Others said no, he had been kicked out of law school, but nobody seemed to know why.

Suzye, who knew everybody in Manitou Springs, said he got the job because his daddy owned the bank, his mother ran the Catholic church, and his uncle was on the school board.

The disturbing picture coalesced in Rachel's mind. A sexual predator in their midst, working among the victims he sought.

"Joey, when did this happen?"

"'Bout forty-'leven times ago."

"Did he grab you or try to touch you?" She glanced in the mirror to see him shaking his head. *No.* Relief flooded her. "This is very important, Joey. Did Jake ask you to do anything for him?"

"Umm hmm." That enthusiastic nod again.

Rachel thought she was going to stop breathing. "What was it?"

"He wanted to take my picture. I said no, 'cause I wanted to swing. Then I runned away."

Rachel could breathe again. Thankfully, no harm had been done so there was nothing that would warrant charges. Still, she would call the sheriff about the incident so he could consider Jake Clement as a possible suspect in the kidnappings. And when she got to school tomorrow, the first thing she would do was investigate why the crossing guard was in the playground giving candy to her son.

"Good boy, Joey. It's very important to do what Gran and I

tell you because we are always trying to keep you safe. Hank is, too."

A quick glance in the mirror showed Joey nodding his head again and Susan shrinking into her seat with her head tucked down.

"Susan, have you or any of your friends ever been approached by the crossing guard?"

"No!" Her daughter's too sharp retort put Rachel on alert, that and the tears that slid down her cheeks.

Oh help. Was this what the magnolias had been warning her about, danger to her children in the very place they should feel most safe?

When she came to the sign over her ranch, she wanted to put her head down on the steering wheel and cry with relief. Gran would be there. Her rock and her best friend. As she navigated the birch-lined driveway, Rachel felt waves of calmness washing through her. Coming home was like slipping off her shoes and sitting in her favorite chair to sip a cup of hot tea.

Gran's ancient pickup was not in the two-car garage, which meant the ladies in her quilting club had so much catching up to do they were still bent over their quilting frames, talking.

In spite of her own selfish needs, she was happy for her grandmother. Victoria needed a break, too. Though she had weathered the years like a champ, losing her only son and daughter-in-law, as well as the love of her life, could not have been as easy as she made it seem.

As Rachel eased her Jeep toward the garage, she was already anticipating a quiet cup of tea. After she'd recharged her batteries enough to be calm and certain, she'd call Rafael and Gracie Vargas to offer her support, then call Hank about Joey's tree house.

Suddenly the empty spot inside Rachel's culinary herb garden caught her attention. Letting the engine idle, she looked closer.

Her garden art was gone, the butterfly Hank had welded together from cast-off pieces of junk metal and given to her for her last birthday. In its place was the unmistakable flicker of a small white card.

"Children, stay in the car." She cut the engine and got out to investigate. An up-close inspection confirmed her suspicions. The card was Justice from the Tarot deck.

Fear made her weak-kneed. She had challenged the Collector on TV, and he had come calling. Had he scoped the garden out last night under the cover of darkness? How had he known she and the children would be in school and Victoria would be at her weekly quilting club? Had he been watching the house to see their pattern? Or had he already been on the premises and merely seized his opportunity?

She could answer any of those speculations with logic. But how had he chosen the only object in her garden that had any real sentimental value to her, a simple, lopsided butterfly made of nuts and bolts and ragged pieces of tin then painted in psychedelic colors that made Rachel smile?

"Now, that's what I wanted to see," Hank had said when he gave her the garden art. Then, a bit self-conscious, he'd added, "Max would be proud of you."

She had cherished that hand-made butterfly, had counted on the rainbow colors to cheer her up every morning, to remind her that she was not a woman alone raising two children. She had stellar backup in the form of her husband's best friend, a kind and capable man trained in martial arts and more than willing to spend his spare time giving her a helping hand.

There is an old saying that you don't appreciate what you have until you've lost it. Losing her garden art was nothing compared to the Vargas family's loss, but still, the gift grew larger and more significant in her mind because it had come from Hank, and because it was now gone and she might never get it back, and because she was so tired of struggle and disappointment she wanted to stretch out on the empty spot in her garden and pound her fists into the earth.

Suddenly the sweet scent of flowers she couldn't quite identify swirled around her.

Sometimes the Fates will send signs that they are not done with you yet.

TWELVE

LOGAN RANCH

Rachel climbed back into her car and Joey kicked the back of the driver's seat. "Mommy! Hurry up and park. I want to play cowboy."

Her son's game of cowboy meant racing into the woods and over the trails he knew so well, trails that would take him through the trees and undergrowth, alternately in and out of her sight.

"Not today, Joey." Not with the Collector possibly still lurking around and the crossing guard offering candy for favors and Lulu Vargas missing. "I thought I'd make popcorn so you and Susan can watch *The Little Mermaid*."

She finished parking and got the children inside to a chorus of protests and a series of negotiations that included letting them play dress-up from her closet so they could be Ariel and Sebastian, the singing crab, while they watched the movie.

After she finally settled them in front of the TV with Sam guarding from his position on the rug, she hurried outside to her herb garden. The Tarot card, Justice, stared up at her, the scales of justice in the queen's left hand and the double-edged sword held aloft in her right hand as threatening to Rachel as if the bogey man himself were standing behind her with a gun to her head.

She wanted to snatch up the card and tear it to pieces. Instead, she went into her kitchen for a pair of disposable gloves and a plastic bag. The sounds of the children's movie plus a quick glance into the den assured her that Joey and Susan hadn't been taken from under her nose.

Returning to her garden, she carefully bagged the Tarot card then sank onto a nearby garden bench. Max was no longer there to be proud of her or provide for her and the kids or protect them.

It was all up to her. She could almost hear her husband's voice.

Buck up, Rach. You've got this.

Under ordinary circumstances, Max would be right. But considering the horrifying string of recent events, she didn't dare leave her family's safety in her own hands.

The first call she made was to the El Paso County Sheriff's Department. She briefly recapped her conversation with Joey in the car that led her to believe the crossing guard could possibly be the Collector, and then she told the sheriff about the theft and the card she'd bagged in her own garden.

"I'll be right there," he said. "Don't touch anything else. Leave the scene exactly as you found it."

Defeat washed over her as she replayed events of the last few days. What else had she said or done wrong? And how could an ordinary person ever know how to behave under extraordinary circumstances? Still, she should have thought before she touched a crime scene. Hadn't she watched enough TV crime dramas with Victoria to know better?

"I'm sorry, Sheriff. I didn't think." She was no Wonder Woman, not even close. She didn't even want to be, for goodness' sake. She just wanted to have a peaceful, ordinary, and sane life.

"That's okay, Rachel. You bagged evidence the right way. Maybe we'll get lucky and find some prints."

She was getting ready to call Hank Carson when her grandmother drove up. Rachel waved her down before she got to the garage and briefed her on the theft as well as Lulu's kidnapping.

"The quilting club heard about Lulu on the noon news. It's just horrible!" Victoria glanced toward the garden. "I wish I'd been here when that snake came crawling around. I'd have given him a taste of old Betsy."

Rachel had a frightening image of her aging grandmother facing the Collector with her equally old shotgun. "I'm glad you weren't. He might have hurt *you*." It was a small blessing her grandmother had been gone. Thinking back, Rachel realized the Collector's reported thefts had always occurred when the owners weren't home. "I'm waiting for the sheriff. Keep the kids inside, Gran. I don't want them to see the law here, especially Susan."

"Don't worry. I won't let them out of my sight."

While Victoria maneuvered her pickup into the garage, Rachel placed her call to Hank. He answered on the second ring. She hadn't realized she was holding her breath till she heard his voice.

"Oh, Hank." She breathed relief. "Thank goodness! I didn't know if you'd be there."

He owned Hank's Charters and Helicopter Tours in Colorado Springs. Though it was a few weeks too early for him to be transporting skiers to the ski areas of the Southern Rocky Mountains, he'd still be very busy flying private charters to Denver as well as doing helicopter tours of Colorado's many spectacular sites, including the High Country, Royal Gorge, Red Canyon, Pikes Peak, and Garden of the Gods.

"Do you have a minute?" she added.

"For you, always. What's up?"

Until she was spilling her soul to Hank, including her fears for her children, she hadn't realized how much she'd needed to confide in someone besides her immediate family. As always, Hank was the perfect sounding board, listening respectfully without inserting his own opinion and showing no impatience, no matter how incoherent she sounded or how she rambled.

"I'll be right there, Rachel."

"I don't want to take you from your work."

"Not a problem. I just hired two new guys to help me take up the slack."

"The kids will be glad to see you."

And so will I.

The thought took her unaware, and something inside her shifted. Her long-held belief that Hank was merely her husband's best friend and a blessed protection for her family faded away, and in its place was a quiet realization that, with Hank, anything might be possible.

THIRTEEN

HANK'S OFFICE | COLORADO SPRINGS, COLORADO

Hank grabbed his Stetson, the iconic brand of cowboy hat no Texan would be without. As he climbed into his truck, he wondered if Rachel would be glad to see him.

He quickly pushed the thought from his mind. Max had been his best buddy, his comrade in arms. Hank had given him a solemn vow that if anything bad happened, he'd take care of Rachel and the children.

That's why he'd chosen to base his charter company in Colorado Springs instead of his home state of Texas three years ago. He'd wanted to be close enough so his promise was more than empty words delivered under high stress. In a world of quick gratification, pop psychology, and frantic but meaningless activity, Hank was determined not only to fulfill his sworn duty to Max but to show a level of care and understanding for his buddy's surviving family that would reflect the true meaning of friendship.

Still, when he'd made the promise, he had no idea of the trap he'd set for himself. Sure, he'd been halfway smitten with Rachel from the moment Max showed him her photo all those years ago. She was gorgeous, no doubt about it. Add a generous heart, a big personality, and a lively sense of humor, and she'd turned out to be the perfect woman for Max.

Who was he kidding? She'd turned out to be the woman nobody else could measure up to in Hank's mind. Since Max's death, he'd seen Rachel at her worst and her best. He'd witnessed every emotion like a neon sign for the world to see, from deep grief to fierce denial to grudging acceptance. But he'd also seen flashes of unbounded joy and deep passion for everything she loved, from her family to the students, to the land that he, Texan born and bred, had also come to love.

In spite of his best intentions to remain strictly friends, he'd failed. Though she still viewed him only as a friend, Rachel was the reason he dated so few women. And those he did take out were doomed to disappoint. He was straddling an uncomfortable fence, and if he didn't get off soon, he was going to end up growing old in a house filled with silence and echoes of what might have been.

When Hank pulled up in Rachel's driveway, he expected to see Sheriff Jeremiah Johnson. What he didn't expect was an unfamiliar Land Rover with New York plates in her yard and a stranger beside her who looked as if he'd been buffed with car wax from head to toe. The blond man had adopted a protective stance over Rachel that should have been reassuring to Hank, but somehow it wasn't.

The man's attentions felt personal, and that got under Hank's skin. When Rachel spotted him and hurried his way, he put the stranger out of his mind. She took up all the space. Nothing else seemed to matter except the worry on her face and the anxiety in her dark eyes.

"Hank. I'm so glad you're here."

He'd take the compliment. Savor it, even. She grabbed his hand and didn't let go as she led him back to her culinary herb garden where she introduced the stranger as Bruce Wyler, a painter and her new renter.

Hank studied the man, trying to read him.

Bruce was as closed-off as if someone had taken a paint brush and applied a thick coat of shellac.

"Rachel was really upset when I got home from sketching." Bruce flashed his smile at her. "I'm glad I was here for her."

Hank couldn't fault the man for giving Rachel the support she needed.

He turned his attention to the sheriff, who was passing the plastic bag containing the Collector's calling card to the forensics expert. The sight made Hank uneasy.

He made up his mind he'd check on her more often. He would definitely start driving by her house a couple of times in the evening just to check things out. Rachel would say no, of course. She was stubborn that way. Still, one of the many things he admired about her was her fierce independence.

Hank turned to the sheriff. "Have they found any forensics yet?"

"Nothing. The Collector never leaves a single piece of evidence. He's one of the most meticulous criminals I've ever encountered."

"Sheriff." The forensics expert, Stella Chaiya, a petite dour-faced woman who was rumored to have been caught smiling only once—when her husband Benz, the owner of the Golden Thai Restaurant, won the trophy for the best coffin in the annual Emma Crawford Coffin Races three years ago. She held up a baggie containing what appeared to be some blond hair and a few fibers. "At last, we got something."

Bruce stuffed his hands into the pockets of his buckskin jacket. "Those are probably mine. I was out here sketching this morning before I left for the Tee Cross Ranch."

Sheriff Johnson scowled. "Anybody see you here?"

"I don't know. Rachel and the children were at school and Mrs. Logan had already left."

"How long were you here?" Jeremiah had pulled a small

spiral bound notepad from his pocket and jotted notes as he questioned the man.

"A couple of hours maybe. But when I'm painting, I don't watch the clock."

"And in all that time you didn't see or hear anybody else?"

"I think there was a car on the road about midday."

"What kind of car?" the sheriff asked.

"I didn't look. I just heard it."

"Probably the mailman," Rachel said. "He usually comes around that time."

Jeremiah Johnson nodded toward the Land Rover. "And that's your car, Mr. Wyler?"

"Yes."

Tension came off Rachel in waves. Hank slid his arm around her, and she leaned against him. He held on to her. Simply held on.

"So, Mr. Wyler," the sheriff said. "How long have you been in this area?" Jeremiah Johnson pulled off his hat and scratched his head as if he were confused. It was all an act. Nothing escaped him, and he was decisive to a fault.

"That's hard to say."

"Why would that be?"

"I've been working on this collection for nearly two years, but for the past five years I've focused on art with a Western perspective. I come and go from the Bronx as needed to capture my subject matter."

Five years seemed an excessive time to work on one collection. Hank had to remind himself that he knew nothing of the way an artist works. But still, years of serving in the military gave you a built-in danger detector. Made you check behind doors and around every corner. Bruce Wyler was a renowned artist with impeccable credentials. But he had easy access to Rachel, the most precious person in this world to Hank. He had to be ever-vigilant, lest he lose her as unexpectedly as he had lost Max.

The sheriff scanned his notebook then eyed his person of interest. "Mr. Wyler, we have a problem here."

The unspoken problem loomed in the garden like a two-ton African elephant. Even the renter—unless he'd lived under a rock and never turned on the TV—had to be aware that the Collector had been operating within the timeframe he just handed the sheriff.

Bruce Wyler rocked back on his heels, completely at ease with himself and the situation. He even flashed one of those polished smiles that made Hank think of some of the actors who had used his charter services for quick sightseeing jaunts or easy access between home and a movie set.

"Let me put your mind at ease," Bruce told the sheriff. "I have the sketchbook to prove what I was doing."

"I'll take a look," the sheriff said. "Now."

Bruce moved off, his polished manners still on full display and his confidence unshaken. Hank couldn't say he liked the man any better for it. He just wanted to get Rachel out of a situation that had her on edge, and he wanted to assure himself that the renter didn't have something worrisome in his background that would make life harder for her. Not paying his bills, for instance. Art seemed a sorry way to make a living.

In Hank's mind, *anybody* this close to Rachel while the Collector was on the prowl needed a closer look. He knew a private investigator who could find out everything he needed to know about the renter. He made a mental note to give him a call.

"Are you done with Rachel?" he asked the sheriff. "She needs to be inside with her children."

Jeremiah Johnson nodded. "While you're inside, take a look around and see if anything else is missing."

Rachel didn't protest when Hank put his arm around her shoulders and led her back to the house.

"Thanks for the rescue, Hank. I was going to ask the sheriff the same thing."

"I know you were."

She gave him a shaky smile. "You're a good friend. And the children need a respite from everything that's happening. Stay for dinner?"

"Of course."

He'd have stayed even if she said it was the dog who needed him. He pulled off his Stetson at the door and hung it on the hat rack in the entry hall.

It looked perfect there. As if it belonged.

FOURTEEN
LOGAN RANCH

Until Hank led her inside her house, Rachel hadn't realized how desperately she needed to get away from the garden.

Bruce Wyler had arrived shortly after her call to Hank. And from that moment the full gravity of her situation had come crashing down on her.

The minute Bruce saw her face, shattered by loss and pinched by fear, he strode over and wrapped her in a hug that felt wonderful and scary at the same time. Wonderful because he was a big handsome man with muscular arms that felt as if they would always keep you safe, and scary because the scent of honeysuckle made a sudden appearance, swirling around the garden, clinging to Rachel's hair and Bruce's jacket, though it was past honeysuckle blooming season and there wasn't a vine for miles around. Victoria had been rigorous about keeping the invasive vine off the ranch.

The fragrance of honeysuckle brings uncertainty.

The scent was a clear warning that the Collector had been there. Was he still on the ranch, hiding in the trees to see the havoc he had unleashed? Waiting to snatch her children?

Bruce sensed her alarm. Still holding her as if she were

made of porcelain and glass, he leaned back to study her. "Rachel, are you all right?"

"I'm distressed." She extracted herself. Naturally, she did. Getting emotionally involved with a renter was the easiest way to lose the rent money she so desperately needed. Plus, she was absolutely not interested in whatever he might imagine he had to offer. "I just discovered some missing garden art and this."

She held up the bagged Tarot card, and was stunned at the play of emotions that flitted across Bruce's face. Comprehension and over-the-top curiosity. Or had her overwrought imagination conjured that?

A more careful study showed the man standing in front of her was simply giving a small smile of encouragement.

"The Collector's calling card must be upsetting for you, Rachel. Are your grandmother and your children okay?"

"Thankfully, they are."

The arrival of the sheriff thankfully put an end to her private interaction with Bruce Wyler, but the faint scent of honeysuckle still swirled around Rachel, climbing up her legs, twining around her arms, and tangling in her hair.

And why not?

Her gift of discerning warnings from scent was always with her.

Now, standing inside her own hallway, Rachel told herself to breathe. Just breathe. Then she let her home fold her in protective arms.

She had always loved this house, unlike her sisters who viewed it as a mausoleum and the ranch as a millstone tying them to a place they couldn't wait to leave. Their grandfather, Finn, who had outlived his only son and his daughter-in-law, knew all three of his granddaughters well. In his will he had left large chunks of stock to Jen and Annie but had bequeathed the house and the ranch to Rachel with the caveat that she would take care of Victoria.

For Rachel, the beloved house held a collection of memories that spanned through time all the way back to childhood—golden summers spent with Jen and Annie playing dress-up with period clothes they'd found in a trunk in the attic; the dappled days of spring when both parents were alive and she could follow her daddy to the barn and see a calf being born; Thanksgiving and Christmas holidays, past and present, where a blazing fire and a box of glass ornaments kept the frozen world at a distance.

But most of all, the love and joy she'd had during her all-too-brief time with Max was still trapped inside the walls. A palpable thing.

Standing beside the hat rack where Hank's Stetson gave off the aroma of sweat and sunshine, Rachel closed her eyes, hoping the joy would soak right through her skin and wash away the recent turmoil, if only for a moment.

"Are you okay?"

Hank's hand on her arm felt right, almost like a cherished memory, a sudden realization she couldn't let herself even consider amidst the current upheaval.

"I am. I just needed to breathe."

"Take your time. I'm here."

She gave herself another moment. When she felt her body shifting into take-charge mode, chin up, shoulders square, she led Hank into the den.

Sam merely lifted his head and sniffed the air, then put his paws back on his forelegs, content nothing was required of him. Not even a bark.

But the children raced toward Hank squealing, their arms wide open. When he scooped them both up in a bear hug, Rachel was momentarily transported back to another time when Max would lift baby Joey in one arm and scoop up Susan with the other. Golden moments. Precious memories.

"How are my two favorite kids?" Hank's big heart and

genuine joy in the children warmed Rachel as if she'd backed up to an open fire.

Susan and Joey began talking at the same time, spilling current events mixed with fear and uncertainty. Her children needed this, the undivided attention of a man they adored and trusted. They even needed time away from the sometimes-smothering love of their mother, just as she needed an occasional respite from them.

Giving Hank a thumbs-up, Rachel left the den and began a systematic search of the downstairs, starting with the office near the front entry.

At first glance, everything looked as it should. Not a thing out of place. But the chill that crept through her, the still-present scent of honeysuckle, and the intuitive sense that someone had been there told a different story. She swept her glance over the room once more. Suddenly she froze.

The spot where Max had placed a small photo of her was empty. It was the last picture he'd ever taken of her, a year before he was killed. She'd been on the trail in the woods, running. When she emerged, her hair clinging to her face in damp curls, her skin dappled with sunlight and shadow, he'd snapped the picture.

Furious at the lingering feeling of invasion still polluting her home, she forced herself to put on a calm face as she hurried back to the den and mouthed to Hank, *found something*. He gave her a thumbs-up then headed outside to fetch the sheriff while Rachel sank onto the sofa between her children.

"Kids, if you'll stay in here with Gran a while longer, I'll have a wonderful surprise for you." She racked her brain to think of something quick and easy.

"I don't want a 'prize," Joey said. "I want to play outside."

As she explained he couldn't go outside yet, she was seized by inspiration and cajoled him with promises to make s'mores.

Rachel wanted to catch the Collector and wipe him off the

face of the map. How *dare* he add fear and necessary lies to the mix of problems she already had to worry about? How *dare* he turn the lives of her innocent children upside down so that nothing was normal and even the ordinary pleasure of building frog houses and reading underneath a canopy of fall leaves was denied to them?

"I can handle things here, Rachel." Gran shooed her away, and she hurried to meet Hank, who was coming through the door with the sheriff and the forensics team.

"This way." She led them into the office and pointed out the spot where her photograph had once stood.

"Is this all you found?" The sheriff was already searching around the bookshelves.

"Yes. But I haven't finished searching the house yet."

"Are you sure you didn't move the photograph somewhere else?"

"Positive."

As the sheriff scanned the bookshelves, he slipped on a plastic glove, reached between the spines of two books, and removed another Tarot card.

"Bingo," he said.

The sight of Justice sent cold chills all over Rachel. The Collector had already snatched two children, Lulu from inside her own home. Terror and fury stormed through her, and she balled her hands into fists. How dare he invade her home, touch her possessions, take things that didn't belong to him! She wanted to scream, cry, kick the furniture.

Overwhelmed, she sank into a chair and lowered her head into her hands. "He's after my children."

When Hank knelt beside the chair and slid his arms around her, she felt as if she were suddenly cocooned in safety. "Rachel could be right," he told the sheriff. "This is personal."

"Maybe. Maybe not. He's taken family photos before." The

sheriff passed off the card to Stella then continued his methodical search for clues.

Rachel's apprehension inched up a notch. What would he find next?

As if Hank had read her mind, he steered her toward the door. "I'll help search the rest of the house."

Rachel was relieved to have him shadowing her as she moved through her home. Though she rarely let herself dwell on the fact that every problem, large and small, was hers to solve and hers alone, she couldn't help but remember what it had been like when Max was there, shouldering the burdens, easing her fears, taking care of things in his quiet, efficient way that made it look easy.

It wasn't. As much as she loved being independent, she sometimes felt overwhelmed by the loneliness and the burden of taking care of every little thing. Sometimes she wondered what it would be like to be part of a couple again. The simple joy of it. The pleasure of touch. The warmth of hugs. The freedom to breathe easy, to laugh often and to know that whatever happened, the two of you would handle it together.

Still, she knew she'd been luckier than most women in her position. She had a home and a supportive, loving family. She also had her husband's best friend, who helped to fill the gaps.

"Hank, thank you for being here. Again. I don't tell you often enough."

"Where else would I be?"

Something in his voice made her search his face. But he had his back to the window, and the bright wash of sunlight obscured his expression. Still, she held his gaze a moment longer, as if she might dive into his ocean eyes and unlock the mysteries hidden in their depths.

"Rachel, you need a security system."

His practical suggestion snapped the spell that had been woven around them. Rachel should have been relieved. The practical side of her knew that. She couldn't risk losing Hank's friendship—especially now—by giving in to feelings that were so new to her she couldn't be certain whether she was turning to him for comfort and security, or whether she was gravitating toward him as if she'd just discovered he was her North Star.

Rachel shoved her personal feelings aside. She and Hank had talked about a security system many times over the past three years. He'd even offered to buy one for her and pay the monthly security monitoring fee, but she was too stubborn to accept that kind of charity. Even from a friend as good as Hank.

"You're right. I need a security system, and I'm saving for that. But right now, Sam is enough."

"Not this time. I'm getting you one tomorrow."

"I can't let you do that…"

"I'm not asking. I promised Max I would keep you safe."

"You've kept that promise. And I don't think Max meant in perpetuity and at your expense."

"The Collector targeted *you*. You need something besides an ancient dog to protect you and the children. If you won't let me do this as a gift, think of it as a loan without interest and with an open-ended pay-back date."

Hank was right. Her *alarm* dog was not adequate, and she couldn't jeopardize her children's safety by being stubborn.

"In that case, thank you."

As they headed upstairs and into Joey's room, she wondered if Sam had been inside the house or in the fenced-in back yard when the intruder came. The doggie door in the kitchen allowed him access to both. Giving him the freedom of the outdoors as well as the shelter of the inside was the only way Rachel could leave him all day. Granted, Victoria was usually here with Sam and would see to his needs, but the doggie door made it possible for her grandmother to do what she wanted without having to worry about taking care of him.

It would also have made it possible for Sam to come inside

while the Collector was here. Had he? If he'd tried to stop the thief, wouldn't there be signs? Scuff marks on the floor? Small objects knocked off side tables?

Rachel re-focused on the task at hand, much harder to do in a room cluttered with Joey's toys and the many treasures he brought inside—bird feathers, rocks that resembled turtles, odd bits of string, sticks that looked like nothing she could imagine.

"Rachel, how did the dog seem when you got home? Was he anxious? Whining?"

"He acted no differently than he usually does."

"I wouldn't pan that off to old age."

Feeling as if she'd been welded to the floor by a bolt of lightning, she paused in the act of searching Joey's closet. "Do you think the Collector is somebody I know?"

"More to the point, somebody *Sam* feels comfortable with. It's worth mentioning to Jeremiah."

"I agree. As soon as we finish checking Joey's room." A quick look in her son's closet showed nothing was amiss.

Her daughter's room was easier. Organized. The bookshelves were overflowing, but otherwise Susan's room revealed no more about her than her own reserved personality.

"That's it." She rolled her shoulders to rid herself of tension.

"I'm going to bunk on your sofa tonight, and I'm going to teach you a few self-defense moves that will be easy for you." Hank draped an arm around her and held on all the way back down the stairs.

Her first instinct was to protest. When he added, "That's not negotiable," the full impact of her situation hit Rachel.

"That would be... great, actually." For the first time that day, she felt like smiling. "By the way, what happened out there with my renter? Did you find out?"

"His notebook sketches proved Bruce was telling the truth about what he was doing, so he's in the clear for now. But in my opinion, we can't rule out anybody. Until we find the Collector, every man in this town should be under scrutiny. Trust no one."

"Hank, I checked Bruce out thoroughly before I rented to him. I would never have someone in my home I didn't trust. He has impeccable credentials and a long history of success and respect in the art world. And he's never been anything except gracious to me and my family."

"Still, I stand by my statement. Nobody is in the clear until this is over."

"I've known most of the men in this town for years—my preacher, my banker, my butcher. I could go on and on. Why on earth would any of those good men, particularly a famous artist, engage in criminal activity?"

"Why does anybody? The psyche is hidden."

"For good reason, Hank. Wouldn't it be terrifying to walk about and see evil intentions showing in a person's face?"

"Maybe we could see it now if we just looked close enough."

That sounded so much like something Max would say that Rachel experienced a moment of déjà vu.

She pushed the argument aside as they went into the office downstairs. Hank was her most trusted friend, and he always had her best interests at heart.

Jeremiah was finishing his work. She and Hank reported their thoughts about the dog's apparent refusal to challenge an intruder.

"Good thinking." Jeremiah jotted some notes. "We'll be done here in a minute and be out of your hair. And, Rachel, we will be following up on your tip about the crossing guard."

"Thanks for coming." Rachel hoped her smile conveyed her deep gratitude. The sheriff and his deputies were some of the hardest working people she knew.

"That's what we're for."

After the sheriff and his team left, Hank said, "What's this about the crossing guard. Jake Clement, right?"

As Rachel told him what Joey had said, he kept his face carefully neutral. Only his eyes betrayed his turmoil.

"I'll look into that, myself. Meanwhile, be on your guard around him, and get ready for some intensive self-defense work after dinner."

"I will." Rachel felt better merely sharing that burden with Hank. "I hate to add one more thing to your plate, but Joey is pestering me about the tree house he seems to think the two of you are going to build..."

"We are. I'll let you in on a little secret."

"What?"

"I'm doing it as much for myself as for him. I always wanted one."

"Hmmm? I believe you're talking about a castle in the trees instead of a few planks across a limb."

"*Planks on a limb*? Madame, where is your imagination? Joey's treehouse is going to be the envy of all his friends." He glanced at his watch. "In fact, we have time to start building today."

"There's something we have to do first. Follow me."

"To the moon and back." When they got to the kitchen, he pretended to be hugely disappointed. "This is not the moon."

"We're making s'mores with the kids."

"That's more like it. Where's my apron?"

He nabbed his favorite, a faded blue bib apron she'd bought many years ago, before children, on a rare vacation she and Max had made to the seacoast of Maine. *Moody's Diner* was printed in white across the front of the bib. It brought back memories that for the first time Rachel realized she could savor without pain. A small miracle.

Her grandmother had told her that the tides of time would gradually wash away the debris of hurt and leave behind precious memories she could collect and enjoy like seashells on the beach.

As she gathered the makings of her children's treat, she glanced out the window. The Collector—unpredictable thief, kidnapper, murderer—had turned his attentions toward her and her family.

Was he coming for her children?

FIFTEEN

Alone at last, Rachel rinsed her coffee cup then stood at her kitchen window gazing at the night sky, grateful her family was safe, grateful Hank was staying overnight, and more than relieved that the day was over. The Collector's visit to her home, piled on top of Lulu's disappearance, made this one of the worst Mondays in her memory.

She needed her older sister. Needed to hear her voice, listen to a good dose of her sound logic. But most of all, she needed to touch base with the sister who had been almost like a mother to her growing up, always there for Rachel and Annie, always taking up the slack left by Delilah's carelessness.

With Hank in the den, Victoria already retired to her room, and both children upstairs waiting for their bedtime stories, Rachel went into her bedroom to call Jen. She wanted her sister's advice on how to handle Susan's secret.

Tanya Beasley did tend to go overboard sometimes, which was typical of young teachers without enough experience to know the difference between ordinary behaviors and alarming ones.

Rachel, who loved pink almost as much as her daughter,

sank into a chair with rose damask cushions and watched out her window as the stars and moon put on a dramatic display of light and shadow across her yard. It seemed impossible that evil could ever get a foothold amidst such beauty.

And yet, cold fingers of fear crept up Rachel's spine and her heart beat too fast, as if eyes were watching her, even in the safety of her own home.

No one was there, of course. The Collector had already come and gone, all the squad cars had vanished, and Bruce was in his basement apartment, doing whatever famous artists do in the evening.

She was just tired, that's all, emotionally drained from an endless day that started with tragedy and ended with personal heartbreak. Still, she scanned her room, looking for anything out of place, any indication that somehow, someone was watching. And waiting.

When her cell phone rang, she nearly jumped out of her chair. It was her younger sister calling from Assisi, Italy, in what would be the early hours of the morning for Annie. She was requesting FaceTime.

Even at three a.m. from the other side of the ocean, Annie was gorgeous, a turquoise-eyed beauty with a thick cascade of wavy auburn hair. Rachel could see the sliver of a moon shining through the window behind her wrought-iron bed.

"Rachel! Are you going hiking?"

Annie rarely said hello. Maybe it was the artist in her who naturally broke every rule. Maybe it was Delilah in her whose intuitions were so urgent she had no time for the small inconveniences of social behavior imposed by society. Maybe she really did inhabit another plane—a glamorous, glorious, magical alternate reality that others could only dream about.

"Not at this time of night. No, I'm not. Hello, Annie. What are you doing up so late?"

"I'm not up. A dream woke me up. Rachel, don't go to the woods. You'll be in danger there."

Other people might write Annie off as a kook, an artist who carried her creativity too far, perhaps even an artist like Van Gogh slowly going mad with his massive talent and the wild swirling of colors and impressions constantly pushing him to put brush to canvas.

"Catch your breath, sis. I'm not going hiking or camping or planning any outdoor activities. What did you see?"

"You were in a forest thick with trees and fog. There was danger everywhere. Especially from the wild things. Birds, I think. And you couldn't get out. Please stay out of the woods, Rachel."

"I will, Annie."

"You promise?"

"I *promise*. Go back to sleep and don't worry. We're all fine here."

"Are you sure? You don't sound fine. Jen told me about the Collector." Annie was like that. As meticulous about personal details as she was about the details in her art.

Rachel reassured her once more. "Hank even gave me a lesson in self-defense after dinner. And he's staying overnight to ensure our safety."

When Annie was finally satisfied, she blew a kiss then ended the connection.

Rachel thought about the acres of forest surrounding her property and the sense of foreboding she'd had since the afternoon. Was Annie's dream about the Collector being on her property today, probably stealing there through the woods, or did it go back to the evening Susan swore she'd seen someone looking at her through the window, maybe someone who had been hiding in the woods beyond?

Sighing, Rachel called Jen's number. Her older sister answered on the first ring.

"Rachel, I was going to call you. I've had those dratted seagulls bashing their brains out against my office windows all day, so you might as well get right to the bad news instead of pussyfooting around with niceties."

"You don't do nice, Jen."

"You've got that right. What's up?"

"The Collector hit my house today, Susan's best friend disappeared last night, and I think she and her friend Wendy are keeping a secret that might be relevant to the kidnapping."

"That explains the seagulls."

Always the peacemaker in the family, Rachel didn't comment. Nor did she tell her sister about Annie's phone call or the floral scents that still swirled through her house. While she constantly fought her past, Jen had always embraced their mother's mystical signs and predictions. So had Annie. In fact, of the three sisters, Annie was most like Delilah Broussard, both in creativity and temperament. She was also high maintenance, just like their mother.

Sometimes it was a relief to Rachel that Annie had moved so far away. But then the minute she felt the unburdening, she felt guilt. Being part of a family was so complicated, it was a wonder anybody ever got married and had children.

"Let me guess, Rachel. You've seen signs."

"I don't want to talk about it. I want to know how to find out about Susan's secret."

"You have to talk to her about the difference between good secrets, like surprise birthday parties and gifts hidden for Christmas, and dangerous secrets that can hurt someone."

"What if she still won't tell me?"

"There's always that possibility. How is she acting?"

"Withdrawn, more so than usual. Upset, which is understandable. She's clinging to that wretched red cape as if Martians are coming to get her and it can ward off spaceships."

"Be patient with her, but firm." Jen sighed. "I don't know why I said that. You don't know how to be firm."

"Sometimes I do."

"Good. Do it more often. Find your inner lioness, Rachel. I found mine a long time ago. I can't tell you how liberating it is."

Jen had the perfect career, the perfect husband, and the perfect pre-teen children. Rachel didn't know what her sister had to be liberated *from*.

For that matter, her own life was messy and sometimes hard, but she wouldn't trade her family and her situation for all the liberation in the world.

"Thanks for the advice, Jen." As Rachel slid her phone back into her pocket, she had the sensation that even her own lamp was listening to her, watching her.

Moving quickly across the room, she slid her hand around the base and the shade, looking to see if she had been bugged. She even searched every surface of her bedside table and the headboard of her bed then moved to look behind every picture frame and trinket on her chest of drawers.

Nothing. She was being skittish, that's all.

Rachel squared her shoulders and said, "Okay, I'm a lioness." Then she went upstairs to tackle the hard work of getting her daughter to talk.

SIXTEEN

Before Rachel began the arduous task of getting Susan to spill secrets, she veered into Joey's room to read his bedtime story.

He beamed at her. "Me and Hank made a floor high in the tree!"

"I know. That's wonderful." She tucked the covers under his chin then selected his bedtime favorite, *Goodnight, Moon*.

He was so tuckered out from working on his tree house, he fell asleep before Rachel could finish the book. She kissed his cheek then went into her daughter's room.

Susan was reading against a pile of pillows, the awful cape over her gown, her earbuds in as she simultaneously listened to music. Rachel sat on the edge of the bed and took her daughter's hand.

"Mom?" Susan jerked the earbuds out. "I didn't hear you come in."

"Do you want me to read you a bedtime story?"

"I quit today. I'm too old."

Her daughter made the pronouncement with the solemnity of someone aged seventy-five instead of seven. Rachel saw her daughter's childhood slipping away while she sat there, helpless to stop it.

"Then let's talk."

"I don't want to. I'm sleepy."

I am a firm mother.

"I know you are, but I need to talk to you." Rachel kicked off her shoes, drew back the covers, and scooted in beside her daughter. "It's been a long time since we had a mother-daughter chat."

Susan rolled her eyes, an all-too-grown-up reaction for her age. "There's nothing to talk about."

"But there is. We all love Lulu and we need to do everything possible to find her. And that includes telling everything we know that might help."

"I don't know anything."

"What about the crossing guard? Joey seems a bit scared of him. Has he ever scared you or Lulu or Wendy?"

"Joey makes up things."

"What kind of things?"

"Jake is nice to everybody, especially me and Wendy and Lulu."

Fear shivered through Rachel. "*How* is he nice to you?"

When her daughter turned away, Rachel cupped her face to bring her back in eye contact. "Sweetheart, look at me. Has the crossing guard ever suggested anything inappropriate to you or Lulu or Wendy?"

"Mom!"

I am a lioness.

"Susan, good secrets like surprise birthday parties are a lot of fun. They're safe, too. But if someone tells you something that might cause bad things to happen, like taking Lulu out of her home, that's a dangerous secret. You should never keep a secret like that."

"I'm *not*!"

"If Lulu or Wendy ever asked you to keep a dangerous secret, you can always tell me, and I won't be mad. You know that, don't you?"

"I just want to go to sleep." Susan rolled away and pulled the covers over her head, a barrier that Rachel couldn't cross without making a big scene.

She kissed her daughter then slipped out of her room and downstairs where Hank waited by the hearth, sipping a glass of wine. He had a fire going and another glass of wine on the coffee table. The soft strain of blues filled the room, her mother's own sultry voice crooning *Come Rain or Come Shine* from the first of the three CDs she recorded before she gave up her career in favor of her own true love.

Hank glanced up from his own glass, took one look at her face, then led her to her favorite chair by the window. He handed her the glass of wine then knelt beside her to pull off her shoes and prop her feet on the leather ottoman.

From the CD player, her mother's lyrics wove a spell around her. *I'm gonna love you, like nobody's loved you.* In that moment, with the magic of moonlight laying a pathway of silver from the window to the Persian rug where Hank still knelt, anything at all seemed possible, even that a heart torpedoed by loss could be made whole again when you least expected it.

"Better?" He studied her face in that intense way Max had when he was checking out her emotional terrain.

"Yes," she said, and it surprised Rachel that she meant it. "I didn't know I needed this little bit of normal until now."

"I'm glad I'm the one sharing it with you." He studied her a heartbeat longer then nabbed his glass from the mantle, sank onto the sofa, and stretched out his long legs.

"Jen would call this the art of living true."

How often had Rachel's older sister told her she had to listen to her heart and her spirit as well as her body? She also said those things were just as important as food, clothing, and shelter. At last, Rachel got a glimmer of what following her heart would be like—the easy conversation, the pleasure of sitting before a fire sharing a glass of wine and enjoying music, the comfort of knowing you are not alone, that the man standing in front of you might just turn out to be the dream you thought you'd lost forever.

"Smart woman, your sister." Hank smiled, the corners of his eyes crinkling from long hours of flying into the face of the sun. "I've always liked her."

"She likes you, too. My whole family does." He quirked an eyebrow at her. "Including me."

It felt good to laugh with him. As if they had read each other's minds, neither of them talked about the day's terrible events. They relaxed into the moment and let Delilah's voice lull them into relaxation.

Hank, always a good raconteur, told stories about some of his tours and the tourists that made Rachel laugh, while the logs in the fire began to burn through. When he got up to stoke them back to life with the poker, a light flashed in Rachel's driveway.

"Hank, did you see that?"

He was already striding toward the window. He stood there for a small eternity. It seemed her heart stopped beating and all the oxygen left the room.

"It's okay." Hank crossed back to the sofa. "It was the renter's vehicle."

Rachel glanced at the clock. It was already eleven.

"Where could he be going this late? And why?"

"Maybe this is normal for him," Hank said. "I've read that artistic people are on different schedules."

"True. I just got a phone call from Annie, and it's three o'clock in the morning in Italy. She has always marched to the beat of her own drum." Rachel stood. "I'd better head to bed. You know where everything is?"

He nodded. "I do. Everything will be fine, Rachel. Don't worry."

She'd headed out the door when a child's distressing cry pierced the night.

"*Mom-my!*"

Both of them bolted.

The cry was followed by Joey, standing at the top of the stairs. "There's a monster in my closet."

Rachel's racing heart slowed a beat. This was an old story. There were always monsters and dragons hiding in Joey's room. Over the years, she'd hit upon the perfect plan to banish them, a bottle bearing the new label *Monster Be Gone*.

"I'll take care of that monster in two seconds flat. Be right back, sweetie."

Rachel went to her bedroom for the monster spray, a bottle of her favorite perfume. Coach Dreams: Sunset. The fragrance reminded her of running through a meadow in summertime. Even the name evoked every beautiful and romantic moment in her life. It wouldn't banish any monsters, but it would certainly make her feel better.

When she returned, Hank was standing at the top of the landing holding Joey. For a moment the sight of them thrust her back in time when life was good, her family was intact, and a future filled with promise spun out before them like a golden ribbon. She quickly swallowed the lump that came into her throat.

"I've got *Monster Be Gone*." She held the bottle aloft and hoped the lilt she'd managed sounded more reassuring to Joey than it did to her own ears. "Let's get rid of that big, bad monster."

She climbed the stairs, her mind more on how this late-night disruption would make Joey grumpy and hard to manage in the morning than on any idea that the monster from her garden and the office might have crept up the stairs and left his dark blot in her son's room.

Hank carried Joey to his room, and Rachel would later blame his broad shoulders and confident stride, so like Max, for her distraction. It seemed need had brought out feelings she'd kept hidden for who knows how long, even from herself.

While he tucked her son into bed, she went to the closet and made a big to-do of banishing the monster with sweeping sprays and stern warnings to *get out of here and don't you come back.*

"There now. All done." As she turned back toward Hank and Joey, she froze.

"Rachel? What is it?"

She was too horror-stricken to speak. All she could do was remain rooted to the spot, staring at the teddy bear in her son's arms. It was not his well-loved Pooh. It wasn't even the one-eyed teddy bear he'd loved on and dragged around since he could crawl.

The bear in Joey's arms was brand new, brown, and much the same size as his babyhood bear, but sporting two button eyes and a stitched-on mouth whose red thread suddenly took on a garish leer that left Rachel drained. She felt as if her life's blood were pooling at her feet.

Daryl Greene had mentioned finding a bear in his son's room before Eddie was kidnapped. Rachel bottled up her screams as she eased toward the bed and sank beside her son. She was shaking so hard, she could barely form words. Hank reached for her hand and held on.

"Joey, where did you get that new bear?"

"There." He pointed toward the closet, recently freed of its monster inhabitants. The closet she'd searched earlier and found nothing amiss.

Hank, quick to catch her drift, lifted Joey off the bed.

"Come on, buddy. Show me and your mommy where you found the bear."

He trotted into the closet then squatted beside a toy chest to the left of the door and lifted the lid. It held the usual collection of miniature cars and Tonka trucks, Legos, balls, fierce plastic lizards and dragons, plus various action figures that make up a little boy's world. In his matter-of-fact way, Joey plucked a card from the jumble of Legos.

"It's a monster with a sword." He dropped Tarot's Justice at Rachel's feet then trotted back to bed, still clutching his new teddy bear. "Read me a story. I'm sleepy."

Rachel could do nothing but stare at the card. Her arms and legs turned to a block of ice. Her mind froze over, refusing to acknowledge the full significance of the teddy bear.

"Rachel?" Hank put his hand on her shoulder. It was fire, a match to her fuse.

Fury poured through her. She smoldered with it. Burned. Nobody was taking her son. *Nobody!*

"How about *The House at Pooh Corner*?" Rachel tried to collect herself, but she didn't know whether she'd be able to hold the book without shaking.

Hank mouthed *you can do it*. Suddenly, she knew she could, because that's the way life worked. You remain strong for your children. *Always*.

Though being brave in the face of fear that would rob her of sleep and cause nightmares lasting into the waking hours was surely easier with someone to share the burden.

She tucked Joey into his covers then sat beside him reading while Hank quietly went about bagging the Tarot card, making it seem he was merely hanging out with them, listening to a bedtime story.

Afterward, she and Hank converged on the den with sleep not even a remote possibility.

"I'll get the card and the bear to the sheriff's office in the morning while you're at school."

"Thank you. I'll put it in the office while I'm getting the children ready for school." She was still trembling with fear and fury. Suddenly, her inner lioness rose up to take charge. "Joey and Susan didn't even get to play outside today because of that psychotic *criminal*. I won't have the Collector deprive my children of one single other thing, even if I have to comb this town, house by house, to find him myself."

Her flash of spunk coaxed a smile from Hank. "I don't recommend that, Rachel, but I plan to give Dustin a call and have him do some nosing around."

Dustin Harper, El Paso County's heartthrob, used to be Sheriff Johnson's best hotshot detective until he decided he could make more money and exercise more control over his life as a private investigator.

Rachel didn't even want to calculate how much time and money Hank was spending on keeping her and her family safe. "Maybe Dustin can find a clue that will lead to Eddie and Lulu and take that depraved maniac down."

"The thing that concerns me most is that the Collector was all over your house."

"Exactly. And we missed the bear first time around. What else did we miss?"

"Your room."

SEVENTEEN

The moment Rachel entered her bedroom again she knew something was different, and terribly wrong. It was *now* filled with the warning scent of magnolias, and she had the eerie sense of being on full display. Someone was watching. But where? How?

Her curtains were wide open. Had *she* left them that way after she'd talked to Jen?

Hank was already at the window closing the gap in the curtains in his matter-of-fact way. There would be no censure for her carelessness, no reminders that she was no longer alone on the ranch with her family. She knew him well. He was like Max in that way, the ultimate protector, just doing his job.

Her conscience pricked her. If he hadn't been so busy looking after them, he would have a family of his own. This was an old argument she had with herself, one she trotted out with depressing regularity.

"I was in here earlier when I talked to Annie and Jen. I checked for listening devices and hidden cameras."

"Good."

"But I don't remember leaving the curtains open."

He made a thorough sweep through the room anyway, and even went into her walk-in closet, something she'd neglected earlier. When he came out, he gave her the all-clear signal, a thumbs-up.

"It looks like everything is fine here."

"Good." Still, she couldn't shake the feeling of being watched. She wrapped her arms around herself to stop from shivering.

Hank pulled her into his arms, and she leaned into him as if he were the only port in the middle of her storm. "I can sleep in here tonight, Rachel." He leaned back to look into her eyes. "Over there in your chair."

She pictured it, all six feet of him hanging off her frilly pink cushion, trying to get comfortable. The ridiculous image took some of the edge off her fear.

"There's no need for you to wreck your sleep. I'll be fine."

"You're sure?"

"Promise."

By the time Rachel was in bed with her own covers tucked under her chin, the old argument with herself circled her brain like a vulture. It was the fragrance of magnolias, still hovering like a ghost, that had her disturbed. It was the awful bear with the ghoulish blood-red grin.

She closed her eyes, then bolted straight up, her scalp prickling and icy fingers of fear climbing her spine.

"Who's there?"

The silence pressed down on her like death itself. She waited, a piano wire stretched too tight, thrumming with fear. At last, she lay down and pulled the sheet over her head. But it did nothing to keep out the heady scent that predicted the worst was yet to come.

EIGHTEEN
THE BAR

He hunkered over his beer, hidden by his disguise. The teddy bear was a masterful touch. Oh yes, it was. The last little thread in a web he'd spun around Rachel Maxey to show her exactly what was in store.

Would she understand the message? Would she see that what he was building, had been building for almost two years, was the perfect home?

All it needed was *her*.

And she'd fallen right into his lap. The cards had told him she was coming.

And there she was Sunday night. On his TV screen. Perfect in every way.

He ordered another beer, the last one before they closed the joint. The Bar, it was called. An unpretentious name for an out-of-the-way place where a man could go unnoticed and hear everything he needed to know if he was smart. He was both of those things, a loner and far more intelligent than anybody would ever suspect.

His mother had made sure nobody ever knew. The old hag. She'd been a master manipulator. The deprivations and the hours he'd spent in the locked closet ensured he would always keep to the shadows, a boy who would take every precaution not to call attention to himself.

Growing up, he had learned that attention brought punishment and home was another name for nightmare.

Wouldn't the old witch be shocked now? His name was practically a household word, nearly as big as the Other. Someday, when the world breathed his name, they would simultaneously think *perfect home*.

He hunched his shoulders and hunkered down over his beer. His thick glasses and his gray toupee slipped forward. He sent a furtive glance around the room before adjusting them and altering his posture. Not too much. He wanted to look like a man nobody would bother to include in any conversation.

He'd chosen a booth directly behind two off-duty deputies. Young. Wet-behind the ears. Bob Smith, his arms and hands tattooed with ink, and Earl "Jonesy" Jones. He'd seen them in the bar many times while he was wearing many different disguises. He knew their habits better than Sheriff Jeremiah Johnson.

After two beers, they began to discuss their work, right on cue.

"Do you think the guy we caught today is the Collector?" Jonesy said.

"Nah. Just some copycat looking for his fifteen minutes of fame."

"That's the dumbest thing I ever heard. Going out to steal stuff you don't want or need just so people will think you're the famous Collector."

His glasses slid again as he bent over his beer. He thought it was dumb of the copycat, too. Didn't the idiot know there was only one man smart enough to become famous and still evade the law?

Anonymity was the key to completing his plan. Perfection took time, patience, and cunning.

"It's a good thing he was so dumb he thought a Tarot deck was a pack of Old Maid cards," Smith said.

He had a big belly laugh for a guy so fit. He was the reason the cops won the Emma Crawford Coffin Races every year at the festival. He looked so silly dressed in a Victorian wedding gown sitting in a homemade casket on wheels while his burly mates at the station pushed him down the middle of the street, the crowd always cheered them to victory.

The Collector poured out the last of his beer. The timing couldn't be better for the Emma Crawford Festival. It was the silliest possible event, but the perfect venue to set the final stage of his plan into action.

In the early history of the town when railroads were being carved out of the Rockies and people were flocking to the healing waters of the springs that had once attracted the Plains Mountain tribes—the Utes, the Cheyenne, and the Arapahoe— a consumptive old maid named Emma Crawford came out West hoping for a cure. She fell in love with a railroad engineer who swore that if she didn't make it, he would haul her coffin up to the top of Red Mountain so she could enjoy a good view of the only place she'd ever found happiness. Years of rain and snow, mudslides, and avalanches finally sent the casket racing back down the mountain. Two young hitchhikers found the bones and the brass name plate from the casket, and the Emma Crawford Coffin Races were born.

The Collector almost salivated at the thought of the huge crowds, the loud music, the chaos, the costumes, the coffin races —all amidst fireworks from Higginbotham Flats. The festival had been expanded this year, almost as if the planning committee had read his mind.

He stifled a chuckle. Next time he'd add a fake mustache to

his disguise. It was much better for hiding his emotions, which were running high tonight. Just thinking of the photo he'd taken from Rachel's office made him giddy. It would do until he had the real thing.

"He could be playing us," Jonesy said. "It might turn out he's either the Collector or somebody in cahoots with him."

"You could be right. He was going to grab that kid if Rachel Maxey hadn't stopped him. That's one gutsy woman. And she gave such a good description, the telephone tip led us right to the construction site where he was working."

"Yeah. One sleazeball down, one to go."

Sleazeball? How dare they insult *him?*

His rage boiled so hot he squeezed the empty beer can till it crumpled. At the sound, both cops twisted to stare. But he knew the art of hiding in plain sight. He did the trick with a quick glance followed by ducking his head like a man too shy to look you in the face, and too meek not to be embarrassed by a small public display of anger.

With one last glance in his direction, the cops paid their bill and walked out with Jonesy teasing Smith about getting home in time to wash the silk bloomers he'd need to wear as a fake Emma in this year's coffin races.

After they were gone, the Collector chuckled outright. It was ten minutes to closing time, and the joint was nearly empty. The two laid-back cops had just confirmed that they'd be too busy during the festival racing their competitors down the street with a fake coffin bearing a fake Victorian Emma to pay any attention to him.

He was so pleased with the way his plans were coming along, he toyed with the idea of leaving a generous tip. Fortunately, his genius kicked in and he left the usual modest amount. Big tips drew attention.

When he left, the bartender didn't even look up. Nobody

noticed when he got into his generic black truck and rolled out of the parking lot.

No, they did not.

But *he* was the famous Collector. And after his next move, this town would be cowering with fear.

NINETEEN

THE HIDEAWAY

The Collector parked in a huge garage beside a white van and an SUV.

After all these years the cards had brought such an unexpected bonus to him, he could hardly believe his good luck. He climbed out of his truck, anticipation zinging in his veins.

By the time he walked into the nondescript house he'd purchased for his purpose, he felt energized and inspired. He ditched the toupee and glasses in a dressing room that held toupees in every color, plus a wide array of mustaches, whiskers, glasses, and enough putty to rebuild his nose and chin if he felt the need. He even had a lockbox filled with fake IDs. It was a display worth bragging about.

"Sheer genius," he muttered, and he didn't get any argument.

Basking in the glow of success and fame, he washed up, brushed his teeth, and gargled with mouthwash then made his way up the stairs to his special place.

"Careful," he murmured. "Quiet." He tiptoed, ever aware of the enormous responsibility of being a father. "Don't wake the children."

His first darling, the little prince he called Mikey, was sound asleep on his bed with a cocker spaniel, a Jack Russell terrier and the Collector's personal favorite, a golden doodle. He'd nabbed it right from under the nose of the big shots at the Tee Cross Ranch.

"That's my good boy, Mikey." The child didn't even stir when he bent over and kissed his cheek. He'd adjusted.

The girl would, too. Tonight though, she was huddled in the corner of her room surrounded by six cats, her eyes red and swollen from crying.

"Daddy's home, Star."

"You're not my daddy and my name's not Star."

"Yes, it is. The sooner you get used to it, the quicker you'll get a real bed and some food."

"I want to go home."

"You *are* home, Star."

"No! I'm *not!*" She glared at him then began a fresh fit of crying.

"You might as well stop that. It won't do you a bit of good. The insulation is top of the line and the house is so remote there's nobody for miles around. Nobody can hear you. Nobody can find you."

A sense of his own greatness washed over him. Even his mother would have approved of his cleverness. Still, he had to differentiate himself from that bad parent.

He was a *good* parent. Yes, he was.

Transforming himself to a gentle father, he smoothed her tangled hair back from her flushed face. Her flinch pained him, as it would any loving parent.

Mikey had been easier to train, more accepting, more loving. For a moment he wondered if he should have taken Susan instead of Lulu. But then, that would be too much. Rachel's own daughter, and a spoiled brat besides.

Joey was more tempting, but the same logic applied. It

would be hard to rename and recondition the children with their own mother on the premises.

No. His family had to be entirely new and unrelated to each other. They had to belong only to *him*. Their love and loyalty had to be only for *him*.

There would be only one daddy. He'd made that clear from the beginning.

"Star, if you behave yourself and stop crying, Daddy will see that you get a nice breakfast in the morning. You might even get some nice toys to play with."

He stood up, aware that towering adults could be intimidating to a child. Still, as much as it pained him to think he had to act like his own mother, he had to show her who was in charge around here.

She scowled at him, defiant. Who knew a seven-year-old girl could be so stubborn?

His anger flared—quick, hot, and destructive. He wanted to lash out at her, hit her so hard her pretty nose split and blood spurted down the front of her nightgown. He wanted to feel the blow in his fists, watch her crumple to the floor and stare up at him with revulsion and horror.

Like that other little girl.

The atmosphere felt charged, silently applauding his hatred, doubling his urge toward violence. He felt validated.

It wasn't the first time he'd had these brutal urges. Oh no, it was not.

How gratifying to turn his red rage loose with balled fists, gritted teeth, and an unexpectedly athletic body that stiffened and expanded until he was Goliath, a giant able to vanquish anyone who stood in his way. How satisfying to feel the terror and admiration he garnered from his audience by revealing a glimpse of the butcher inside who was capable of unspeakable things.

Still, the Collector prided himself on going unnoticed in

public by the people he saw every day, by sliding under their radar while they acknowledged him with a friendly smile and a nod of recognition of his public persona. He took great pride in his very ordinariness. He enjoyed a wicked sort of glee that you could look at him until your eyes crossed and you grew faint from hunger, and you'd never notice the demon he kept leashed and chained deep inside.

He hadn't wanted to inherit it from her, the wicked witch who bore him. At first, he'd fought against it; but then he realized the power it gave him, the prestige.

Feeling invincible, he reined in the beast but kept his stern façade and voice. A powerful lesson to his audience.

Don't cross me.

"Star, if you don't behave, not only will I not feed you, but I'll take away the cats and leave you here all by yourself for the rats to gnaw on."

He glanced into the far corners of the room as if an army of rats waited behind the walls to do his bidding. Come to think of it, that might be a good idea. It would be easy to bring them inside.

He smiled, thinking of the pleasure it would give him to punish her with rodents, starved till they were ravenous for anything that moved.

Suddenly her defiance vanished, and she gave him a terrified stare. Oh well. She'd learn. Just maybe not as fast as he'd like.

The girl needed a mother's touch. She needed Rachel to tame her, and he needed Rachel to tame his beast.

Who knew? As much as Rachel already admired him, they might have a child sooner than he'd planned. Forget easing her into her role. Her future had already been decided based on her ability to bear as many children as she was told. Her fate was sealed.

He smiled as he envisioned himself molding a dozen new

beings in his image, sturdy babies with Rachel's good looks and his brain. She had many child-bearing years left in her. Maybe even two dozen. She was of sturdy stock. She could handle it.

Some of his offspring would be girls. Oh yes, they would. They'd be head and shoulders above their peers, brilliant masterminds straight from his family's gene pool, equally at home with charm and evil.

He didn't need the sniveling brat in the corner. One snap of her neck would do it. He could almost feel her life ebbing away under his hands. The exhilaration and power of it all...

His fists clenched and unclenched. Should he or shouldn't he?

"Do it." Evil whispering in his ear, soft and enticing. "Go ahead and do it."

When he squatted beside her, she shied away.

"Now, now. Daddy's not going to hurt you."

Not much. Then it will be over.

He stroked her hair then fitted his hands gently around the neck. It was slender, delicate, the veins pulsing with all that beautiful red blood.

"Now." The whisper of evil held both admiration and urgency. "It will be empowering."

Wait. Maybe it would be more satisfying to use a knife.

But then there would be the mess, the disposal, the room for error. He couldn't take a chance, not right before his big coup.

He was a patient man. He knew the art of biding his time. He also understood the necessity of proving that he, and only he, was in charge.

"Not yet," he said.

When he released her, the Collector congratulated himself. As always, his timing was superb.

"Goodnight, Star. If you know what's good for you, you'll remember what Daddy said."

There. Don't say he didn't warn her. He was the perfect

daddy, yes, he was, and Rachel would complete his perfect family.

Soon. Very soon.

TWENTY
LOGAN RANCH

Hank got up before dawn, long before Rachel and her family stirred, and set out for a run that would give him a chance to check every inch of Rachel's property. No small task.

With military precision, he searched for signs of an intruder: broken branches, a campsite deep in the woods on the outer reaches of her property, tire tracks and shoe tracks that shouldn't be there. His usual run took far longer because of the thoroughness of his search.

By the time he got home, Rachel's vehicle was gone, and so was the renter's.

Hank entered through the kitchen door and went straight to the coffee pot. Victoria was already at the table with her coffee and the newspaper spread out before her.

"I'm glad you could join me." She smiled at him and folded the newspaper. "Sit down and we'll have a little chat."

Such a leisurely pace was a luxury for him, partially because he was always rushing off to work, but mostly because there was nobody in his house to share coffee and conversation.

Victoria was always good company. Hank looked forward to a chat before he left for the sheriff's office with the Tarot card he and Rachel had found in Joey's room last night, as well as the teddy bear that had terrified her.

"You want another cup, Victoria?"

"No thanks. I'm good."

He settled into the chair beside her, but more than that, he sank into the comfortable feeling of Rachel's kitchen. This was a real home. Love was a palpable thing here. He could almost imagine that if he stuck his tongue out, he could catch it and savor it all day long.

If he weren't careful his soft side would be showing. Wouldn't the guys who flew for his tour company have a heyday cutting a tough aviator down to size?

Victoria studied him so long, he felt foolish for forgetting her sharp intellect. "Did you sleep well last night?"

"My years in the military taught me to sleep anywhere, but Rachel was having a tough time." He told Victoria about the teddy bear and the card in Joey's toy box. "I'm taking them to the sheriff's office in a few minutes."

"What I'm thinking is that this house felt mighty good last night with you in it. Maybe you ought to stay another night or two. Even better, I give my stamp of approval if you want to move in."

"Thanks, Victoria. Don't think I haven't thought about it. But you know that's up to Rachel."

"I reckon she won't ever say anything about the matter unless you quit pussyfooting around and *tell* her how you feel."

Did it show? Hank schooled his emotions. He was a careful man who prided himself on strategic planning and good timing. He wasn't spontaneous like Max, and his feelings for Rachel were too tangled up in that long-ago friendship with her husband for him to be clear on the future.

And he certainly didn't intend to say anything about the relationship that would mislead Victoria. Under the guise of sipping his coffee, he retreated into silence.

"My Finn swept me off my feet. You might want to do the same with my granddaughter. I won't be here forever to take care of her, you know."

He almost chuckled at that. Rachel had told him many times the provisions of her grandfather's will. Of course she didn't see taking care of her grandmother as anything except an honor and a joy, and he suspected the two women actually took care of each other. Still, he played along with the older woman's fantasy that she was the one doing all the caretaking.

"You're going to live to a hundred."

"That's my plan, but what if I don't?"

Hank was dancing around a conversation that had taken a very personal turn, and he knew it. He didn't want to announce feelings he'd shoved to the back of his mind for at least two of the last three years. And yet he didn't want to shut the door on any possibilities. That kind of waffling was a cowardly thing to do, especially with Victoria Logan, the most straight-talking woman he'd ever known.

"I'm staying until I can get Rachel's security system installed. Right now, I can't think of anything except the safety of Rachel and the children."

"You could take a page out of Finn's book. He was a good man to imitate."

"Rachel has told me about Mr. Logan. I'm sorry I never knew him. But after the dust settles on this Collector business, who knows what might happen?" He escaped to refill his cup then joined her back at the table. "Are you going to be okay here by yourself while I'm gone?"

"If anybody comes after this old bag of bones, I'll blow them to Kingdom Come with old Betsy."

He downed his second cup then leaned down to kiss her on the cheek before he left the kitchen, already regretting he'd added a qualifier to the statement of his intent. *Might* was a word for wimps and cowards. He didn't like to think of himself that way.

Hank veered by Rachel's office for the teddy bear she had bagged and left on the desk. As he picked it up, he felt the same surge he used to experience in the military when he climbed into his helicopter and flew off to face the enemy.

But, this time, the enemy had no identity.

As Hank got into his truck and headed to the sheriff's office, the sight of the toy filled him with icy determination. He was going to hunt the Collector down and personally see to it that he never came near another child.

TWENTY-ONE

EL PASO COUNTY SHERIFF'S DEPARTMENT | COLORADO SPRINGS

The El Paso County Sheriff's Department oversaw the largest county in Colorado. Accordingly, their offices and their huge staff in Colorado Springs reflected the scope and importance of the work they did.

Major crimes were always referred from the small Manitou Springs Police Department to Sheriff Jeremiah Johnson. This was the first time in years the quaint little town better known for its hiking trails and healing natural fountains had experienced back-to-back kidnappings and a bizarre crime spree such as the one credited to the Collector.

When Hank told the officer out front that he had more evidence on the Collector, he was escorted straight into the sheriff's office.

"Pull up a chair." The sheriff crossed to his credenza. "Coffee?"

"No thanks. I've had two with Rachel's grandmother."

"How's the family doing?"

"You know Victoria. Tough as nails. Rachel's very much like her."

"What brings you here, Hank?"

Hank pulled the baggie from his pocket, slid the Tarot card across the desk, and then set the teddy bear beside the card.

"A teddy bear?"

After Hank told the sheriff the circumstances surrounding the bear and the latest Tarot card, Jeremiah said, "This case is making me gray." He punched the intercom to call his forensics expert into the office. "Stella, I need you to run out and see what you can find at the Logan Ranch in Joey's room, especially around the toy box. I'll need photos, prints, the whole nine yards." He handed her the teddy bear. "And find the manufacturer on this."

Alarm crossed her face. "There was one of these in Eddie's room before he vanished."

"We missed this one when we were at the ranch yesterday. Joey found it in his toy box last night."

Hank waited till Stella was gone to launch his own investigation.

"Sheriff, everything the Collector did at Rachel's house says to me that he had a very personal interest in her. Are you going to put a security detail on her house?"

"I can't, not on what I have so far. The Collector's been in other houses and taken personal items, including family photos. Our department is stretched thin as it is. We've got a bunch of unexplained dead cattle on half a dozen ranches and everybody who misplaces something calls us to say it was the Collector."

"Can you increase the patrol cars going through her neighborhood?"

"I can do that. But right now, our priority is finding two kidnapped kids. We're working with the Denver police on similarities between the Langley boy and our missing children."

Hank nodded. "Maybe Rachel's recollection of the man in the park will help catch the man responsible for these heinous crimes."

"We caught her guy last night. It looks like it's going to be a dead end, though there's a slim possibility he's some kind of partner to the Collector."

"Who is he?"

"Just a twisted junkie copycat criminal with delusions of grandeur. A kid in his twenties who has already thrown his life away." The sheriff steepled his fingers. "He was fired from the same construction company where Daryl Greene and Rafael Vargas work. That raises all kinds of red flags. We're taking a closer look at everybody who works there."

Hank made a mental note to have Dustin look into the construction company's male employees. "Have you made any more progress in finding the Collector?"

"The best thing we have so far is the Tarot cards." The sheriff inspected the one in the baggie, then scooted it back across the desk. "You see those stains and the yellowed card stock? Every card the Collector has left behind has been like that."

Hank studied what appeared to be coffee stains on the well-used card. "It looks antique. Even the artwork seems to be an older style."

"The owner down at the Purple Mystic shop said this type of card was used in the seventies, and they are very hard to come by. You'd have to go someplace online like eBay or Etsy or else find them in an antique shop."

"You think the Collector is old? Someone who dabbles in the mystic arts?"

"Could be... Or else somebody in his family did and passed the cards on to him. We're checking that angle now, and we've got eyes all over town looking for unusual behavior from males that fit our suspect's description—purchase of food like kids' cereal and the other junk they eat, buying children's clothing, particularly a little girl's coat and shoes since Lulu was taken in her nightgown."

"Good luck." Hank stood and shook the man's hand. "I

appreciate everything you're doing. If I can help in any way, let me know."

"We are not at the point where we can call in an air support chopper, but if you'd be willing to do an air search, you might spot something that would be helpful."

"You've got it." He'd do anything to keep Rachel and her family safe. It was not only a personal mission, it was a sacred duty, sworn to a fallen comrade in arms and best friend. "What, specifically, should I look for?"

"Any signs of these two children." Jeremiah handed Hank a flyer with the missing children's photos along with a description of the clothes they were wearing when they were taken: blue jeans and a yellow hoodie with Kermit the Frog on the front for Edward Greene; a pink ruffled nightgown featuring fairy tale princesses for Lulu Vargas. "And map out any houses that are remote enough to serve as a hideout."

"Have there been reports of any particular vehicle used by the Collector?"

"Nothing consistent." Jeremiah shook his head. "There's just so little evidence in this case. We need a break of some kind."

"I'll do my best." Hank promised.

But would it be good enough?

TWENTY-TWO
COLORADO SPRINGS

The question haunted Hank on the drive to his office. Not even the golden October day airbrushing the skies and painting the mountains in festival colors could keep Hank from thinking that no matter how carefully he searched from the air, it might be too late for the missing children.

Their loss would be a personal heartbreak for him. He'd grown up under the wide skies and rolling plains of Texas, the oldest of six boys, the one his blue-collar parents counted on to keep his younger siblings out of trouble. And safe. He was the mature one, the dependable one, the son most likely to do better than the grueling hours and low pay of his father, a beat cop, and his mother, a factory-assembly-line worker.

All that changed under a hot blue sky in August when the brothers went to the creek behind their house. Their dad had strung a rope to a sturdy oak limb overhanging the water. Their favorite game was vying to see who could swing out, then let go and stay underwater the longest.

It was a foolish game. A dangerous game. Hank, at thirteen, knew it. But in his first teen year, he was still a little kid, longing to be grownup while still clinging to his childhood.

He was an expert with the rope and usually won the contest. But his twelve-year-old brother, George, and the nine-year-old twins, Johnny and Jimmy, had shot up like beansprouts that summer and were giving him a run for his money. The competition got so fierce, only one person was paying attention to six-year-old Benny. His eight-year-old brother, Bob, who had no hope of winning the game.

Bob, who spoke the three words that changed Hank's life.

"Benny's down under."

By the time Hank got his baby brother out of the water, he was blue and cold and so far past his last breath there was no hope of reviving him.

On that boiling day by the creek, Hank swore he would never let another person die on his watch.

And he hadn't. Until Max. And then the ones who came after, all those brave boys on the killing fields of Afghanistan, fighting to keep America safe. And free. If only they had known the thing they loved most about their country was slowly slipping away on the home front, freedom siphoned off while nobody was looking, and a way of life slowly draining away like tomato soup through a sieve.

He would fight to the death to find the lost children and to keep Rachel and her family safe.

Hank put in a call to Dustin Harper, the private eye he had engaged after the Collector first paid her a call.

"Do you have anything yet on Bruce Wyler?"

"I've substantiated all his claims to fame you find on the internet. He's an only child. His dad, Michael Wyler, is a prominent orthopedic surgeon, still living. His mother is deceased. She was a high society maven who chaired multiple charity organizations. She had her hand in a lot of pies."

"Find out how she died and specifically what groups interested her. Also, I have something else for you."

"Shoot."

"I want you to take a look at all the male employees at Pikes Peak Construction Company and then dig into Manitou Springs and Colorado Springs residents who might have been deep into mysticism. Specifically, anyone within the past fifty years who read Tarot cards."

Dustin whistled. "That's a big order. But I'm your man."

Hank's next call went to a top-of-the-line home security company to expedite shipping of the components for their system to Rachel's house. He would install it himself. It couldn't be any harder than flying fighter jets while dodging enemy fire.

Hank glanced at his watch. Half past ten. By eleven, he'd be back at his office complex, gearing up to take one of his Eco-Star helicopters into the air.

He said a quick prayer for the lost innocent children.

"Hang on. I'm coming."

TWENTY-THREE

MANITOU SPRINGS ELEMENTARY SCHOOL

In spite of Rachel's unsuccessful talk with Susan last night about not keeping secrets, she gripped the steering wheel of her car this morning, determined to be a lioness and a firm mother who wouldn't take no for an answer.

Joey complained all the way to school about having to leave home ten minutes early. He complained that he didn't get enough sleep, he didn't get to kiss his teddy bear and his dog goodbye, he didn't get to see Hank, and he didn't have time to run outside and check on his new tree house.

His grousing was good-natured and easy to handle. All Rachel had to do was say, "Umm hmm... sorry... we'll make up for it when we get home."

On the other hand, Susan sat in the back seat of the car as silent as a closed fist. Every time Rachel tried to catch her eye in the rearview mirror, she looked away. A sure sign of guilt. She knew something she wasn't telling.

Both of them were relieved to pull into the parking lot and start the school day where they wouldn't see each other except from a distance across the cafeteria or the playground for the next seven hours.

After getting Joey settled, Rachel found his teacher, Beatrice Masters, in the teacher's lounge. She was a tall, rawboned woman who looked as if she should be striding across a polo field in riding boots and urging a fast horse toward the goal line. In reality, she was a middle-aged, unmarried daughter of two Presbyterian ministers, and she was legendary for her even temperament and kindness to children.

She was alone, thank goodness, enjoying a cup of black coffee.

"Bea, do you have a minute?"

"Hello, Rachel. I do! It's eight minutes to the bell and I'm having a second cup. Join me?"

"I will." Rachel had been too keyed up for coffee when she left home. Part of that was due to the Collector's visit, but the rest had to do with the faint floral scent that was still hiding in the folds of her curtains, underneath her lingerie in the chest of drawers, and even in the steam coming from her bathroom showerhead.

"You look serious, hon. Is this about Susan? I know Lulu was her best friend."

"No. In fact, it's about Joey."

"Oh, he's a charmer, never a minute's trouble. I hope I haven't done something to upset him."

"No. He worships the ground you walk on."

Bea's laughter was full-bodied and welcome, like a brisk breeze coming down from Pikes Peak. "The quicksand is more like it."

"I'm concerned about the crossing guard. Joey mentioned that Jake tried to give him candy and take his picture, and I don't recall any reason that would have happened. Apparently, he didn't touch Joey or cause him any harm, but in light of Lulu's and Eddie's kidnappings, I did report Jake to the sheriff as a possible suspect."

"Oh dear. I suppose you didn't get the note I sent home?"

"No, but it wouldn't be the first time. Joey is my child most like Pigpen in the *Peanuts* cartoon. Everywhere he goes, he leaves a trail of forgotten things."

"I know that, and I should have told you. The children and I are creating keepsake books, and I asked Jake to help me with the photos. His mother and I have been friends since college. He's an excellent amateur photographer, and he loves children. He brought candy as little treats." Bea chuckled. "But I do remember Joey refusing both. We had to sneak and get a candid shot of him."

Rachel felt cautiously optimistic. The fact that Bea vouched for the crossing guard was almost proof that he was not a predator. But even the most discerning people can sometimes be fooled.

"I have to do that at home, too. Joey hates having his picture taken."

After chatting a while longer, she thanked Bea and headed back to her classroom.

She smelled them before she saw them, two dozen red roses. They sat in a gold florist's vase on her desk, sending off the scent of rose petals and disaster so thick it clogged Rachel's throat and gave her a headache.

On top of that, her children were revved up, milling about the room as if someone had used a cattle prod.

"Miss Maxey, look what you got!"

"They *stink*. Can we open a window?"

"Is it your birthday, Miss Maxey?"

"Miss Maxey! Miss Maxey! Can I have one to take home?"

The bow around the vase was huge, shades of pink and purple, both garish and full of meaning. Pink was Rachel's favorite color, and purple was the color of royalty. There was nothing attached to the bow except a bit of string where the card had been cut off. A small white envelope was taped to the side of the vase.

Rachel pulled it off, and out slipped the card. A Tarot card. Yellow with age. Not Justice this time, but the Queen of Hearts. She was trapped in a spell of horror, dire predictions, and fear swirling through her with tornadic force.

The school bell saved her. She slid the card into her pants pocket then turned to face her class.

"Children, take your seats." There was an excited scramble. Every seat was filled. Every face beloved and familiar. All her students were accounted for. "Now, did anyone see who delivered the flowers?"

Hands went up all over the room.

"Okay, children! One at a time." Rachel pointed them out, one by one.

"I did! I did! It was a tall man with dark hair."

"No! He was short with *gray* hair."

"He had glasses! And a great big nose."

No help there. "Did he say anything?"

"NOOOO!" they shouted in unison.

Throwing the offensive bouquet away would have upset the children and destroyed evidence. Rachel had no choice but to get her children into the reading circle and leave the roses sitting there like the blood-red eye of an evil witch who had promised to cut out your heart.

She took her first off-duty time to visit the principal's office, roses in hand and the story of their mysterious arrival at the ready.

Dr. Evelyn Slater was a large woman with firehouse-red hair some said was from a bottle of dye, while others said it was a wig. A thirty-year veteran of teaching, she had gone back to school to earn a doctorate so she could continue her work in education as an administrator.

Her advice to Rachel was chilling, but not unexpected. According to the news, the flowers had been reported stolen this morning, taken right off the front porch of a resident in Manitou Springs, where the delivery guy had left them.

Dr. Slater told Rachel to leave the flowers and the card for the police.

"I've already touched everything."

"Anybody would, Rachel. It's only natural. Just put them on the credenza over there."

While Rachel stowed the evidence, Dr. Slater pulled up the school's security tapes.

"We've already seen these, as we routinely do. I don't know how the delivery man slipped through unless this is him." She stopped the tape on a fuzzy image. "Do you recognize that man?"

Nobody could. The blurry tape showed a nondescript person in a janitor's uniform pushing a large cart. It looked as if the camera's lens had been greased with Vaseline. He—or she—was not identifiable in any way except size.

The person on the fuzzy tape appeared to be the same size as the crossing guard. A shiver ran through Rachel.

"This person is a similar build to Jake Clement. Did you notice that, Dr. Slater?"

"I didn't. I only know the school's janitor was not scheduled to arrive until thirty minutes after this tape was made." She rewound the footage and leaned closer to watch. "You're right. But I just can't believe that's anything except a coincidence. Jake's record here is impeccable. Do you notice anything else?"'

"I'm sorry. No. I can't identify that person."

"Okay. When the officers get here, we'll send a substitute to your room and bring you in here so they can talk to you."

"I don't know anything except what I've told you this morning and what I told the sheriff yesterday about the break-in at my house."

"I'll make sure they know that. Hopefully, they will only keep you a few minutes."

Dr. Slater always looked out for the welfare of her teachers as well as her children, one of the reasons Rachel loved working with her.

As she went back to her classroom, Rachel found herself watching for any glimpse of Jake, skulking around in the hallways where he didn't belong. Suddenly, the scent of magnolias overwhelmed her, and she glimpsed the crossing guard down the hall, at the water fountain.

She headed that way, and he hurried off.

"Wait!" she called, chasing after him. "I want to talk to you."

But he vanished around a corner. Rachel stood in the empty hallway, her heart hammering too hard and the scent of danger still wafting around her.

She balled her hands into fists. "Coward! You can run, but you can't hide. I'm watching you."

TWENTY-FOUR

COLORADO SPRINGS

Hank's Eco-Star helicopters were perfect for touring, but equally great for a search. The Fenestron tail rotor guaranteed a quiet ride that wouldn't draw attention, and the wraparound windows assured an unfettered view of the terrain below.

He logged in his flight as six p.m. Zulu time, the universal time kept in Greenwich, London, and used by pilots around the world because they frequently crossed so many time zones.

As Hank lifted the helicopter over the crags and peaks of the Rockies, he felt the sense of exhilaration that always accompanied taking up a chopper. The beauty of God's green earth seen from the air filled him with awe every single time. It was incomprehensible to him how anyone lucky enough to be in such a paradise could stoop to evil.

He banked his plane left and headed toward open ranch land, the most likely place he'd find a cabin remote enough to hide a criminal who continued to wreak havoc on two cities in the surrounding area.

His hours-long search yielded four houses between Manitou Springs and Colorado Springs that were so remote he'd missed them the first time over. Though there were no signs of the missing children, nor was there anything to indicate the Collector might have taken them to these places, Hank took aerial shots before returning to his office and marking a map for his office assistant to scan and email to Sheriff Johnson.

He still had a long day ahead. Glancing at the clock, he put in a quick call to Rachel. He could hear the strain of her school day in her *hello*.

"That bad, huh, Rach?"

"It shows?"

"A little. What's up?"

"You aren't going to believe this."

When she told him about the roses, a fresh stab of fear pierced him.

"I can be there in about thirty minutes."

"Absolutely not! You have a business to run, and I'm not about to let this raving lunatic make me and the children feel like prisoners in my own home. Besides, Gran has her shotgun."

"But can she *use* it?"

"Don't ever underestimate Victoria Logan. You do *exactly* what you had planned to do. I mean that, Hank."

"Yes, ma'am."

"Your Texas is showing." He could hear a smile in her voice. "What did you find out from Sheriff Johnson today?"

He gave her a quick recap of his conversation with the sheriff and his air search. "I have a couple of chopper tours and then an evening charter in the turbo-prop to Denver, so I'll be late coming back tonight. I'll use my key."

He'd had it since Max died. Though this would be only the second time he'd used it. The first was when Rachel called in the middle of the night, frantic because Joey had decided to "fly" down the banister in his Superman cape to get his own glass of water. Fortunately, the midnight run to the ER turned up nothing more serious than a broken collarbone.

After the call, Hank grabbed a quick sandwich and coffee,

then geared back up and took to the air again. Denver was an easy run, the weather was beautiful, and the tourists easy to please.

By the time he had finished his day's work and got back to Rachel's ranch, it was almost eleven. A Harvest moon, fat and golden, lit his way to her house. She'd left the porch light burning. Such a small thing, and yet the sight of it touched Hank in ways he could barely explain. Seeing it, he felt as if something essential was missing from his life, and had been missing all these years.

When he parked, he noticed the renter's Land Rover was there. His mood dampened somewhat as he retrieved Rachel's key. He was in the process of fitting it into the lock when the front door swung open.

There she stood. Rachel, her hair loose, her feet bare, her fuzzy pink robe belted around her narrow waist. Backlit by the lamp on the hall table, she looked like a Botticelli painting, "Idealized Portrait of a Lady," her hair a mass of black curls instead of red-gold. She was missing only the ribbons, beads, and feathers.

"I waited up for you," she said. Then she took his hand and led him into the den where logs crackled in the fire.

He never knew this was exactly what he'd been hoping for until he sank into the sofa and became almost overwhelmed by a sense of coming home. Rachel sat beside him, close enough that he could smell a hint of her floral shampoo still caught in her hair, the scent of her dusky rose skin that seemed permanently imprinted with an intoxicating fragrance.

Though he would have been content to do nothing but breathe in the same air as this glorious woman, she was electrified, lit up with the bad news of roses and the even more disastrous implications of the Queen of Hearts Tarot card. She wanted to hear again, blow by blow, Jeremiah Johnson's explanation of the ancient Tarot cards the Collector used.

She tapped her lower lip with a fingernail painted deep rose. It had a mesmerizing effect on him. Glossy nail to soft-looking lips. Satin. Or maybe velvet.

Hank shook his head. He had been in the air too long. Or under stress too long. Or in denial too long. He was about two seconds away from kissing her.

"I don't know." A tangle of curls fell over her left eye, and she raked her hair back. "There's something I heard once about Tarot cards. Some terrible tragedy."

"Maybe Victoria knows?"

"I didn't want to mention anything to her about the roses, but word got all over school, and, of course, the children told her the minute we got home. But when I asked if she'd ever heard of anything connected to Tarot cards, she said she couldn't recall."

"You've had a long day. Why don't you just sit back and relax a bit?"

"It has been stressful. My head hurts all the way to the roots of my hair."

"Lean back and I'll massage your scalp."

This was where Rachel always balked, where she stiffened up like a soldier going into battle and proclaimed her undying independence. Miraculously, she leaned into him, a yielding bundle of soft robe and soft woman. He sank his fingertips through her mass of glossy hair and began to massage her scalp.

Her sigh was long and drawn out, almost like a song, one of those sultry blues ballads Delilah had once used to bring men to their knees. Hank was almost on his knees, putty, melted butter, a river of dark honey flowing ever toward Rachel.

Finally, she sighed then gave him a sideways glance. His heart almost stopped.

"It's getting late," she said. "I should go." And then she slipped away.

It took Hank five minutes to get himself back under control.

TWENTY-FIVE
LOGAN RANCH

Rachel sat straight up in her bed, her heart hammering in her chest, awakened by an urgency that coursed through her like a river of fire. Her skin crawled as if fingertips were sliding through her hair and face, down her throat and beyond. She could feel eyes, watching her.

"Who's there?"

The room was dark, not even a sliver of moonlight showing through curtains she'd drawn so close they overlapped. Add the sudden fragrance of magnolias, and the strong sense that she was being watched sent prickles of fear down her spine.

She snapped on her beside lamp and looked at the screen of her cell phone. Two a.m. And the cloying scent of waxy blossoms more at home on the riverbanks of the Mississippi than in the mountains of Colorado drifted through the bedroom, taunting her. Her mother's voice whispered through her, a warning from the grave.

Harbingers of evil use the witching hours between midnight and two to show themselves...

Rachel battled the urge to wake Hank. Instead, she inspected behind the curtains, inside her closet, and even behind the shower curtain in her bathroom, though nobody could possibly have seen her on the bed from that angle.

Empty. Everything was empty. Just Rachel and her fears, standing in the middle of her bedroom in the wee hours of the morning.

"I have to stop this."

Still, as she crawled back into bed, she still had the sensation of eyes watching her.

The next morning when the alarm on her cell phone went off, Rachel hit snooze, though when she finally got out of bed, she deeply regretted her moment of weakness. Not only had the extra bit of sleep done nothing to make her feel better, but she was now starting her day racing to catch up.

Bruce Wyler was sitting at the kitchen table, drinking a cup of coffee.

"Well, good morning," he said, all smiles.

The sun slanting through the window made a halo around his hair, highlighting his handsome face and a gleam of interest in his eyes.

She nodded at him, too frustrated to reply. Her house was off-limits to him, and the last thing she needed was to lose her rent money by having to discourage the personal interest of her renter. Her glance swung from him to her grandmother, standing at the sink with her back to Rachel. She never even turned around.

"Is that you, Rachel?"

"It's me, Gran."

Victoria turned toward her, and Rachel's heart sank. A florist's cellophane wrapping, the kind available at grocery stores, lay on the counter behind her, and in her hands were two dozen roses. Pink. Arranged in one of the Mason jars they kept in the pantry, though neither of them had canned tomatoes since Max died.

Had the Collector sent them to her house?

"Look what Bruce brought for you!" Gran set the flowers on the bar, then rearranged a few blossoms. "Isn't that nice?"

"I wanted to make up to you for what happened in the garden." He stood up, uncertain now. "I hope I'm not overstepping my bounds."

She was only moderately relieved the roses hadn't come from the Collector, and her face showed her dismay. Obviously. Her sister Jen was the only one of the Logan girls who had learned to school her thoughts.

"It's okay," she told Bruce. How did you thank someone for roses you didn't even want without encouraging him?

"Rachel, it was embarrassing to be caught in the middle of the theft in your garden, but I'm glad I could be there for you. The roses are my way of letting you know how grateful I am to be staying in your charming apartment where I can work in peace."

Her grandmother smiled at him, obviously impressed by his comments.

"Isn't that nice?" Victoria said. "He told me the same thing when he knocked on the door this morning."

"That's very thoughtful, Bruce. Thank you."

Rachel stood in the doorway, not offering him a second cup of coffee, not suggesting he might stay for breakfast. Roses or no roses. She didn't want to encourage bending the rules of their agreement. She'd made it clear that the family quarters were private, and that she would only be in his apartment to collect his sheets and towels for the laundry.

"Right, I'll be going then. I hope you have a good day, Rachel."

On the way out, Bruce put his hand on her shoulder, just a simple touch, and yet she felt uncomfortable. Shaking it off would be rude, but enduring it felt like some sort of capitulation. She waited until the front door slammed behind him before she poured her coffee.

"Gran, where's Hank?"

"He left before you got up. Said he had a long day."

"Did he say when he would be back?" Rachel felt selfish to the core for even asking. He had his life. She had hers.

"This evening. He said be sure to tell you he would return after he dropped off his charter group in Denver."

The previous evening by the fire drifted into her mind. What struck her most was the elation she'd felt when Hank walked through the door last night and her current relief that he'd be returning tonight. Nor could she ignore her ease in confiding in him, his genuine concern for the missing children, and his selfless involvement in trying to find the hiding place of the Collector.

She crossed to the roses, sitting on the breakfast bar like an accusation. Bruce had left no card. *Good.* At least she didn't have to contend with uncomfortable intentions declared in writing.

"Gran, do you remember when I asked you about the Tarot cards? I seem to remember something awful happened, related to cards. It might have even been when Mother left to visit her relatives and didn't come back for months."

At the mention of her mother, Rachel got a strong whiff of the spices Delilah used to keep in a sachet bag near her bed.

Charms to ward off evil...

"*Pshaw.* That didn't mean a thing. The Bohemian was always pulling stunts like that." Victoria's pursed lips showed exactly what she thought of her daughter-in-law. "Besides, I don't know how I could possibly recall anything from that long ago. At my age, I'm not a walking encyclopedia, you know."

Rachel didn't have time to pursue the subject. She didn't even have time to reassure Victoria not to worry about the Tarot cards. She gave her a quick kiss, grabbed a muffin, then headed off to dress and herd her kids into the car.

As usual, Joey was talkative on the way to school, and Susan was reserved. Rachel caught her daughter's eye in the rearview mirror.

"Susan, have you thought any more about what Lulu told you and Wendy?"

"MOM! I already told you. I don't know!" She ducked her head, but not before Rachel saw her tears.

"I didn't mean to upset you, sweetheart. Just think about it and let me know if you remember anything."

The school seemed to be floating in mist this morning, though there wasn't a single cloud in the sky or wisp of fog on the ground. As she parked, the scent of Delilah's evil-defying potion filled the car, though Rachel was the only one to notice.

Trapped by the past, she watched Joey and Susan merge with the other children heading toward the school's entrance. If you didn't know better, you'd think it was an ordinary school day in Manitou Springs.

But if you were Rachel, caught in her mother's shadow, paralyzed with scent and surrounded by mist, you'd see how the crossing guard hurried to take Susan's arm, how he leaned down to smile at something she said, how he held on to her just a bit too long.

And then you'd see the wide smile Susan flashed him, full of innocence and trust. You'd see her borne along by child-like faith that every adult in her small world was there for the sole purpose of providing her needs and keeping her safe.

Was Jake Clement the secret Lulu had asked Susan and Wendy to keep?

Rachel watched until both her children were safely inside the school. When she turned to watch the crossing guard again, he had vanished.

Sighing, she stepped from her car. Thankfully, the mist and the fragrance of spices didn't follow her.

Still, for the first time since she'd been teaching, Rachel dreaded walking into the schoolhouse. What would be waiting for her on her desk? How was she to tell Tanya that her own daughter wouldn't confide in her? How was she going to deal with a child who knew something that might lead the police to find Lulu?

TWENTY-SIX

MANITOU SPRINGS ELEMENTARY SCHOOL

The Collector vibrated with anticipation.

Across from the school where Rachel taught there was a neighborhood park filled with hiding places. Behind the toilets. Hunkered down in the shrubbery near the swings where the children often play. All those lovely, lovely children.

His favorite spot was in the thick grove of birch trees, still hanging on to their leaves. The canopy of red and gold swayed over him like lovers dancing. Like him dancing with the woman he had chosen to honor above all others. A woman truly worthy of raising a family. Not like his wretched bag of a mother who deserved every bit of fire and damnation heaped on her head.

There she was, *his* woman, beautiful from head to toe. Oh yes, she was. And he had an unfettered view of her as she walked into the schoolhouse. Glorious walk. That of a sensual woman so exactly right for his purposes, he couldn't contain himself.

He salivated. Actually licked the drool from his own lips.

"She's perfect in every way," he murmured.

His thundering heart nearly burst out of his chest.

"Yes, she is."

She paused and tilted her head sideways as if she sensed her lover was near.

"Soon I'll bring her home."

The agony and the ecstasy!

"Yes, indeed. She will be the crowning achievement!"

Rachel was at the schoolhouse door now. *Turn, turn.*

When she turned back around and smiled, he knew it was all for him. Oh yes, it was. She was already halfway in love with him.

The roses had done their work. Oh yes, they had. Though he had never been married, had never even dated, he knew how to please a woman. Hadn't he spent most of his life sharpening his mind and toning his body for just this moment?

When the time came, Rachel would be so captivated, she'd fall into his arms like a ripe plum. Oh yes, she would!

Happy day!

TWENTY-SEVEN

Rachel glanced at the school clock on the wall. Five minutes till three.

Thank goodness. Rain had threatened all day, matching her gloomy mood. The day had been additionally difficult because the children were still apprehensive about Lulu's disappearance but at the same time, revved up by the Emma Crawford Festival.

Incomprehensibly, the committee had decided to start it tomorrow evening instead of Friday. To what end, Rachel didn't know. It seemed a foolhardy decision, particularly in view of the local kidnappings.

Her own children wouldn't want to miss a minute of the festivities. Rachel could only console herself with the idea that there would be a huge police presence due to the kidnappings, and the crowd would be filled with other concerned parents keeping a close eye on the children.

Still, she didn't like the idea of that much exposure.

After the school bell rang and they'd finally settled into the car, Joey immediately began lobbying for an early start at the Emma Crawford Festival.

"I want to go early and eat three hot dogs!" he cried.

"*Ewww*." Susan held her nose in pretend horror.

"Maybe two, Joey. Three will make you sick."

"Vampires don't get sick."

His vampire costume had been hanging front and center in his closet since Jen had sent it in September, a hand-me-down from her son, Tommy.

"Can I spend the night with Wendy?" Susan said.

"Not on a school night. We've talked about this."

"Not tomorrow. Friday?"

Rachel couldn't bear the thought of having Susan out of her sight overnight. What if Lulu wasn't enough for the kidnapper? What if he wanted all three girls? If he was local, he'd surely seen them together, either at the park or on the school playgrounds or even at each other's houses.

The overly protective side of her hoped the impending storm lasted long enough to cancel the festival.

"I don't think an overnight play date is a good idea right now, honey."

Susan teared up. "You never let me do what I want!"

"I know it seems that way, especially since Sunday, but I promise you, everything's going to get better soon, Susan. How about we pop some corn and have some hot chocolate when we get home?"

Anything to keep them inside. This hovering mother-hen stance was such a reversal of the opinion she'd held merely three days ago that Rachel wanted to scream. The Collector might as well have moved into their home and taken his place at the head of the table. She was so mad at him, she found herself holding the steering wheel in a death grip.

When Joey yelled, "Yes!" Rachel startled, and her mind swung back to the popcorn.

"Susan, what about you? Does that sound good?"

Finally, Susan gave her grudging agreement.

Rachel didn't even mention that they'd also be watching another children's movie. When would this madness ever end? And how was she possibly going to have a sane minute trying to keep her children close at a festival that would last throughout the weekend?

She called Gran from the car and told her to put the hot chocolate on. They made it Mayan style, real chocolate squares melted in a double boiler, then a dash of cinnamon and a touch of red pepper added along with the milk and a bit of half-and-half for richness.

Hank often said he'd already become addicted. She'd be sure to make an extra cup of chocolate he could zap in the microwave when he got home.

The minute they walked in the door, Gran hugged all three of them as if she hadn't seen them in weeks and might not see them again for another month. And wasn't that the beauty of love? You can never get or give enough hugs.

"Hot chocolate's almost ready."

"Did you make enough for Hank?"

"Of course. He's family."

Rachel didn't even let herself think about that comment. Instead, she glanced at the clock. Almost four. The clock was her enemy today.

She had time for only a few sips before she slipped out of the kitchen and down the basement stairs. She had promised her renter she would gather his linens and towels from the hamper every Wednesday and Saturday at four.

When she inserted her key into the lock of Bruce's apartment, the scent of magnolias assaulted her. Her mother's warning from the grave made Rachel pause, more than a little apprehensive.

TWENTY-EIGHT

BASEMENT APARTMENT | LOGAN RANCH

Rachel didn't know what to expect when she used her key to enter Bruce's apartment. Art supplies everywhere? Spatters of oil and acrylic paints on the furniture? More flowers?

She pushed the door open, and for a moment, she stood in the doorway, simply breathing. It was spotless. The bed was made, the dishes were out of sight, and nothing marred the surface of the counters in the kitchenette or any of the tables, not even a stray paint brush, or a page from his artist's sketchbook.

What had she expected? Artistic chaos? Crushed beer cans littering the floor and water rings on the tables? One of Joey's imaginary monsters jumping from the closet?

Get a grip. She was so upset by the Collector's invasion of her home, she could hardly think straight.

Still chiding herself, she went straight to the hamper and gathered Bruce's sheets and towels. There was nothing left to do but go back upstairs, toss them into the washing machine, and be done with it. Then she'd return Saturday afternoon with them folded and clean.

Simple.

"Move it." She said this aloud to herself, trying to get her feet to cooperate.

But the faint, sweet scent had followed her inside and was rising from the desk. The pull was so strong she dropped the laundry on the sofa.

The magnolias always know.

An impending sense of danger made her heart hammer and her throat dry.

"I will not give in to this again. I *won't*."

Nothing is as it seems.

She covered her ears to block out the sound of her mother's voice, but Rachel had never been able to stand up to Delilah. Not then and not now.

She tiptoed over to the small oak desk as if it might turn into an ogre at any minute and bite her hand off. She'd take a quick glance. Just one. And then she'd be done with foolishness once and for all. If necessary, she would keep the dreaded scents away by stuffing Vicks Vapor Rub up her nose.

She glanced around the top of the desk. Charcoal pencils in a holder, neat as could be. Closed sketchbook on the blotter in the center of the desk. Simple tools of his trade. Nothing amiss there.

Still, she reached toward the sketchbook, opened it, then stood there flooded by equal parts guilt and suspicion. The charcoal sketch staring up from the page was undoubtedly her. Same hair and eyes, same mouth.

She turned the page, then another and another. Her image filled every page, and one of them was of her sleeping. It was so realistic, exactly the way she slept on her back with both arms thrown above her head, that she wondered if he'd crept upstairs and watched her in the middle of the night. Or had he managed to install hidden cameras?

Memories of being watched flooded her. The creepy feeling. The strong convictions. The all-too-real sensation of having her privacy stolen.

But *why*? Why any of this?

Had Bruce also taken her favorite ornament from her garden and the photograph from her office? Terrified, she sank into the desk chair and leaned over, heaving. She broke out in a cold sweat and raced into the bathroom to swab her face. Her hands shook so hard she could barely hold the towel to her face.

How *dare* he do this? How *dare* he sneak in the house while her children were sleeping? How *dare* he invade her personal space and watch her at her most vulnerable?

Disgust and fury replaced her fear. She tore back to his desk and jerked open the drawer. Paperclips, pencil stubs, pens, a roll of stamps, envelopes. Scotch tape.

A sound outside vaulted her from behind the desk. Grabbing the pile of linens off the sofa, she bolted toward the window and peered out. The sound made her jump again. It was only a tree limb, slapping against the window. Relief flooded her. The wind had picked up. The rain that had threatened all day wouldn't be long coming. And it was going to be fierce.

Good.

Maybe it really would rain out that dratted festival. At the very least, it would give her another excuse to keep her children inside, safe from the clutches of the Collector.

Still trembling with fury, she dumped the laundry then returned to finish her search of the desk. At the back of the bottom drawer, she spotted a terrifying sight. A deck of Tarot cards.

Was *Bruce* the one who had kidnapped the children?

With a growing sense of horror, Rachel stared down at the cards. Snatches of her conversation with Hank played through her mind.

"Yellowing card stock... from the seventies... tattered edges... spattered with stains..."

The cards Bruce had tucked into the desk were new. Still, they were there, four decks, all wrapped in cellophane. Beside them was a slim volume titled, *How to Read Tarot Cards*.

Was her renter just curious about the local boogey man, or was he doing research for himself because he *was* the bogey man?

Spurred by her discoveries, Rachel dug deeper in the drawer. Her next find chilled her to the bone. Underneath the Tarot instruction book was a stack of biographies on some of the most heinous serial killers in history: John Wayne Gacy, Jack the Ripper, Son of Sam, Ted Bundy. Her hands shook as she pulled her iPhone from her pocket and snapped pictures of the contents of the desk drawer. Then she flipped back through Bruce's sketchbook, snapping the charcoal likenesses of herself.

By the time she'd finished, rain rattled the windows like demons trying to get inside.

Her feet magically carried her upstairs and her better angels locked the apartment and basement doors behind her. They must have. Her hands were shaking too badly to have performed even the simplest task.

Victoria met her at the head of the stairs.

"You look like you've seen a ghost."

"I think my renter might be the Collector," Rachel gasped.

Victoria's usual take-charge expression collapsed with horror. "How is that possible? You checked him out!"

"I know. I know..." Rachel glanced around, frantic, uncertain. How could she have brought the most feared man in Manitou Springs into her own home? "Where are the children?"

"Upstairs with Sam."

If she weren't so distraught, the sounds would have told her that. Susan's imperious princess voice and Joey's growls announced they were already practicing vampire and princess in their costumes.

Still shaking, Rachel dropped the laundry then grabbed a chair from the kitchen to wedge under the knob of the door going down to the basement.

Without a word, Gran gathered the clothes and carried them into the laundry room. In short order, the sounds of the washing machine filtered back to Rachel, followed by the reappearance of Victoria, her face a map of concern.

"Let's go where we can have more privacy."

Rachel wrapped an arm around her grandmother and led her to the kitchen. She didn't want their conversation drifting up the stairs to her children. She was close to collapsing into a terrified heap.

Slashing rains and dark clouds had plunged the house into early darkness. Gran went about the kitchen snapping on lights while Rachel zapped her chocolate milk in the microwave, never mind that it would never taste as good as straight from the pan. Afterward she huddled at the kitchen table, chilled by the storm, hugging her mug and telling her grandmother what she'd found in Bruce's apartment.

Victoria's rage grew with every revelation. "If my beloved Finn were living, he'd run that skunk off our ranch with a horse whip. I might just do it, myself."

"I wish you could, but it's not that easy to get rid of a renter, Gran. He has a signed contract. Current laws make it impossible for me just to go to Bruce Wyler and ask him to leave."

"What about all that evidence?"

"He's an artist. He'll explain away the drawings of me in a heartbeat. And it's not against the law to read books about serial killers or to have Tarot cards in your desk. Everything I found proves exactly *nothing*." Rachel felt as defeated as if the storm were in her kitchen, destroying her home and intending to drown her and her family.

"If Hank were here, he'd know what to do," Gran said.

"But he's not."

Victoria brooded, leaving her chocolate untouched. "Bruce Wyler's all show and no substance. I never did like him."

"Why didn't you tell me?"

"A broke-down horse can stay in the same stable as a thoroughbred. You need the rent money."

"Not if I'm putting my children at risk. Has he done anything suspicious I don't already know about? Anything you've seen while I've been at school?"

"Not a thing. He never even knocks on the doors trying to get in here on the pretext of asking me a question. The only time was when he brought the roses."

"Maybe Bruce is obsessive about his subjects, and I just happen to be one of them?" Rachel was grasping at straws, trying to justify what she'd seen in the desperate hope that the Collector wasn't in her very own basement. "I could be wrong about him. It's easy to think the worst when you're scared."

Rachel raked her hands through her hair. Driving rain battered at the windows with deadly intent, and jagged streaks of lightning sliced the sky. The electrically charged air added to her fear. She kept seeing the stack of horrible books she'd found in the renter's desk, and the exact likeness of her sleeping...

"I keep wondering why he would have *four decks* of Tarot cards in his desk," she said.

"Maybe he's obsessed with the Collector, too? Augusta says lots of people get that way about celebrities, even if they earned their fame doing awful things."

"You could be right, Gran." Rachel felt a faint glimmer of hope. The new angle was perfectly logical. Maybe Bruce was merely an eccentric artist, renting her apartment. Or was he? "But I keep thinking there's something I'm forgetting. Something about those cards..."

"There used to be two or three women around here who read cards. Seems like your mama knew one of them."

"Who was she?"

"I can't remember now."

"Do you remember anything at all about the relationship, how old Mom was, or where she might have met someone like that?"

"It was too long ago. Much as I hate to admit it, my memory's not what it used to be." Her grandmother shook her head. "For that matter, my body's not, either. Can you stop by the drugstore after school tomorrow and get me a good laxative?"

"I'll go now."

"Not in this storm. I'm not that bad off."

"Are you sure?"

"Quit looking at me like that, Rachel. I'm old and irregular, not *dying*!"

Suddenly, all the lights went out. The children screamed, the dog barked, and Rachel had the creeping feeling that this was not an act of nature but the act of an unnatural human being with a twisted mind.

"Gran, don't move."

As Rachel blundered through the darkness toward the stairs, she thought she heard the rattle of the doorknob to the basement door. But she had no time for that now. Her children were still screaming.

Before she could reach the bottom step, they were already tumbling down the staircase, followed by Sam. Rachel gathered her crew and herded them toward the kitchen. Gran had already lit candles and set them on the table and the kitchen counters. Everybody looked ghostly in the flickering light, as if the storm and the events of the past few days had stolen their identities and turned them into mere shadows of themselves.

Amidst the chaos, somebody started pounding on the front

door so hard it sounded like a group of giants trying to get inside.

"Rachel!"

Bruce. Terror zinged through her.

"RACHEL!"

What on earth was he doing out in the storm instead of letting himself into his own apartment?

The pounding escalated, followed by another shout. "Let me in!"

"What am I going to do?" she whispered to Gran.

"Let him stand out there and let the lightning get him."

"Gran!" Rachel's mind whirled with possible solutions, none of them good. "Take the children and Sam back upstairs and lock yourselves in Joey's room and barricade the door. Call Hank. He should be here any minute."

"I don't like this," Gran said.

"I don't either, but it's the best I can do. I signed a rental contract with him. A landlord can't just leave a tenant in a dangerous thunderstorm."

Rachel waited until they were upstairs then groped her way through the dark house toward the front door. "Bruce," she called, "what are you doing out there?"

"I forgot my key. Let me in. The lightning's getting really bad out here."

"Just a minute." She didn't recall seeing his key in the apartment. What if he was lying? What if that had been him trying to get into the house through the basement door?

A clap of thunder followed by a sharp crack of lightning told her that he might really be struck and killed by a stray bolt. Colorado had the highest number of deaths by lightning strikes of any state. Though most of them occurred in the spring and summer months, there had been many in October. She could see the national headlines: *Rachel Maxey Responsible for Death of Famous Artist.*

What if she was wrong about him being the Collector? The phrase *innocent until proven guilty* went through her mind.

Another boom rattled the windows. She couldn't postpone the decision. And Hank would soon be here.

"Rachel!"

"Okay. I've got it."

Consoled by the thought that Hank would be home any minute, she slid back the chain and twisted the deadbolt.

Was she about to let an innocent man into her home or a madman?

TWENTY-NINE

DENVER INTERNATIONAL AIRPORT | DENVER, COLORADO

All flights leaving Denver had been canceled. With the runway visual range below fifteen hundred meters, the danger of deadly collisions by planes during take-off was a risk no pilot or airport would take.

Hank cradled his coffee cup and debated whether to call Rachel, or wait for a weather update first. Earlier reports predicted delays of no more than two hours, but the storm lashing the windows of the pilot's lounge told another story. Lightning bolts zigzagged across the sky, showcasing the state's deadly history of storm-related fatalities.

Pete Armstrong, an older pilot with a smaller charter company in Colorado Springs, strolled into the lounge and paused beside Hank. "Hey, Carson. You might as well grab supper before the stranded passengers fill up the restaurants, and then nab a cot while you still can."

"I'm hoping to get out of here in the next hour."

"Not a chance, buddy. Latest report says this front is not going anywhere tonight, and we'll still be socked in early tomorrow with heavy fog."

Pete had fifteen years more experience than Hank and a stellar safety record. His word was as good as law.

Still, leaving Rachel and her family alone to face whatever the Collector had in mind next left a knot in Hank's stomach. Even if he went into the airport to find a restaurant, he wouldn't be able to digest a bite.

"Thanks, Pete."

"Not a problem. If you want any sleep, you'd better throw your gear on a bunk far away from mine. I had spaghetti. It makes me snore like a freight train."

Everything made Pete snore, but Hank didn't point that out. He stowed his gear on a cot in the sleeping section two bunks away from the black backpack emblazoned with PILOT PETE in red letters then left the lounge. But food was not on his mind. He wound through the corridors till he found a quiet spot underneath a set of stairs where he could talk to Rachel and have a chance of being heard above the chatter and frequent announcements of flight information that filled the airport.

He connected on the first ring. But all he could hear on her end of the line was background noise from the storm and the sound of a door shutting.

"Rachel?"

In the background, he could just about make out a man's voice.

"Sorry, I'm dripping on your floor..."

The voice had Bruce Wyler's distinctive East Coast accent. Straining to hear more, his bodyguard instincts went into overdrive.

"Rachel, what's happening there?"

"It's just Bruce." The chipper voice wasn't typical of Rachel. It was Rachel being wound-up and nervous. "He got caught in the storm without his key."

There was a little hitch in her breath. One of the many little telling signs about Rachel he knew so well. She was more than nervous. She was scared.

"Rachel, listen carefully. Tell him it's me, that you have to take my call and he should stay in the hall while you get a towel so he can dry off. Then secure Victoria and the children and get in your bathroom and tell me exactly what's happening."

As he waited for her to follow his instructions, his mind whirled in a dozen different directions. Who could he call to protect her? Maybe the sheriff could spare a patrol car, but would the sight of it set off the man who could easily be the Collector?

"Hank?" she said. He heard the door shut and the click of a lock. "I sent Gran and the kids upstairs with Sam before I let Bruce inside. I'm in the bathroom now."

"Where's Wyler?"

"He's still standing in the hall."

"Do you need help right now?"

"I don't know..."

This was not Rachel being independent. It was the woman he knew so well being utterly alone and uncertain about what to do.

"Talk to me, Rach."

As she told of what she'd discovered in her renter's room, Hank felt himself defaulting back to military days when a sniper waited behind every burned-out building and seventy-five percent of the escape routes were littered with explosives that could as easily end your life as blow off your arms and legs.

Rachel's description of the sketch of her sleeping was particularly disturbing.

"How is Wyler acting now?"

"No different from always, really." She was breathing too hard. "It's just me. I can't forget the images of what I saw. I'm projecting all those serial killers onto him. If he really is the Collector, he's going to pick up on my fear and..."

"Take a deep breath, count to three and exhale. Slowly... and again." He could hear her breathing begin to return to normal. "Better now?"

"Yes. Where are you? When will you be here?"

"Still in Denver. I can't fly out in this weather."

"Oh no!"

"Rachel, listen. Take Wyler a towel. Tell him I got stuck in storm-related traffic but will be there any minute, and then you send him straight to his apartment."

"I propped a kitchen chair against the basement door. He's going to see that and know something's going on."

"Tell him it wouldn't stay shut when you came up with his laundry, and that was your way of fixing it."

"I'm an emotional mess, Hank. I don't know if he'll believe me."

"Pour on the charm. You can do this. Remember the self-defense moves I taught you?"

"Yes."

"If he makes a move, use them."

"I will."

"Good. He knows I'm coming, so I don't think you'll need them. After he leaves, check your bedroom again for hidden cameras. Now, go before he gets suspicious. As soon as we hang up, I'll call the sheriff to send a patrol car."

"Okay. I can do it. I'll be fine."

"Call me back the minute you get Wyler back in the basement. And if you find cameras, let me know."

"I will."

After she'd ended the call, Hank stood in the shadows under the stairway hanging on to the phone as if he could tether her to safety by the force of his will. It shouldn't take her more than ten minutes to get the renter out of the hall and back into his apartment. Fifteen at the most.

He called Sheriff Johnson. Rachel's discoveries in the basement were more than enough for him to send a car to stakeout her house. Hank sank into a hard plastic chair he spotted near the wall and leaned back to wait.

It was going to be one of the longest nights of his life.

THIRTY
LOGAN RANCH

When Rachel got back to the hall, the power had come back on.

Bruce was still waiting, but not where she had left him. He'd moved farther inside and was standing in front of the hall table staring up at the only professional portrait she had of her small family.

It had been hand-painted after Joey's birth. She was seated, holding her baby boy in one arm with her other wrapped around Susan. Max stood behind them, splendidly dressed in his uniform and flashing his smile that always lit up a room.

The sight of the renter's greedy eyes drinking in this scene sent shivers through her.

"Great picture. The perfect family." Bruce turned to smile at her. "Are you taking them to the festival?"

Was he just making small talk, or did he have an ulterior motive? He was staring at her with a quizzical expression. If she didn't say something, he was going to get suspicious.

"Yes. They wouldn't miss it."

"I always wanted a family like that but never seemed to have the time. Maybe someday I will."

"Maybe so. Families are wonderful."

"It'll be too late for my mother to see it, God rest her soul, but my dad will be happy to see his son finally doing something normal, like raising kids, instead of trekking all over the country with a canvas and a box of paints."

The word *normal* sliced through Rachel with the efficiency of a surgeon's blade. The contents of Bruce's desk drawer announced loud and clear that he was anything but normal.

"I brought you a towel." She thrust it at him as if he were a flaming bonfire that might burn her house down any minute. "You must be cold from all that rain."

"I am. Thanks for the towel." He peered at her through wheat-colored hair that, dampened, didn't even look natural. In fact, everything about the man standing in her hallway now made her think of a hollow shell who had conveniently filled himself up with the attitudes and opinions he thought might belong to a famous artist.

"A fire would be nice," he added "but there's no fireplace downstairs."

She'd as soon cozy in front a fire with a rattler as invite him into her den.

"I'd invite you to join me in the den, but I've got to get in the kitchen and get busy now that the power's back on. Hank will be here any minute, and he'll be starving."

"Where is he?"

Was Bruce suspicious? Curious?

Rachel realized she was still as tightly wound as a woman getting ready for fight or flight. She forced herself to relax and give him what she hoped was an easy smile.

"He got caught in traffic because of the storm, as I imagine you did. He holed up a bit in the laundromat down the road to call me." She glanced at her watch, trying to exude confidence. "He should be pulling up any minute."

Bruce studied her so long, a hot flush crept into her cheeks. She felt guilty and vulnerable, all at the same time. And more than a little alarmed. Was it her overwrought imagination, or was his look predatory?

"Does this mean there's something going on between you two? Not that I could blame the man."

First the pink roses, and now this. Horror shuddered through her.

The images in his sketchbook played through her mind. Maybe she could dampen Bruce's obsession by telling him she definitely had something going with Hank. Or maybe such an admission would make him mad or set off some other bizarre behavior that would be even worse than what she'd already discovered.

Her anxiety rose by the minute, and then she heard the sound of a car engine coming up her driveway.

Rescued!

Bruce angled himself so he could look out the window and stiffened. "I've kept you from dinner preparations long enough. If you have a spare key, I'll just hurry off for a hot shower and a good book."

As Rachel escorted him toward the basement stairs and gave him a spare key, she thanked her lucky stars for the flashing blue lights she'd seen through her front windows and for Hank who had called the sheriff to her rescue.

When she next saw Hank, she would even thank him for the breathing lessons that allowed her to get through a smooth explanation of a door that wouldn't shut properly and the kitchen chair that held it in place.

As soon as Bruce was through the door and his footsteps had receded on the basement stairs, Rachel propped the chair into place once more and raced upstairs to check on her family.

The children tumbled into her arms, and she held them close. "Gran, we're all going to sleep up here tonight. You can sleep with Susan, and I'll sleep with Joey."

Victoria followed Rachel into the hallway. "What's going on?"

"Bruce is in the basement and a patrol car is stationed outside the house. Hank's grounded in Denver, but he'll be back tomorrow. I'll bring your things upstairs when I come back. Don't let the children out of your sight."

By the time she got to the kitchen, Rachel felt as if she had run a marathon. If Bruce was standing in his apartment with his head tilted, listening for sounds of her movements, he would have a good idea where she was.

Leaning against the island, she called Hank.

"He's in his apartment and a patrol car just pulled up. Gran and the kids are fine."

"And you?"

"I'm okay. I can do this, Hank."

"That's the best news I've had all day."

Rachel pocketed her cell phone and went into her bedroom to check for hidden cameras. The utter quietness felt creepy. She switched on her small wall-hung TV for company and set about searching all the places she and Hank had already looked.

What had they missed?

She was checking her picture frames when a bulletin on the late-night news torpedoed her. The skeletal remains of six-year-old Caroline Hankins had been found in the same landfill in Denver where a forklift driver had discovered the body of the Langley boy. Caroline had been taken from her home only three months after the boy vanished.

Rachel slumped to her bed, so overwhelmed by a mother's fear for her children, she could barely breathe. Grabbing her TV's remote control, she turned up the volume.

"The seven-year mystery of the kidnappings of the Langley and Hankins children might never have been solved if the city had not decided to clear a section of the landfill for a new administration office."

The camera switched to both sets of parents, heartbroken by the loss of all hope but grateful they could now bury the remains of their children.

Rachel cried as a split screen showed a photo of a smiling child on her swing, her face as delicate as a magnolia bloom. Next to it was a heartbreaking shot of two men bearing a gurney that held the small bones of the little girl only a year younger than her own daughter.

"In a stunning twist," the reporter added, "our sources tell us evidence was unearthed with Caroline Hankins that links her murder to the infamous Collector of Manitou Springs, Colorado."

Her search for hidden cameras forgotten, Rachel collapsed onto her bed and muffled her anguish with a pillow.

But terror leaves no time for sorrow. She got up, washed her face, and gathered the things she would need for her family to sleep upstairs. Safe.

She hoped.

THIRTY-ONE

It was not yet daylight when Rachel left her family sleeping and hurried downstairs to dress and call her older sister.

Jen didn't even say *hello*.

"I heard about that poor Hankins kid last night, but the news just confirmed all the warning signs I've had from the seagulls. They're bashing themselves on my windshield now. You're in danger, Rachel."

"It's my children who are at risk. I've *got* to get rid of my renter." She told her sister about her discoveries in his apartment. Jen's husband was a lawyer. He'd know how to evict him.

"I'll talk to him and see if he can come up with an angle, but leases in the U.S. are notoriously hard to break. You can't just evict him. The courts have gone bonkers, even ruling for the renter when the owner is clearly being harmed. Is everybody okay?"

Rachel said *yes*, though how could she be okay when she couldn't remove a renter who was possibly kidnapping and killing children, and the man she counted on for protection and every other good thing in her life was grounded by fog, hundreds of miles away?

Sighing, she glanced out the window. The two deputies who'd arrived last night in the middle of the storm were still out there, silently guarding her house.

She poured coffee into two Styrofoam cups and went outside. She didn't recognize either of them. The younger one, sitting on the driver's side, powered down his window. Tattoos were inked all across his hands. His name tag read Bob Smith, but in spite of the uniform and the ordinary name, she had a sixth sense that there was far more to him than met the eye.

"I thought you could use a cup." She handed the coffee through the window to a simultaneous chorus of *thank you*. "If you're hungry, we'll have pancakes in about twenty minutes. I'll tell Gran to make extra."

The older of the two leaned forward. He was a handsome young man with a bald head that resembled a bowling ball. "Thank you, but we're about done here. Unless you need us for anything else, we'll be leaving soon."

"We're all fine, here. Thank you for everything. I'm sorry you had to come."

"Don't ever apologize, miss," Bob Smith said. "We'd much rather come and find you okay than not get the call until the following day then arrive and find you missing or dead."

Rachel wrapped her arms around herself to stave off a shiver as well as the early morning chill. Was it the mention of death or was it her sixth sense kicking in again?

"Thank you, again."

"If you need us tonight at the festival, we'll be there along with cops on practically every corner of town." The older guy with the strange foghorn voice put on his sunglasses and waved as she left.

Rachel went back inside, dreading a festival that required cops on every corner. As she headed toward a kitchen filled with the aroma of pancakes and the morning chatter of Gran and the children, her cell phone rang.

It was Hank.

"Everything okay there, Rachel?"

"As well as it can be." She gave him a rundown of a quiet night where Bruce never reappeared. "They found the bones of Caroline Hankins in Denver. I'm so scared for my children I hardly know which way to turn."

"It was all over the news out here. I'm going to get home as soon as I can. I don't want you to leave for the festival until I get there. Better yet, don't go."

"The children have looked forward to it for weeks, and I just *hate* to see the Collector take this away from them." She repeated her conversation with the surveillance team, including the news of beefed-up security for the festival. "We'll be very careful. Gran and I won't let the children out of our sight."

"The fog's lifted here, but air traffic will keep me grounded for at least another hour, then I'll have a very long day re-scheduling the tours and charters I missed. But I promise I'll be back as soon as I can."

"Not a problem. A lot of other parents will be there watching out for the children, and I don't plan to stay long anyhow."

"You be very careful, Rachel. I'll call when I'm headed your way tonight."

"Promise?"

"I promise."

Tonight seemed one of Joey's forty-'leven days away, and her promise seemed impossible to keep.

Because how can you be careful to avoid the dangers you never see coming?

THIRTY-TWO

MANITOU SPRINGS DRUG STORE

After her call to Hank ended, Rachel was caught up in a whirlwind that lasted throughout the school day and beyond with errands. By five o'clock the children were so cranky, and she was so harried, she almost forgot about getting her grandmother's items as well as her own. She made one last stop by the drugstore downtown.

Leaving the children in the car was not an option. They tagged along with her, complaining with every breath as she purchased her grandmother's laxatives and a bottle of fiber gelatin capsules. When she dropped them into her tote bag, Joey tugged her hand.

"Now can we look at toys?"

"Just for a minute. And I'm not buying a thing. Your toybox is overflowing."

"Yeah, but my bear runned away."

Rachel rolled her eyes. That's how she had explained the missing bear the Collector had left. *He went on a big adventure while you were at school. When he comes back, I'll bet he will have amazing stories to tell.*

The things a mother will do to keep her child safe.

Joey dragged her around the corner to look at miniature trucks, pointing out at least six that he wanted for Christmas. Then Susan insisted on getting some snacks at the other side of the store.

As Rachel headed down the snack aisle with the children, she spotted the mailman holding two bags of potato chips.

He smiled. "I can't decide between plain and barbecue flavored. What do you kids think?"

"That one!" they chorused, pointing to the bag in his right hand.

"Barbecue, it is." He set the other bag back on the shelf. "I guess you're excited about the festival tonight?"

As he listened patiently while they told him about their costumes, Rachel felt a renewed hope that once the Collector was caught, her hometown would once again return to normal where neighbors helped each other and good people took the time to make children feel seen and heard.

"Have fun tonight." He waved as he headed to the cash register.

As she got in the car, Rachel regretted she hadn't asked him if he would be there. She blamed it on stress.

When they got home, the children raced upstairs to get into costumes, never mind that they wouldn't be going to the festival until after Victoria had watched *FAME*. Fortunately, it aired at five, and the children were mollified by Rachel's promise that they would arrive in time for the coffin races, then eat supper at the festival afterward.

When the opening credits for *FAME* blazed across the screen and Augusta Harper's signature blues music filled the den, Joey and Susan were too busy arguing over hot dogs versus hamburgers to complain about having to wait for Victoria's favorite show to end.

Rachel pushed aside the terror of the last few days and

allowed herself to relax and enjoy an ordinary evening with her family.

"Oh look. Augusta's got her guitar!" Gran beamed at Rachel, and that smile, so beloved, made the day's chaos feel less overwhelming. "I hope she plays something."

The author had been born in Cleveland, Mississippi, the cradle of blues. She often credited the pain and suffering in the plaintive Delta Blues for the rich, evocative writing that had made her famous.

Suddenly, Rachel found herself wondering how much pain and suffering her own mother had endured in order to pour so much soul and heartbreak into the blues ballads she sang.

When Augusta kicked back her sequined gown, propped her signature red garden boots on a stool, and announced she was going to sing "Why Ain't You Dead Yet" by an obscure songwriter called Li'l Rosie, Rachel caught her breath.

There was an old music notebook with yellowing pages tucked in the bottom drawer of her desk. It contained blues songs, both lyrics and melodies, composed under the name Li'l Rosie. The titles—"Ain't No Use Cryin", "Solo Livin Blues", "Lonesome Road Blues", "Walkin Blues", "Don't Mess With Me", and "Why Ain't You Dead Yet"—as well as the musical notations and lyrics were written in Delilah's slanting hand.

When Augusta cut loose strumming and singing, the TV audience went wild. So did Rachel's grandmother, never knowing she was cheering to a blues lament composed by her own daughter-in-law.

Riveted, Rachel listened to the song, the words as familiar to her as the list of students in her gradebook.

Woke up this mornin' feelin' low down and sad.
Said I woke up this mornin' feelin' low down and sad.
My pants got a hole and my music's turned bad.

That was only the first verse. The others were equally mournful.

Delilah had once told Rachel *a novel is a story told in three hundred pages and a song is a story told in three minutes.* This song told a story of loss, poverty, and heartache.

Rachel wanted to go back in time and hug her mother. She wanted to hear the stories of her childhood in the dark bayous and forbidding backwaters of the Mississippi. She wanted to go with her mother on those infrequent visits to New Orleans instead of staying blithely behind under the care of the happy-go-lucky Irishman who was her father and the loving vigilance of grandparents who doted on her.

If Rachel had learned anything from the havoc the Collector had visited on her hometown, it was the importance of family. Would her mother's parents and family have loved her and her sisters? Why had they never been part of Rachel's life growing up? She couldn't imagine a world in which Victoria would give up seeing her grandchildren and great-grandchildren and making every effort to ensure their safety.

Why had she and her sisters never inquired about them, never thought of the forgotten relatives as part of the family?

She made a mental note to talk to Jen about it. And Annie, too, if she would ever stay in one spot long enough to answer Rachel's calls. Granted, she almost never called Annie, telling herself her baby sister preferred it that way. But did she?

She would have to ask Jen.

As her grandmother ranted away at the contestants on TV, even going so far as to call one of them a *heifer* and another *meaner than a sidewinder,* Rachel found herself thinking about how often she depended on Jen for advice. Especially since Max's death. It seemed Rachel was afraid to make an important move that hadn't been sanctioned first by her older sister. Jen had grown so important in Rachel's mind she might as well be Wonder Woman.

"I have to find my own inner Wonder Woman."

She looked up to see if Gran had noticed her talking to herself, but Victoria was too enamored with her show to notice.

Rachel turned back to her grading. If she were lucky, she'd be finished by the time the show ended, and she wouldn't have to sit up late after the festival to complete the job.

She was on the final paper when her grandmother said, "Oh no. I can't believe it!"

Rachel looked up just in time to see the hometown favorite graciously accepting his elimination and congratulating the remaining two contestants.

As the credits rolled, Rachel marked the last paper and then began the task of getting her children to wear coats over their costumes. In the Rockies, temperatures dropped rapidly and dramatically after the sun went down, and the last rays of sunlight were already painting her windows. Additionally, the previous night's storm had ushered in a cold front that foretold snow wasn't too far behind.

Rachel donned her own coat and grabbed her tote bag. But as she climbed into her car with her family, she detected the faint scent of magnolias once again.

The icy fingers of fear marched down her spine, and she almost ushered her family back into the house. She could picture it: Joey having an epic meltdown, Susan pouting, Victoria stoic but caught in the middle.

Consoling herself that Hank would soon meet her there, Rachel started the car. But the warning scent of magnolias stayed with her all the way to the festival.

THIRTY-THREE

EMMA CRAWFORD COFFIN RACES AND FESTIVAL | MANITOU SPRINGS, COLORADO

The crush of people in downtown Manitou Springs was exactly what the Collector had expected.

They milled about like cattle in the center of town underneath the iconic clock topped by a statue of Hebe, cupbearer to the gods of Mount Olympus. It had been built to celebrate the town's booming industry, bottled mineral water.

A stage had been set up near the clock for the band, the West Side Rhythm Kings. The beat of their music was so loud it thrummed through the Collector like his beloved murder of crows. He felt himself filling up with power, growing stronger by the minute.

Just thinking about his own prowess sent him scurrying with the crowd to the park where beer from Bristol Brewery and shots of tequila from Agave Underground flowed as freely as crow's blood. Another week of drinking the blood from his feathered demon friends, and he would be omnipotent. Oh yes, he would.

He tossed back the shots of tequila, one after the other, and a hot burst of power bloomed through him as sharp and bright as the sights and sounds filling his vision. Swirling dancers, gaudy homemade caskets on wheels, hordes of women in Victorian splendor heading toward Miramoat Castle to pay respects to the ghoulish faux, Emma, laid out in her wedding gown for her annual wake.

But where was *she*? His love, his future?

He wound his way back through the throngs, unnoticed, invisible. Oh yes, he was. Nobody saw his powerful black wings. Nobody noticed his sharp beak, capable of ripping you apart with one tear. Nobody called him by name. Nobody saw the aura of terrible beauty and complete destruction that hovered over him like the eye of a Category 5 hurricane.

The cards had foretold this night, and now here it was. His own personal hunting ground.

More than twenty-five years since its inception, the Emma Crawford Festival had grown to attract tourists from all over the world, making this the kind of crowd the Collector had dreamed about. The cards had not only foretold the masses of people, but Pikes Peak, looming above the festival. It was a giant phallic symbol, a proper monument to the Collector who would father a dynasty of such pure grace and pure evil the world would quiver at the sound of his name. Oh yes, they would.

Streetlights and lights pouring from the downtown businesses and strung along the booths of vendors provided so much illumination the Collector might have been fooled into thinking he was standing in broad daylight.

Still, *she* was nowhere to be seen. The light of his life. His soulmate.

A darkness rose in him, as black as the alleys and the occasional dark spot along the sidewalk where people had gone out of business during hard times or had chosen to close their stores and go home early. He peered in the shadows, looking for her. There was nothing to see except the fleeting shapes of a few stray cats and dogs scavenging for scraps.

He wanted to caw at the moon, beat his feathered chest,

ruffle his wings and soar to the treetops so he could use his X-ray yellow eyes to spot her in the crowd. She would be his. Oh yes, she would.

He licked a drop of tequila from his lips in anticipation.

"It's a great night to catch a finely feathered bird." Making the boast aloud gave him a sense of power.

Lately, that's how he had come to think of Rachel Maxey. A glorious bird of many colors who would fluff her royal plumage at the sight of him and scream with delight as he spread his black wings over her, fierce and powerful, omnipotent even. Capable of performing heroic feats and founding a famous dynasty.

"She's a catch. Absolutely gorgeous."

He couldn't get enough of spying on her.

"Oh yes, indeed, she is."

She even invaded his dreams.

"Irresistible. I can hardly wait."

She would be the queen mother, all because of his cleverness at finding her, wooing her, courting her. And now his patience at taking her.

Suddenly, miraculously, there she was! On the other side of the street.

He stood on his tiptoes to get a better look. She towered above her grandmother, an old lady slowly shrinking into her cowboy boots, and her two children, who were nothing to the Collector. Nothing at all. A nuisance. If they presented an obstacle, he would crush them and throw them away like trash.

His children with her would be far superior. Oh yes, they would!

"She's going to make a dozen beautiful children. Maybe more. Yes, she is."

He licked his lips in anticipation, too excited to contain himself. A glance at the crowd told him no one was paying any attention to him, or his boasts.

"I could take her now."

There was a flurry at the starting line of the race.

"But, wait."

Those silly homemade caskets—plexiglass and corrugated metal and cast-off pieces of wood painted psychedelic colors that glowed under the streetlamps—were lining up at the starting point, getting ready to come trundling down the street on their rickety wheels, carrying a ridiculous collection of Emmas dressed in Victorian wedding gowns.

The councilmen from City Hall, who always did well in the race, pushed their casket down the street. Inside was their chairman of the board, playing the hapless bride. He looked absurd with his white satin gown splitting at the seams and his three-day growth of beard making him look like a grizzly bear wearing a yellow wig.

The crowd cheered and screamed as they took an early lead in the race.

"With all this excitement I could grab her now."

He craned his neck so he could spot *her*.

"Wait. Not yet."

The crowd closed in around Rachel, effectively hemming her in as the casket from the sheriff's department came whizzing by, a stupid concoction decorated with pumpkins, skeletons, and orange and black streamers. None other than Sheriff Jeremiah Johnson was dressed up as Emma, his lips painted a garish red and his ham-sized hand over his satin chest where the officers had stitched a giant red heart.

"Who's manning this stupid festival? All the cops are in the coffin races."

The Collector glanced around. No matter which direction he looked, he could see uniforms.

"Where did all these cops come from?"

His own question was nothing more than thinking aloud. The Collector knew. Of course he did. He was so famous, so dangerous, so respected and feared, the city of Manitou Springs had called in support from the surrounding area. The place was teeming with fit men and women just itching to be the one to take *him* down.

He felt himself growing stronger, fiercer. He felt the ripple of muscle and feather along his backbone. He felt the blood of his own vicious murder of crows pulsing through him.

Every day he shot four of them. Yes, he did. Stripped their feathers, drained their blood, then drank it from a cup. Warm. Powerful. Evil. Amazing. Yes, it was.

The firefighters' coffin, his favorite, blood red, whipped the crowd into a frenzy. Not surprising. Didn't they know red was the color of rage?

And lust.

He felt his own lust rising as he glanced over the crowd toward the magnificent woman now totally hemmed in by enthusiastic festival-goers.

The Collector never took unnecessary chances. He would have been caught long ago if he acted on impulse instead of careful calculation.

While the coffin races were exactly the distraction he had counted on, they also offered impediments he had not calculated, ones that were impossible to overcome.

"She will have to wait."

Oh yes, she would.

"But what if I could separate her from the crowd?"

His perfect instincts kicked in. He wasn't about to take foolhardy chances when he was so close to achieving his dream.

The Collector ruffled his feathers as big as he dared on this over-crowded street where anybody could be looking. Anybody at all.

"Wait. The perfect moment will come, and she's worth waiting for."

Oh yes, she was!

The all-powerful black feathered king had spoken. He slipped away into the darkness.

THIRTY-FOUR

Rachel had found a parking place close to the main activities of the festival, and ushered her family to the center of the town to watch the coffin races. As the garish coffins whizzed by, she scanned the area for anything or anybody who would set off alarms. Relieved to see so many parents she knew, as well as Tanya Beasley, she moved her family toward Susan's second-grade teacher for extra security.

"Huge crowd," Tanya said, then exclaimed over the children's costumes and moved to flank them in a protective gesture that made Rachel feel better.

"Thanks, Tanya." Rachel gave her a grateful smile.

She hadn't expected a crowd this big on a weeknight. Though she knew there would be extra security, nothing had prepared her for the sight of so many cops. In addition to the local police, there were also officers from Colorado Springs. Law enforcement personnel were visible on every street corner and around the perimeters of the various venues, including the picnic tables where she would have dinner with her family.

Alarm skittered through her. They had geared up for the worst. In a crowd this size, anything could happen.

By the time the coffin races were over, Rachel's son was jumping up and down, proclaiming to be starving.

"You are most certainly not *starving*, Joey." He looked angelic, even in his vampire suit. Better yet, he and Susan were safe.

Her son nodded vigorously, his cowlick bobbing. "I am. I could eat a *horse*."

Rachel's mother's heart melted. "All right, then. I'll be back as soon as I can with food, but the lines will be long. You have to be patient." She turned to Tanya. "Do you mind staying here with Gran and the children while I'm gone?"

"Not at all. Why don't I take them to the picnic area and find a table before they're all taken?"

"Great. I'll get your food, too, while I'm at it. What do you want?"

"Nothing thanks. A couple of former classmates have driven from Denver and will be joining me shortly."

As Rachel headed toward the food kiosks, she noticed other parents keeping a tight rein and a close eye on their children. Was this going to forever be the way of the changing world?

As she slid into a long line at the hot dog stand, she sincerely hoped not.

"Great night for the festival." The male voice coming from behind her was familiar.

Rachel turned to see the mailman. He wore a black down jacket with the hood pulled over his thinning hair to ward off the cold. Everything about him shouted timid and uncertain—his smile, his slightly stooped posture, even the tilt of his head.

Poor man. In the six years she'd known him, she'd never seen him with a friend or family member.

"Yes, it certainly is. How are you doing this evening, Charles?"

"I'm well, thank you, Miss Rachel. I just stopped by for a bite to eat before I head home. It's been a long day."

There was something courtly about his manners, and a bit old-fashioned, like those of a much older man. But he couldn't be more than ten or twelve years older than her. Maybe she could introduce him to the new teacher at the elementary school. She was a lonely widow, just about his age, and every bit as nice.

Before she could say anything more to Charles, she found herself at the head of the line facing an impatient-looking woman who told her to hurry up and order.

"People are waiting," the woman snapped.

Rachel placed her order then shot an apologetic smile over her shoulder to the mailman. Shortly afterwards, she was balancing a large order on a flimsy paper tray.

"Have a good evening, Charles."

He nodded as she made her way through the hustle and bustle at the food kiosks, around the corner, and back to her family. She spotted Tanya, waving her over.

A quick survey told her nothing new was happening inside the roped-off area where folding tables had been set up in the middle of the street. Joey had removed his jacket, but Rachel decided not to insist he put it back on. Who knew what a little boy's thermostat was like? She'd have to rely on his common sense to make him retreat into downy warmth if he got too cold.

"Thanks for staying, Tanya."

"Not a problem." She left to join her friends, who had arrived and staked out a spot two tables over. As Rachel divided the food, a group of wandering minstrels, high school kids, some of whom she knew, stopped by their table to serenade them. After they left, a band of clowns, unrecognizable in all their makeup, strolled among the tables, juggling balls and making balloon animals.

Rachel couldn't make out any of them behind the grease paint, outlandish wigs, and garish costumes. Some of them even wore elaborate carnival masks. Feeling more than a little uncomfortable, she eased her chair closer to her children. Across the table, Victoria did the same.

When a tall clown with a particularly deep voice reached toward Joey, she tensed, ready to spring into action.

"A dog balloon just for you, little Dracula," he said.

Joey was so excited he grabbed for the balloon animal and dropped his half-eaten hot dog. Nothing can melt down quicker than a hungry, overly excited four-year-old whose supper was scattered across the pavement.

"It's okay. It was an accident." Rachel scooped up the ruined food in a napkin. "I'll get you another one."

Fortunately, the clowns had dispersed and there were no other entertainers nearby whose heavy makeup and gaudy masks hid their true intent. The nearby tables were filled with other families, some with one parent, some with two, all of them with children excited to be out on a school night wearing costumes and eating fast food.

And fortunately, Tanya was still close by. But then Rachel spotted Bruce Wyler standing on the sidewalk beyond, staring in her direction. Cold chills ran all over her.

"Gran, I'm going to get Joey another hot dog. Keep an eye on Bruce Wyler while I'm gone."

"Don't worry. He won't get past me again."

"Good. I'll be back as soon as I can. If the line is long, it might take half an hour. Are you okay with that?"

"Certainly. I'm still so mad about our local boy being put off my favorite TV show tonight I could spit nails and jump over fences."

It felt good to laugh.

"Okay. If you need anything just send Susan over there to fetch Tanya Beasley."

Just to make sure she could count on Tanya, Rachel stopped by her table and asked if she'd keep an eye on her family.

"Of course. I'll be right here, Rachel." She stuck her feet out from under the table. "I'm wearing these cute new boots that are too tight. My feet are so sore they'll have to take a backhoe to remove me from this spot. Take your time." She grabbed Rachel's hand. "And don't worry. I won't let your children out of my sight until you're back."

As Rachel started to leave, she noticed her renter, still standing in the same spot as if he'd been watching her for quite some time. Had he?

The next question was, *why* would he? Anybody that young and famous certainly had better pickings than a schoolteacher with her own family. Memories of what she'd found in his room made her shiver.

"Tanya, this might sound paranoid but the blond man near the clock tower is the artist who rents my apartment, Bruce Wyler. I don't trust him, so please make sure he doesn't come near Gran and the children."

"I can do that. I'll put my mean schoolteacher hat on."

"Thanks. And if you see Jake Clement, keep him away from my family, too."

"Jake? Why?"

"I have my reasons. I'll tell you about them tomorrow at school."

"Okay. Don't worry. I've got this."

Beyond the picnic area, Rachel joined a large, jostling crowd inching past the strolling musicians and the street vendors in the direction of the food booths. Even in the crowd, she had the strong sense that she was being watched.

Rachel whirled and almost bumped into none other than the crossing guard. Icy fingers slid down her spine.

"Jake, are you following me?"

"No!" He looked alarmed and then sheepish. "Well, yes, actually. I saw you and thought I'd catch up and say hi."

What was this all about? Through the years she'd seen him

at school fund-raisers, sporting events and other school functions, and he had never sought her out to say *hi.*

"I can't stay to chat, Jake." Rachel made her greeting as cool as possible, and tried to move around him.

Jack side-stepped and blocked her, then leaned so close, her skin crawled. "You look especially pretty tonight."

Her danger meter went into fire-alarm mode. *Don't show fear.* A quick scan showed a cop on the corner, within shouting distance.

She relaxed a bit, but she wasn't about to acknowledge his compliment. If this was a clumsy prelude to asking her out, she wasn't going to give him the least bit of encouragement. Besides, she didn't trust him, not one little bit, as her Southern mother would say.

Was it her children he wanted? The sudden thought almost paralyzed her. She made a mental note to call the sheriff as soon as she got back to her family and see if he'd found a clue that would tie Jake Clement to the Collector.

If he kept deliberately blocking her, she'd report that, too, she didn't care how insignificant it sounded. She was tired of being scared, tired of looking over her shoulder, sick to death of the evil that held everybody in her town hostage.

"I have to go. I'm on an errand to replace Joey's hotdog." Rachel tried to move around him again, and he grabbed her arm. Panic shot through her.

"Cute kid." His smile looked predatory. "So is Susan."

Her skin crawled. "Kids are always cute. And precious. I hope they catch the scumbag taking them."

She shook off his arm and bolted. He called after her, but she kept running. She veered toward the hot dog stand and glanced over her shoulder. Jake was walking in the other direction.

Rachel leaned over, trying to calm down and catch her

breath. But her heart was hammering so hard, she had to gulp for air.

Finally, she was able to stand upright again. But until the Collector was caught, this nightmare was far from over.

THIRTY-FIVE

Still shaken, Rachel headed to the hotdog stand.

"Rachel." She whirled in the direction of the person calling her name and saw the mailman, sitting on the curb with his head on his knees and two large sacks at his feet.

What fresh nightmare was this? A heart attack? A mugging?

She headed in his direction, scanning the area for signs of foul play. "Charles?" she said. He looked up, ashen-faced and sickly. "Are you okay? Do you need me to get a doctor?"

"Rachel..." His breathing sounded labored. "I'll be all right in a minute. I get these spells sometimes."

She sat down beside him and felt his forehead as if he were one of her children. "You don't have a fever. I'll get you some water."

"No, I think I'll be okay if I rest here a bit." He gave her a wan smile.

"I'll sit with you until you feel better."

"You're very kind, Miss Rachel."

"Not a problem." There was no way she could walk off and just leave him sitting on the sidewalk, maybe having an attack of some kind that might kill him. "Is there somebody with you? I saw a deputy back a few yards beside the hamburger stand. I could ask him to page someone for you?"

"No." He stood up, a bit wobbly. "But if you'd help me get to my vehicle with this food, I'd really appreciate it."

"Sure." Rachel grabbed the two bags then offered her arm. "Lean on me." He leaned on her more heavily than she'd imagined. "Where's your car?"

"Not far. I'll show you."

They passed all the well-lit lots that were nearby, and even the ones that were moderately close. As the sidewalks became more uneven and the streetlights more infrequent, her hopes began to sag. He was parked farther away than she'd imagined. But that was the nature of the Emma Crawford Coffin Races and Festival. Parking was always a problem.

She was going to be very late getting back to her family with Joey's hotdog. Still, there was no way she could get her phone out of her pocket now without slowing them down. Her consolation was that Tanya would take care of her family until she got back. And Hank should be arriving soon.

The long walk was beginning to take a toll on Charles, whose breathing became more labored. That, plus the increasing darkness, ramped up her unease.

"Charles, do you need me to call for an ambulance?"

"No. I'm fine."

"You don't sound fine. Maybe we should sit down and rest a bit?" It would give her a chance to call Victoria.

"I said, I'm *fine*! Keep going."

His snappish reply set off the first alarm bells. The parking lot they approached was unkempt, shadowed by shrub brush and darkened by streetlamps with burned-out bulbs. Rachel felt the first shiver of fear.

Trust no one. Hank's warning echoed through her.

What had she done?

Rachel fought back her fear. Her natural inclination to help had overruled her survival instincts and her common sense. Everyone knew the Collector was constantly upping his evil game. Had he gone from taking children to kidnapping women?

Seized by a new terror, she wished she could rewind time and be back on the street fetching one of the many deputies to help the mailman.

Was she in jeopardy? Were her children going to be left motherless as well as fatherless?

She tried to school her growing fear. "Charles, how far is your car?"

"Just a few more feet."

Okay, he sounded normal again. She'd known him for *years*. She could do this. Still, as they entered the shadow of an ancient tree with overhanging branches, chills formed along her arms and the back of her neck, and they had nothing to do with rapidly dropping temperatures.

The air was filled with the unmistakable scent of magnolias.

Rachel tried to convince herself the floral warning was conjured up by her own fear, but the scent intensified. It clung to her hair and her skin, wafted up from the earth. It even wound around her nose and mouth, threatening to smother her.

She fought for breath. She fought for control.

Charles was watching her. Waiting.

"Great," she said. There was a false-chipper note in her voice, the one that meant she was now scared out of her socks. "I believe you can make it by yourself now. Joey's probably crying that I'm not back with his food."

"Joey can wait."

Was it her imagination, or did his voice harden? Did he tighten his grip?

"But he's just a little boy..."

The scent of magnolias became more insistent. Suddenly, a stiff wind shivered the branches above her, sending red leaves raining like blood at her feet. The wind moaned and the air became so heavy with the sweet fragrance of magnolia blossoms that Rachel could almost see her own mother shimmering in the dark.

Run. Run.

Urgency ripped through Rachel like a blade, but she was frozen in place, rooted to the spot with terror.

Run. Now.

Her mind whirred. She was taller by a good two inches, and judging by everything she'd seen, she was in much better shape. She could outrun him. But she had to be smart about it.

She calculated the way he was holding her. The only way to get loose was to jerk toward his weak point, not his palm, but the fingers that circled her wrist.

Rachel took a deep breath then dropped the plastic bags. When they burst at Charles' feet, she jerked her wrist out of his grip.

She was free! And running!

"Stop right now!" he screamed. "Come back here!"

Let him scream. She was a good three lengths ahead of him now, and gaining. She thought about screaming, but it would be a waste of breath. She had seen no one in this area for the last five blocks. There was no one to hear her, no one to see.

The scent of magnolias swirled around her, and leaves were flying off all the trees as if they had been caught in a sudden storm.

And wasn't that true? The Collector had unleashed a storm of evil, and she was trapped dead in the eye with the blood-colored leaves.

She could hear him behind her, pounding across the pavement. Clearly nothing was wrong with him. It had all been an act.

No time for regrets. She was almost out of the parking lot. The minute she hit the sidewalk, she would be home free. A straight shot toward streetlights and festival lights. People. Cops. Blessed relief.

Her toe caught in a crack, and she fought for balance. There was nothing to grab except air. Nothing to break her fall. She was headed face down. A blow that could kill her.

"No!" she cried.

She twisted her face away from the pavement, twisted her entire body mid-air. Her side glanced off the pavement, but she was still rolling. Rachel landed on her back on a sorry patch of grass at the edge of the parking lot.

The blow knocked her breath out, and she lay there, winded, listening to the mailman coming closer.

He towered over her, his features twisted with rage.

"If you've hurt yourself so that you're no good to me, I'm going to have to kill you."

"No. Please..."

His hand cut off the rest of her sentence. The rag that closed over her mouth and nose smelled of dirt, chemicals, and evil.

Rachel pushed him with all her strength. But the darkness was already overtaking her.

Wait. This can't be happening.

What would her children do without her? Who would...

With the suddenness of snuffing out a light, the world went black.

THIRTY-SIX

HANK'S OFFICE

Hank stood in his office in Colorado Springs listening as his call to Rachel went to voicemail. It was his third attempt in the last thirty minutes. Why wasn't she answering her phone?

He made one more futile attempt then listened to the hollow sound of ringing. He was debating whether to head out to the festival and hope she would call to give their location during his fifteen-minute drive when the screen of his mobile phone lit up.

"Victoria! I've been trying to reach Rachel. Where are you guys?"

"At the tables in front of the Purple Mystic. Oh, Hank. I'm worried sick. I don't know where Rachel is."

The bottom dropped out of his world.

"What's going on?" He could hear the children crying in the background. "Tell me everything."

As Victoria told him a rambling and almost incoherent story of Joey's hot dog and Rachel's errand to replace it, he raced to his black Ford Expedition and tore off toward Manitou Springs.

"How long has she been gone?"

"More than an hour. Closer to an hour and a half. I know I

should have called you sooner, but I thought she got stuck in a long line at the hot dog stand..."

Rachel would never leave her children and Victoria that long at a festival she'd been fearful of attending in the first place. His instincts, coupled with the thefts on her property, told Hank she'd been taken.

He mentally kicked himself. He should have canceled his last two tours. He should have been there with her.

"Is anyone nearby that you know and can trust?"

"Yes." She named a teacher he'd heard Rachel mention before. "Good. Ask her to get Sheriff Johnson and tell him everything. I'll be there in less than ten minutes."

By the time Hank reached downtown, the sheriff and the police chief had their officers fanned out, searching for clues and asking questions.

A third-grade teacher who vanished from the Emma Crawford Festival, leaving her children and her grandmother behind, was big news. Rachel's role in foiling a kidnapping plus her turn on the *Sunday Night Special* talk show had put her in the spotlight.

As word of her disappearance spread, so did panic and morbid curiosity. Parents screamed the names of children who had wandered away, and the older festival-goers scurried to gather their belongings and leave for the safety of their homes. Every person with a cell phone and visions of going viral had their phone out filming, adding to the chaos.

Even the beefed-up security forces at the festival were stretched to the limit to prevent the panicked crowd from becoming a dangerous mob. The forces included the El Paso County Sheriff's Department, who handled all the serious crimes in Manitou Springs that were beyond the capabilities of the town's much smaller police department.

Sheriff Jeremiah Johnson, a man whose many years of experience and stellar record in law enforcement made him one of the most respected men in Colorado, wasted no time ditching the rules regarding missing persons and marshaling all forces in a search for Rachel.

Rachel's staunch young teaching cohort, Tanya Beasley, sat on a picnic bench with her boots off, rubbing her socked feet while she told him the news. Rachel's children huddled against Victoria, Joey looking wide-eyed and scared, Susan, sobbing and distraught.

Though Hank's first instinct was to join the search, he knelt beside the children. Rachel would have wanted it that way. She'd made it abundantly clear that her children always came first.

"Joey, Susan, I want you to know that we will find your mom. We won't stop looking until we do. Okay?"

Joey nodded, but Susan cried even harder. Hank opened his arms and she tumbled toward him.

"It's my fault!" She was crying as if she might never stop.

"It's not your fault, Susan."

"It *is!*"

Her whole body shook with her conviction and her sobs. Hank felt helpless against this assault of grief.

"I've got this," Tanya told Hank, then she leaned toward Susan, sympathy and love clearly written on her face. "None of this is your fault, but it's okay to cry. I understand how upset you are. Is there anything you want to tell me?"

Susan nodded, then buried her head back on Hank's shoulder.

Tanya stroked her hair. "It's okay. No matter what you say, none of this is your fault. Okay, Susan?"

"'K." She sniffed, then wiped her eyes.

"Do you want to talk to me now?"

"Mrs. Beasley, me and Wendy kept a secret."

Tanya still stroked the child's hair. "It's okay. You can tell me."

"Lulu's mom wouldn't let her eat candy on account of Juanita."

"Her older sister has Type 1 diabetes and is insulin dependent," Tanya told Hank. "Susan, what else did Lulu tell you?"

"She told me and Wendy she had a friend who was going to give her all the candy she wanted."

Ice filled Hank's veins. This was an old story that never ended well.

Tanya squatted beside Susan, rigid with urgency. "What friend? Was it the crossing guard?"

"I don't know. Lulu didn't say."

"Did she say anything at all about him?" Tanya said. "What he looked like? Where or when he was going to give her candy?"

"Soon. That's all she said. She was going to get the candy soon." Susan ducked her head. "She was going to share it with me and Wendy."

"You did the right thing by telling me, Susan." Tanya hugged her. "I'm proud of you."

Lulu's recent kidnapping was suddenly the elephant in their midst, the secret she'd told prior to her disappearance a massive clue to her kidnapper.

Tanya exchanged a glance with Hank that said it all. The detectives working Lulu's case could now work from the angle of finding the man who had promised candy to a child, someone she knew, someone she trusted.

"Do your thing, Hank," Tanya said. "I'll let the sheriff know everything. Including Rachel's suspicions of the crossing guard and the fact that her renter was here stalking her."

"Thanks, Tanya." The wind picked up as the expected cold front spread its icy fingers over the festival crowd. Victoria was shivering. The last thing they needed was for her to get sick.

"Victoria, I'm going to take you and the children home then come back here and join the search."

"I'll get us home, Hank. I have a set of keys to Rachel's car."

"Are you sure?" He studied her closely for any signs of fading. "It's late and very dark outside."

"I was driving John Deere tractors before you were even born." She spoke with asperity. "I'm like Queen Elizabeth, God rest her soul. I can fix them, too! The day I can't get my great-grandchildren out of the weather is the day I'll be six feet under."

"Good. I'll just see you to the car."

As they walked to the parking lot, Victoria didn't falter a step. Then she drove off, steady as a rock.

"That is one remarkable woman." Jeremiah Johnson had come up behind him. "Tanya Beasley told me where to find you."

"Any news?"

"The hot dog vendor remembered Rachel's first visit but didn't recall seeing her a second time. Nobody near the concession stands remembered seeing her at all."

That was not surprising considering the large crowd, most of them in costume, even the adults.

Plus, Rachel wasn't the kind of woman to call attention to herself. To Hank, she was a stand-out, tall, elegant, and classically beautiful, especially when she let her hair down and it swirled in wild curls around her face. Most of the time she tamed it in a tight bun and opted to wear little to no makeup and dress in a way that made her inconspicuous.

"Whoever took her probably did it between her first and second visits to the hot dog stand," the sheriff added.

Hank balled his hands into fists just thinking about Rachel's terror the moment she realized she was being kidnapped.

"Tell me what you want me to do."

"Air search the minute it's light enough to see, obviously. Meanwhile, we can use all hands on deck tonight."

It was nearly two a.m. when Hank got back to Rachel's ranch. He had left only because Jeremiah told him he wouldn't be fit to fly in the morning if he didn't get some sleep. Even then he hadn't left the festival before the sheriff promised they would do everything in their power to find Rachel.

Law enforcement in El Paso County was good, better than good, but Hank knew the sheriff and his deputies were already overburdened with an unexpected crime wave and not nearly enough resources.

After checking to see that Victoria and the children were safe in their beds, Hank went into Rachel's bedroom. It smelled like her, that heady combination of exotic florals that seemed to be always caught in her hair and clinging to her skin.

He snapped on the lights and stood in the middle of the floor, looking and thinking. The room had already been swept for recording devices. What had they missed?

He put himself in the mind of the unhinged artist who had sketched her sleeping. His best view would be... *There.* In the vent over her bed.

Hank balanced himself on the springy mattress, reached up, and removed the vent. And there it was, a tiny camera, the lens trained straight down to where Rachel would have been curled under her covers, her hair spread across the pillow, her lips curved into a smile as she dreamed.

He went to the kitchen and returned with disposable plastic gloves and a plastic bag. The forensics team might be able to lift prints from the camera. Though Hank didn't need a team to tell him who had put it there. The obvious answer was either that slick maniac who rented her apartment downstairs or the Collector, who had obviously been all over Rachel's house.

His cell phone rang, nearly toppling him from the unstable mattress. A broken neck wouldn't do. On steady ground once more, he glanced at his screen. It was Jeremiah Johnson.

"Hank, we found Rachel's cell phone."

Hank tamped down his excitement. He knew the discovery could as easily portend bad news as good.

"Where?"

"Soda Springs Park."

"Did you find out anything in her call timeline?"

"We've got forensics working on it."

"Did you find anything else?"

Hank was afraid to ask the questions swirling through his mind. Any blood, hair, bits of clothing? Any signs of struggle? He wouldn't even let himself think of finding her body. He wouldn't let himself go down the path that this could be rape or murder, instead of another kidnapping.

"Last night's rain did us a big favor. We found tire tracks near the phone. It appears someone drove through, paused without coming to a complete stop then headed east. They were probably tossing the phone... and a Tarot card. We're keeping this card under wraps to avoid escalating panic in the city and to keep the Collector as much in the dark as possible. We can't afford to tip him off that we're closing in. Not with Rachel and those children still in his possession."

The chilling words filled Hank with the same icy determination he'd felt before entering the killing fields of war.

"I've found something at the ranch," he told the sheriff. "A hidden camera in Rachel's bedroom. I didn't put any more prints on it."

"Good. Leave it with Victoria. I'll send forensics by to pick it up so you can get in the air in the morning without delay."

Hank grabbed a blanket and pillow then made his way to the den, his mind whirling. He would be relentless. He would search every square inch of Colorado if he had to, and then beyond. Nobody was going to deprive Joey and Susan of the only parent they had. Nobody was going to harm the woman he valued above all others and get by with it.

A determination unlike anything he had ever known filled him up. He became a glacier with half its power hidden from the naked eye, capable of great and terrible destruction, an immovable wall of ice that would strike terror into the soul of the wicked.

Heaven help the man who had taken Rachel.

THIRTY-SEVEN

THE HIDEAWAY

She was coming to.

Charles went to the bathroom to check that he'd wiped off the last bits of white powder he'd used to create a sickly parlor. Things had worked out better than he had imagined. His clever planning had paid off. Finding Rachel so quickly in the crowd the first evening of the festival and then having her come back to the food vendors when her kid dropped his hot dog had to be providence.

The cards had foretold it, and now she was his. Oh yes, she was.

He adjusted his toupee and patted it smooth. The wavy brown hair gave him a dapper touch. When she saw him with all this hair, she was going to admire him extravagantly, perhaps even swoon.

He wanted to look his best for his bride, and tonight he'd succeeded in spades. In fact, with this toupee, there was no telling what heroic feats he could achieve on his honeymoon night.

Satisfied, he went back into the bedroom and sat beside her bed—*their* bed. He watched to see his beloved's first reaction to her new home. Would she appreciate the white candles he had lit all around the room, the red roses, three dozen of them, the canopy of netting he'd hung so the bed looked like something that might have belonged to Queen Elizabeth the First. The Virgin Queen.

Rachel would be his virgin. He would call her Elizabeth, symbolic of starting his new family with a woman he'd made pure by his love.

She opened her eyes and turned her head this way and that, surveying the room. Finally, her gaze landed on him, and he was thrilled by what he saw.

She was not panicked. Oh no, she was not. In fact, she gave him a beautiful smile, obviously in appreciation of his handsomeness. And his hair.

Charles congratulated himself. Choosing her was brilliant. Genius, actually. His ability to read her like a book only added to his excitement.

"Where am I?"

"Home." He bent over her and smoothed her hair back from her forehead. His hand sliding over her skin was only a preview of the delights to come. "I fixed it up just for you, Elizabeth."

A small frown marred her brow, but it was only temporary. The smile that followed was more than enough for him to forgive her small lapse in manners. In fact, he would forgive her anything if only she hadn't hurt herself. Everything he'd seen from her indicated she already loved him in some way. Maybe not the deep commitment of a wife to her husband, but that would come in time. All the signs were there. And the cards never lied.

"Elizabeth, I know you tried to run from me because you were a little bit confused. I expected that because of the way it was necessary for me to bring you here. I forgive you on one condition."

"What's that?"

"That you did not hurt yourself in a way that makes it impossible for you to bear my children."

Her blush of modesty was exactly what he would expect from a woman of her class and upbringing. Modesty was a rare quality, and one he treasured in his Elizabeth.

"I'm sorry, Charles. I didn't mean to run. I *was* confused."

"I know, sweetheart." He leaned over her and kissed her left hand. "You have a skinned left knee and some minor scratches and bruising on your left hand, but I've already treated those with the proper cleansing and antibiotic creams."

"Thanks."

"That's vulgar and beneath you. Say, thank you, Charles."

"Thank you, Charles."

"That's better."

If he had been able to have his usual blood-of-four-crows drink that evening, he'd have taken her on the spot whether or not she was fertile, just for the sport of it. But he didn't have any time to waste. His plan for the future was elaborate, and its success depended on almost split-second timing.

"I'm going to examine you now, Elizabeth." Her blush proved she was modest. Seeing the color bloom across her cheeks was almost as good as a passionate kiss.

As he reached to pull the covers off her, she shrank back, once again proving her modesty. He waited, letting her get over her shyness.

"I know how important this is to you, Charles." She took a deep breath. "Shouldn't you get a doctor?"

"Sweetheart, I *am* a doctor." Almost. He had gone to medical school long enough to acquire the basic knowledge he needed. What he hadn't learned in those two years of torture, he had finished learning from the medical books he had stolen before he burned down the library. "Just let me know if anything hurts."

Her reaction to his hands on her abdomen was instantaneous and extremely gratifying. If he had not been able to compartmentalize, to separate the clinical from the physical he might have started his dynasty that very moment. But he was not a man of impulse. Everything he had worked for hinged on ensuring his dynasty.

If Rachel proved to be incapable of bearing children, he would dispose of her as easily as he'd dispatched those two kids in Denver and the crows who provided his elixir of immortality. He could always go to Plan B—Dawn Williams.

"Any pain here?" He moved his hands around her abdomen. "Or here?"

When she gave her head a negative shake each time he asked the question, he felt like leaping off the bed and dancing around the room with his wings spread. He felt like flying to the sky and screaming his news to the world.

"This is wonderful news, Elizabeth. You are in topnotch condition! Now, we can begin our life together."

The charming blush she gave him said it all. She was ready. Eager.

"I love that we're starting it with flowers." Her voice was soft and seductive as she admired the roses he had so carefully stolen just for her. "Thank you, Charles."

"Call me Charlie."

"Charlie. It has a nice ring."

The thrill of having her say the name he'd longed to hear all his life filled him with such pleasure he felt ten feet tall.

"Say it again. My name."

"Charlie."

Soft. Seductive. A wife's voice crooning to her beloved husband.

He almost removed her ropes. She was spread-eagled on the four-poster, her wrists bound to the headboard and her ankles bound to the footboard. A gag had been totally unnecessary. Even on the trip home.

He had knocked her out long enough for the drive to his cabin, plus the time it took to get her upstairs and tied down so there was no possibility of escape. In fact, even if he decided to remove the ropes, Rachel had no hope of leaving him. He'd prepared the upstairs of his cabin so well it would take a small army to breach his security measures.

And though she was taller, she would be no match for his strength. His basement was better equipped than any gym he'd ever seen. When he'd leaned on her as she helped him to his van, he knew she'd felt only a fraction of the strength in his body.

She would be no match physically. Oh no, she would not. Still, there was something animal-like in her, some deeply buried passion he couldn't wait to tame in their wedding bed.

He leaned close so he could watch her face for lies. "Are you comfortable, darling?"

"Yes."

She didn't flinch. In fact, she settled her head more solidly on the pillow.

My, my, she is a fast learner. Oh yes, she is.

If she kept this up, he could remove the restraints.

"Would you like me to release you from the ropes?"

"It's up to you, Charlie."

Even better. Tonight would definitely be their honeymoon night. Excitement spread through him faster than a flash flood in a box canyon.

"What would you say if I left you tied up all night?"

She hesitated. Still, she showed no fear and not a hint of the revulsion he had seen on the faces of so many women through the years, including his own mother.

"If you decided to keep me bound, I'd be worried about who would take care of our children."

Ah, clever woman.

She understood that everything he'd done had been all for

the sake of creating a perfect family. He had known she'd make the perfect mother. Another feather in his cap.

"I'm taking care of them. I'm a good daddy."

"Yes, you are. Thank you, Charlie."

He moved closer, studying every inch of her with avid anticipation and judging her reaction. She still didn't flinch. In fact, his stare aroused her. He could see it in the flush that crept into her cheeks, the way her body tensed against the ropes.

Splendid! She was ready for him. Yes, she was.

It would be a simple and easy matter to leave her in ropes while he ensured a future generation of little Charlies. As he mulled over the pros and cons, he watched her face. Her expression was soft and trusting. No fear. No uncertainty.

It was more than acceptance. It was instant loyalty to him. Charlie. The unexpectedly clever man nobody ever noticed who had quietly and steadily built himself the perfect home by taking the perfect possessions from other people who didn't deserve them.

Such a woman should have a wedding night to remember.

"Elizabeth, I'm going to untie you now."

"Thank you."

How clever and quick she is to respond to her new name!

"Before I loosen your bonds, there are certain instructions you have to follow. Can you do that?"

"Yes."

"After I untie you, go to the bathroom and take a shower. You'll find everything you need. Your honeymoon peignoir set is hanging on a hook over the back of the door. It's white and just your size." She watched him closely, hanging on his every word, breathless with anticipation.

"Thank you."

"Take all the time you need, darling. I'll be waiting for you." He bent toward the ropes on her right wrist.

"Charlie, wait!"

He didn't like to be kept waiting. When he set out to do a thing, he was the kind of man who always followed through with his plans. No hesitation. No deviation.

Still, she'd given him no reason to be angry. No reason to suspect she was anything except his compliant bride.

"We spilled your food at the festival, and I've had very little to eat. Is there a kitchen in this lovely home where I could fix us a nice cup of hot chocolate before we... proceed?"

Oh, how he loved a modest woman.

They were always so eager to please.

It was an unexpected bonus that, already, Elizabeth knew a woman's place was to take care of her man.

He salivated at seeing her reaction to the red blender, compliments of the snooty Kimmells, who never spoke to him, not in all the years he'd delivered their mail; the matching coffee maker he'd taken from the Brewsters, who had actually turned him in to his boss for stepping on Mrs. Brewster's prize petunias; the homey red-checkered tea towels from the mean old woman everybody called "Snookie" except the neighborhood children, who called her a witch and rolled her house with toilet tissue every Halloween.

And there was so much more. The perfectly stocked shelves and pantry, the meticulous way he'd lined up the canned goods, the care he'd taken to keep alive the Phalaenopsis orchid he'd taken from the ritzy old lady in Manitou Springs who had a private greenhouse and was hoarding all varieties of orchids so ordinary people had to pay more than they were worth in order to have even one on their windowsills.

His wife would appreciate his cleverness and his Robin Hood sensibilities.

Oh yes, she will.

Now that he had given it some thought, the kitchen was the perfect place to begin his marriage. Especially tonight while the children were sleeping off the sedatives he'd given them. He'd even knocked the dogs out, clever man that he was. He'd given all of them so much medicine it would take a herd of elephants to wake them.

Growing up, he'd always longed to have a kitchen like those of the few boys who occasionally befriended him for brief periods of time. Their kitchens were cozy, the hub of their home, the place where casual conversation and laughter flowed with the ease of foolish Emma Crawford's casket sliding down the side of Red Mountain so many years ago after decades of snow and rain unearthed it from its resting place.

Judging from a handful of visits to other homes during his childhood, good kitchen rapport was pivotal to a good marriage. He'd observed many major decisions being made in front of a hot stove.

"I have the perfect kitchen for you."

"A *perfect* kitchen?" His new wife smiled at him. "That's wonderful. Thank you."

He'd never had anyone express gratitude to him as often as his Elizabeth. Beaming, he kissed her full on the mouth.

Heavenly bliss.

She was better than perfect. She was an angel.

There was no way he would let anybody else have her. *Ever.* She was *his,* and his alone. He would father all the children himself. He was more than capable.

Pumped up with satisfaction and renewed resolve, he untied the knots and set his wife free.

THIRTY-EIGHT

When the mailman untied her, Rachel wanted to reach up and wipe her mouth where he'd kissed her. She wanted to spit on him, scream at him, and claw his face.

He was genuinely unhinged. She'd identified him as the Collector from the stolen goods spread around the room, items reported missing from his alter ego's long string of thefts—the Vargases' blue crystal clock on the mantle, the unusual antique spittoon on the hearth that had belonged to Wendy's great-grandfather, the distinctive watercolor print on the wall, a rose garden painted by a local artist.

Even worse, she could see madness in his eyes and his expression—flat and devoid of all emotion, even when he used endearments.

The bedroom had no windows, a glaring sign of his derangement. What kind of animal could live in a room without *windows?*

Obviously, the answer was the kind of madman with so many delusions Rachel had a hard time figuring out which was worse, the thought of a wedding night with him or the thought of bearing his children. She tried not to think of the women who had been captives of madmen through the years, the ones who had escaped and the ones who had endured for years before they were finally set free, empty inside, broken and unrecognizable.

The latter was unthinkable. She refused to be his victim. The Collector had stolen her, but he would *never* take her heart, her soul, and her mind. She would use every resource at her disposal, every ounce of her courage, determination, and spirit to deny him the thing he wanted most: a new family created at the cost of destroying the people he had kidnapped to use for his sick purpose.

But she would never win by struggle. The Collector was too strong, and his hideout appeared to be a fortress. The only way to survive was to play along with him and wait for her chance when he let his guard down.

She schooled her emotions, made herself smile as he helped her out of the bed. So far, her instincts to play along with him had worked. She had not only escaped his anger, but her guess had paid off. She had learned that Lulu Vargas and Eddie Greene were okay. At least, she hoped. She hadn't yet seen or heard any evidence that they were here.

"Elizabeth, can you stand?"

She would *never* be his Elizabeth. But Rachel hid her rebellion and made herself smile at him.

The odious Collector still had his hands on her, and she was standing there in her socked feet. She wanted to shake him off and run, but where would that take her except to the other side of a coffin-like space where the door was locked by not one but three deadbolts.

"I can, Charlie," She made herself put a purr in her voice. "If you could give me a minute, I'd like to freshen up in the bathroom before we go into our kitchen."

"Of course, darling. Take your time."

He had a vulnerability. Hearing his name as an endearment made him more agreeable and easier to manipulate.

She tried to act casual as she retrieved her tote bag from the chair where he'd left it along with her overcoat, her scarf, and her boots. It was a miracle she still had the bag. He must believe this horrible place was so well fortified, it was impossible to escape.

Rachel struggled to keep her hopes up. She thought about getting her boots, too, but that might set him off. There was no telling what he would do if he thought she was trying to escape.

She flashed him what she hoped was a timid but grateful smile then went into the adjoining bathroom, also windowless. Her cell phone wouldn't be in her bag. He was too smart for that. But would everything else?

As she closed the bathroom door, a quick glance at her watch told her the Collector had probably only knocked her out long enough to get her to his house and tie her to the bed. He'd wanted a wedding night, and that would be no fun with a comatose woman. He hadn't left himself enough time for a thorough search of her bag. And he certainly wouldn't have anticipated the nature of her after-school errands.

The bathroom was large with new fixtures, including double sinks in front of a mirror that covered one entire wall. But there was no lock on the door. There was not even a chair she could push against it. Even worse, the revealing white lace gown and negligee hanging on an over-the-door rack screamed of the horrors that lay ahead.

Rachel thought she was going to be sick. She filled a paper cup and drank until she settled down. Her hope of survival depended on keeping her wits about her.

When had he renovated the jail-like cabin? It had to be long before she'd had her fifteen minutes of fame on *Sunday Night Special with Dawn Williams*.

Rachel pictured him delivering mail to her mailbox every

day. How long had he been watching her, making his diabolical plan?

He had been her carrier since Susan was a year old. She remembered well the first day he'd driven the route. She'd walked to the mailbox with her baby on her hip to post a letter to her sister Annie just as he drove up.

He had handed the mail through the car window, and she'd said, "You must be new."

"Just started the job today."

When they'd exchanged introductions, she had no idea she had set herself and her family on a path toward destruction. She had no idea he would one day terrorize the entire town.

Rachel turned on the water again to cover the sound of her activities. The woman staring back at her from the mirror was as pale as a cake of soap, with eyes that were overly bright and hot red splotches of anger on her cheeks. She splashed her face to help cool it down, then left the water running while she rummaged in her large tote. The bag containing her grandmother's chocolate-flavored laxative and the little bottle of psyllium fiber in gelatin capsules was still tucked into the bottom of her voluminous tote bag. She'd never been more grateful for being a teacher with a huge bag full of supplies.

She removed the squares of laxative from their foil wrappers, folded them into a tissue from one of the individual packs in her purse and tucked them into a large pocket of her loosely-fitting cargo pants. Then she carefully separated some of the gel caps and poured the psyllium husks into the foil wrappers from the laxatives.

A tap on the door caused her to spill granulated fiber on the floor.

"Elizabeth, are you okay in there?"

"I'm fine. I'll be out in just a minute."

She cleaned the mess with tissue then tossed it along with the empty gel caps into the toilet and flushed. She hastily stuffed the rest of Victoria's laxatives back into the bottom of her tote bag, and as an afterthought, slashed on a fresh coat of lip gloss.

There. She was ready to face the psychopath on the other side of the door. Pasting a smile on her face, she opened it and stepped through.

"You face is still wet." He leaned in to wipe her cheek.

For an awful moment she thought he was going to kiss her again. She didn't know if she had enough mental strength to keep from gagging this time.

Instead, he took her hand and led her toward the door.

Panic seized her. What if she hadn't fooled him at all? What if he saw straight through her hastily devised plan to escape? What if he decided to take her somewhere and kill her?

She considered trying to jerk her hand away, but there was nowhere to go, nowhere to hide. With each step her terror grew.

What was behind that door?

THIRTY-NINE

Rachel's heart hammered as she went through the bedroom door. She was in a dimly lit hallway with plush carpeting so thick her sock-feet sank deeply into the pile, and the mailman appeared to be in the same creepy but upbeat mood of a new groom on his wedding night.

A quick glance down the hall showed a door with multiple locks. Did it lead to freedom? She buried her urge to jerk free and fling herself at the door.

On their march in the opposite direction, they passed two doors, directly across from each other. Both were padlocked. Though she strained to hear, there was not a sound coming from behind, either.

The hall spilled them into a huge open living space. Bright red sofa and chairs, garish in the lamplight, were arranged in a circle around a wide-screen TV, which hung above a fireplace. Bookcases lined the walls on each side of the hearth, and several family photographs reported missing in his various thefts were grouped among the books. A couple of paintings that looked vaguely familiar hung on the wall adjacent to the fireplace.

She tossed her tote bag casually onto the sofa. He'd never

suspect the treat she made had anything in it except ingredients from his own pantry.

The den was separated from the kitchen by a bar with four stools. There was not a sign of a window anywhere.

Rachel's hopes fell. Then, suddenly, beyond the kitchen, barely visible in the glow of a lamp on the bar, she spotted a small glimmer of light. It was coming from what appeared to be a sliding glass door. A breakfast table and four chairs sat in front of it.

Where did it lead? A rooftop patio? Or was it merely a wide expanse of glass that led nowhere but made her long for the freedom of whatever lay beyond?

Rachel could feel the tension in the Collector's fingers as he tightened his grip. The air was thick with his expectations. She could almost taste them, the sharp bitterness of evil.

"It's lovely." She made her voice warm and inviting. It took massive effort and more courage than she'd ever known she had.

"I did it for you."

Sick pervert.

"I know. Thank you."

"Let me get the lights."

He dropped her hand and was halfway to the light switch before she called to him.

"Wait. Could you please leave them dim?"

When he turned, his face was closing up, suspicion rising.

Oh help. She felt her panic rising. Only the thought of getting back home to her children brought it under control.

"It's so much more romantic that way, sweetheart," she crooned. "Especially considering this is our honeymoon night."

"Of course, darling."

"Why don't you sit down there at the bar and let me make the hot chocolate?"

She was relieved when he sank onto a bar stool. The light would be in his eyes and she'd be in virtual darkness in the kitchen. She forced herself to walk back and caress his face and shoulder before she went into the kitchen.

He almost purred. She nearly gagged.

"Charlie, would you mind telling me where the pans and mugs are located, and the cocoa and sugar and spices? I don't want to waste our time together searching."

"The pans are in the cabinet to the left of the stove, and the rest is inside the pantry on the left."

Even better.

"Oh, and Elizabeth, there's an apron for you hanging on a hook just inside the pantry door."

"Thank you."

"You're welcome, darling." He continued to talk as she headed to the pantry. "In the morning, you'll find some pretty dresses in our bedroom closet. I want my wife to look perfect at all times. No slacks and blue jeans and whatever that is you're wearing. Understood?"

Rachel shook with fury. Every fiber in her body rebelled at being remolded by this depraved man.

"I understand. How very generous of you."

She was glad her back was turned and the kitchen was dim so he couldn't see her gritted teeth. As she headed into the pantry, she decided she'd like nothing better than to bang him over the head with the large can of peaches sitting on the top shelf of the pantry.

Patience.

She couldn't afford to make any rash moves until she knew exactly where the children were, what weapons she had in that claustrophobic, locked-down apartment, and how she might lead them all to safety.

She put on the apron then made herself pop out of the pantry and strike a little pose for him.

"Ta-daa!"

"Bravo, darling!"

He made the hairs on her neck stand on end. She hated him on such a visceral level, she wondered that he didn't see it and guess she was putting on a performance.

Back in the shelter of the pantry she dumped enough laxatives and psyllium husks into his mug to fell a hippopotamus. Then she set the mugs and the rest of the supplies on a red plastic tray she found tucked behind a cereal box and marched out to make a potent mug of chocolate.

She set the tray on the counter beside the stove. He immediately hopped off his stool.

"I'll bring the mugs over here, darling."

"No!" She scrambled to think of something. "Please keep your seat, sweetheart." The term of endearment did the trick. He plopped back onto the stool. "The secret to my hot chocolate is the spices I add at the end." She grabbed the bottles of cinnamon and hot pepper for him to see. "It's an old Mayan recipe, and..."

She almost told him how much her children and her grandmother loved it. That would be a major mistake. He had given her a new identity so there would be no reminders to him of her other life.

"I want it to be something special for you to remember our wedding night," she added. "A new tradition just for the two of us."

"I like that. You're the most exciting woman I've ever known."

Wait till you taste this chocolate.

She chatted to him the entire time she made the chocolate, partially from nerves, but mostly to keep him in a satisfied stupor over there by the bar. She peppered the conversation with frequent endearments and soft trills of laughter.

It worked so well, he was a wad of satisfied contentment by the time she handed him a lethal mug of chocolate. Cinnamon floated on the top to camouflage the taste. She'd even found a bag of miniature marshmallows to further counteract the bitter taste of chocolate-flavored laxative.

She lifted her own mug. "Here's to us, sweetheart."

"To us, and a most beautiful start to the perfect marriage."

He took a big gulp, obviously in a hurry to get to the intimate portion of what Rachel hoped would be the worst night of his life.

"Do you like it?" She gave him the coy smile of an eager bride.

"It's splendid." He gulped down some more of the toxic brew. "What is that unusual flavor?"

"Red pepper. The Mayans say it enhances the taste of the chocolate.... and the libido." She made herself look down as if her own modesty had overcome her. "I'm so glad you approve."

"If you do everything as well as you make this hot chocolate, I'll be your captive for life."

He grinned hugely at her. Leered, actually. And then he finished his drink in one gulp.

She'd given him such a massive dose, he was already looking a little green. Rachel grabbed a napkin from the holder and leaned toward him.

"Sweetheart, you have a little bit of chocolate..."

He bolted, grabbing his grumbling stomach with one hand and his backside with the other. Judging by the sounds he made, both voluntarily and involuntarily, he lost his unfortunate race to the bathroom.

She covered her mouth with the napkin to hide any tell-tale signs of her own desperate hope that her cobbled-together plan was working. As soon as he was out of sight, she dug into her tote for travel-sized room spray—a must-have for every teacher—and the personal military-grade flashlight Max had insisted she carry at all times.

Her heart racing, she hurried toward the sliding door and began to flash the SOS signal. Would anybody see? Was there a neighbor close enough to see her distress code in the dark?

She shoved against the door, but it wouldn't budge, even after she jiggled the lock. No telling what he'd done to it.

Out of nowhere, the scent of magnolias swirled around her, their warning screaming through her with the urgency of an avalanche in the Colorado mountains that buried people alive.

Danger. Danger. Everywhere.

Pressed against the glass, struggling against a sense of overwhelming defeat, Rachel strained to see into the darkness beyond. Shapes of the forest loomed before her, a section of yard illuminated by the moon. She dragged a kitchen chair to stand on, trained her light high into the darkness and saw a strange gathering of dark birds in a large tree separate from the others.

Rachel pointed her light higher and turned on her SOS signal. Three quick flashes, three slow.

Wait. Repeat.

There was nothing beyond the door except darkness. She felt the soul-numbing return of desperation.

Was that a sound behind her? She whirled and almost toppled from her chair, but there was nothing to hear except the whir from the refrigerator that signaled the ice maker was doing its job.

Still, she didn't dare risk being found out. She thought about stowing her tote bag in the pantry deep behind bags of dog and cat food, but he knew she had it. Taking a clue from *The Purloined Letter,* she left it in plain sight on the red sofa. Then she girded herself to march toward the bedroom and check on the mailman.

Thanks to her, he should be really sick by now. But even in that condition, he might still pose a threat. And when he got over it, would he realize what she'd done? Would he kill her? Bury her in some hidden canyon where her bones would not be found for seven years, like those of the poor children in Denver?

Rachel began to shake and had to bend over to take deep breaths. Finally, she was able to continue her cautious march toward the bedroom.

As she passed the doors in the hallway, she listened for any signs of the kidnapped children. There was nothing except rustling movements and a sound very much like Sam thumping his tail.

The dogs the Collector had stolen?

The door to the bedroom suite came into view, and Rachel braced herself before she went inside. The sounds coming from the bathroom said loud and clear her plan was working beyond her wildest expectations. As she waited for the gastric explosions to subside, she had the feeling she was in the midst of an absurd grade B movie, a combination of farce and horror that would end in two hours so she could get back to her real life.

When the sounds stopped, she knocked on the bathroom door.

"Charlie, sweetheart? Are you all right?"

"*No*! I'm sick in here!"

His reply showed he'd lost control. He was no longer the arrogant man, so sure of himself that he had untied her and allowed her to keep her tote bag.

A small glimmer of hope took the edge off Rachel's fear. "Oh dear. I'm so sorry." She covered her mouth with her hand as if he might magically see through the door and witness her small burst of triumph. If she could survive the night, she'd think of something else tomorrow. She *would*. "It must be the red pepper I put in our chocolate. Next time I'll leave it out. Some people can't tolerate hot stuff. I'm really sorry, sweetheart."

"I know you are, darling. We'll have to postpone our honeymoon night. I hope you're not too disappointed."

His quick pivot toward his evil scheme resurrected her fear. It was going to take more than a heavy dose of laxatives to escape from the Collector. She struggled to keep from running toward the door at the end of the hall and clawing at the locks.

"Oh, of *course* I am. But don't you worry about me, Charlie. You're worth waiting for."

"Darling, do you mind sleeping on the sofa?"

She would be thrilled if she weren't scared she was going to die—and those poor, hapless children along with her.

"It will be a sacrifice, but I'll do anything to help you, Charlie."

"You'll find bed linens in the storage drawers of the coffee table."

"Okay."

There were the unmistakable sounds of a digestive system in distress. "I'm going to have to ask you to leave now, Elizabeth."

"Goodnight, then." She lowered her voice to a seductive purr. "I'll see you in the morning, sweetheart."

"Goodnight, dar..."

The rest of the Collector's sentence was swallowed up in his current emergency.

Rachel stood outside the door, collecting herself. Then she made her way to her bed on the sofa. She had won, for now, but the victory brought no relief. The Collector would recover from tonight's fiasco.

But what fresh terror would tomorrow bring?

FORTY

LOGAN RANCH

After a night of very little sleep, Hank was up when the first ray of light pierced the windows of Rachel's den. He folded his blanket then went into the hall bathroom to freshen up before heading for the coffee pot.

Victoria was already at the kitchen table, hanging on to a cup as if it were the only thing anchoring her to life on earth. She looked so care-worn and pale that Hank worried she might collapse.

"Are you okay?" He slid in beside her.

"I couldn't sleep." She shook her head as if she couldn't believe what was happening. "I've already called Jen. I tried Annie, but I couldn't get her. Jen wants you to call her before the children wake up."

Rachel's sister, Dr. Jennifer Logan Turner, was already in his iPhone contacts. Savvy, efficient, and extremely intelligent, she'd insisted on being his emergency contact for all things concerning her Colorado family.

Though it wasn't likely the children would be up for a while after the trauma of their mother disappearing at the festival,

Hank grabbed a mug of coffee then stepped onto the covered back patio to talk where they wouldn't hear.

Jen answered on the first ring and got right to the point.

"Hank, you should have called me last night. I could have already been there on the red eye."

"Victoria was holding out hope they'd find Rachel last night. We both were."

"Listen to me now. Don't pull any punches when you talk to the children. Tell them the truth about everything. Children are resilient, and they worry more about the things they *don't* know and understand, than the things they do. Got it?"

"Yes." He'd learned that from being around Rachel. Last night, he and Victoria had been very clear to the children about what had happened.

"I couldn't get a flight to Colorado Springs so I'm going to book into Denver tonight on a seven o'clock flight. I expect you to be there with bells on and whisk me back to the ranch in one of your fancy planes."

"You don't have to come, Jen. The sheriff's posting round-the-clock protection for Victoria and the children."

"I'm coming. Benjamin can take care of the children. Not that the twins need any help. I'd be a sorry excuse for a mother if a couple of twelve-year-olds didn't have enough independence to take care of themselves." Jen finally paused her non-stop diatribe to take a breath. "Soon as I get my ticket, I'll text my flight info. You just be at the airport. I don't want to rent a car and drive."

"I'll be there."

Hank was glad to know she was coming to help, especially considering Victoria's age and the uncertainty of the situation.

"Oh, and Hank, I've been thinking a lot about the way this cretin you call the Collector works, and I remembered that Mom consulted a Tarot card reader before Rachel and I were born. I heard Gran talking about it when we were kids. Considering this maniac is leaving Tarot cards everywhere, I think it's significant."

"So do I. But Rachel said your grandmother can't remember anything about it."

"When I get there, she will. I always had a way of rankling her so bad she could remember every little transgression by anybody in the family, especially Mom and me. You'll see."

Hank went back into the kitchen to let Victoria know Jeremiah would be sending someone to pick up the evidence he'd found in Rachel's room and to tell her of Jen's plans.

Victoria nodded her approval. "She's as tough as they come. Much as I hate to have her bossing me around, I'm glad she'll be here to help."

"I'm heading out now to do another air search."

"What about breakfast? I could rustle up some pancakes?"

She barely looked able to get out of her chair. He made a mental note to send one of his office assistants over to stay with her and the children today.

"I'll grab a doughnut at the office."

His office manager, Wanda June Luckett, Alabama born and bred, made sure there was a fresh supply at all times, plus a fresh pot of coffee.

"I'll see you this evening after I pick up Jen." He scrawled his office number on a note pad. "If you need me and I don't answer my phone, call Wanda June. She'll know how to get in touch with me."

As he went back into the den, he spotted a photo of Victoria's son Patrick with his wife Delilah and their three daughters. All of them got their Creole mother's regal beauty, but only Jen inherited her mother's fierce look of a warrior.

In his truck on the way to Colorado Springs it occurred to him that he didn't need a photo to remember how Rachel looked. She was imprinted on his heart, and had been for a very long time.

. . .

Hank's office was abuzz with news about Rachel's disappearance. The office staff was gathered around the TV listening to KKTV-TV's own Dawn Williams explain how Rachel had become a local celebrity by her act of bravery in Soda Springs Park.

He was getting ready to turn away so he could suit up and start an air search when Dawn said, "Up next is another celebrity, artist Bruce Wyler, who has been staying with Rachel Maxey."

While she listed the artist's accomplishments, Hank balled his hands in fists. The implication would have everybody in her viewing audience thinking Rachel had a romantic attachment with that scumbag. He waited to see if they'd clarify the relationship, or stick to the more sensational misinformation.

Wyler strode onto the set as if he owned it. His blond hair looked even more fake under the television lights. Was it *dyed*?

Dawn leaned toward her TV guest with an earnest look on her face. "Bruce, I know you're devastated by Rachel's disappearance. As someone who is as close to her as her grandmother and her two children, what can you tell me about Rachel Logan Maxey?"

"She's a beautiful and loving woman, completely devoted to her family and those of us she considers her dearest friends."

Several of Hank's staff who knew of his long-time friendship with Rachel turned to study his reaction. He just shrugged.

Let the man make a fool of himself. When Hank found Rachel, she'd set the record straight with Dawn Williams in a New York minute. The one thing he hated more than insincerity and posturing was outright lies.

"Have you seen anything that indicated someone would want to harm her?" Dawn asked her guest.

"No. To the contrary, Rachel is universally loved."

"There was an official report filed of a theft at her home." Dawn Williams held up what appeared to be a new Justice Tarot card. "The thief left his calling card at the scene. Wouldn't that indicate the Collector had her in his sights?"

"Isn't all theft personal? The Collector did take a garden ornament, but he's been taking insignificant things for two years now. There's absolutely no reason he would take Rachel Maxey."

"He took her photograph, too."

Hank couldn't tell from the renter's reaction whether this was news to him. If he did already know, he put on a good act of pretending surprise. He leaned toward Dawn, his face filled with sincerity.

"If the information I've read is true, he's taken photographs before. And isn't a family photo just an indication of the Collector's domesticity and longing for the comfort of a family?" Bruce sat back in his chair with the satisfied look of an authority who had just dropped a gem of wisdom. "Dawn, I agree this is an unconventional way to furnish one's home... and perhaps even a bit bizarre to the general public, but as an artist who has traveled the world, I can tell you I've seen things many times worse than what your famous Collector is doing."

"From your perspective as a world-famous artist, what is your assessment of the Collector?"

Bruce treated his TV audience with a smile that had probably charmed his fans around the globe. "Your Collector will go down in history as one of the world's most notorious criminals."

"Wow!" Dawn leaned back in her chair, clearly pleased at the unexpected turn her interview had taken.

Hank was disgusted. He'd seen enough of Bruce's spin and his private life to know the artist was clearly not normal. Still, he stayed through the commercial break to see what else he could learn.

After the ad for the Purple Mystic finished, Dawn got right to the chase.

"Bruce, is there anything else you want to say to our viewing audience?"

"Yes. Rachel Maxey has become very..." He hesitated, seeming to choke up for a moment. "Important to me. I'm offering a ten-thousand-dollar reward for any information that leads to her safe return."

A few in Hank's staff cheered, not realizing that Bruce Wyler had just made the sheriff's job much harder. People would crawl out of the woodwork to get their hands on the money. Sheriff Johnson's office would be flooded with calls that would send his deputies chasing false leads in every direction.

As Hank left to suit up, he called the private investigator he'd employed. "Dustin, have you found anything yet on the Tarot cards?"

"I have a few names of readers, but so far, nothing going back as far as you suggested."

"Keep digging. And keep digging into Bruce Wyler's background. I want to know details about his childhood, his mother's death, his relationships, and anything else that is pertinent."

There was no need to add, *Work as fast as you can.* The PI was well aware of the urgency.

Once Hank was in the air, he headed straight to the cabins in the isolated areas he'd already mapped out. Instinct told him there was something he'd missed, some small detail that could be the break they needed to find Rachel and the missing children.

Flying in the early morning gave him a different perspective from his late afternoon search. The angle of the sun revealed things that had previously been in shadow.

The first and second cabins showed nothing new, but when he flew low over the third, he saw a rooftop garden that hadn't been visible on his evening flight. While a Denver ordinance a couple of years back had mandated more sustainable green areas in the big city's high-rises to help clean the air, they were not common in the vast reaches of the state where dense forests more than did the job.

Hank banked left and turned for another pass over the bright canopy of leaves protecting the unusual rooftop garden. Suddenly, he saw a flash of light, too bright to be the reflection off a window. He circled and flew back as low as he dared.

There it was again, barely visible through the dense leaves. An unmistakable blip of light. Could it be the sun striking a mirror? People often hung mirrored baubles in their gardens.

Could this garden also hold the butterfly he'd made for Rachel? There was little chance of seeing it from the air, especially through the trees. Still, Hank had to try. With desperate hope as his co-pilot, he made another run over the cabin.

But the light had vanished. Whatever secrets the garden held were well hidden by a canopy of red and gold leaves.

"Hang on, Rachel. I'm coming."

Undaunted, Hank continued his search in ever-widening circles in the dome of a blue sky that seemed to go on forever.

FORTY-ONE

THE HIDEAWAY

It was still very early when the sound of helicopter blades catapulted Rachel awake on the sofa where she lay on a lumpy pillow in a wad of unfamiliar blankets.

Hank!

He was searching for her! It had to be him.

Grabbing her flashlight from her tote she raced toward the window, but a flinch of pain slowed her down. The pavement had torn her cargo pants and plowed up the skin on her left leg, which had apparently taken the brunt of her fall when she went down.

Finally, she got to the door and flashed the SOS signal. The sound of the chopper was already receding.

"Oh no, no, no," she whispered. "Come back..."

As if there were a magical cord binding her to Hank, the chopper whirred close again, dipping so low she could see a portion of the logo on the side of the chopper through the mass of fall leaves. It was definitely Hank.

Desperate, Rachel flashed the signal again. This time she trained the light toward the cockpit.

Please. Please. Please.

Would Hank see it through the treetops? Would he see the entire light sequence or catch just a glance? She squeezed her eyes shut and willed him to understand. Her concentration was so great she almost missed the sounds.

A door slamming. He was awake. And if he saw her sending SOS signals, his revenge would be unspeakable.

Rachel palmed her flashlight then tried to gain control of her shaking hands and runaway terror. Too late, she wondered if the Collector kept cameras hidden all over the place.

She pivoted and caught a glimpse of the Collector standing in front of one of the two doors in the hallway beyond the den and kitchen area. The yipping of dogs was followed by three of them bursting through the door and trailing after Charles until they were all out of sight.

Of course, she'd forgotten about the dogs. Obviously they couldn't be left inside all day long. They'd have to have food and water. But how long would that take?

She hurried back to the den and slid the flashlight into her tote. Then she folded her bedding and stowed it in the drawers under the coffee table. As she straightened back up, she saw her own face staring at her from the bookshelves.

It was the photo the Collector had stolen. He'd placed her inside an ornate heart-shaped frame gilded with faux rubies and diamonds. She wanted to smash it against the wall. Max had chosen the original simple silver frame.

"Elizabeth? What have you been doing?"

She whirled to face him. He looked awful. His face sported a greenish pallor, and his stomach still gurgled. He was carrying a coat hanger holding a frumpy house dress in a print that looked as if it belonged on a dish towel.

She flashed him a smile intended to dazzle, but it didn't work. He looked grumpy, out of sorts, and more than a little suspicious.

"Oh, Charlie! Good morning. I was just folding my bedding. Are you feeling better?"

"Some." He stalked past her and peered out the sliding glass doors. "Did you hear a helicopter out here?"

"There was some sort of noise, but I didn't notice what it was. I was too busy stowing my bed linens."

His stare felt as if he were peeling back layers of her skin. She made herself approach him with a smile, reach out and caress his face.

"I like to keep a tidy house for my husband."

"Well, now. That's better." He handed her the tacky dress. "Get dressed and cook breakfast. I don't want to ever see you in a man's britches again."

Relief swamped her. If she could keep up the game, maybe this was not going to be her day to die. "Whatever you say, sweetheart."

"You'll find shoes and everything you need in our bedroom closet, and makeup and perfume in the bathroom." His voice softened. "Fix yourself up pretty."

"I'll try. I want to please you, Charlie."

"Take your time. I don't have to be at work until ten-thirty."

The good news washed through her like a healing balm. She hoped he'd be gone all day.

Rachel found the undergarments in the closet, skimpy, lacy things she'd imagine in a brothel. The shoes were four-inch stilettos, the kind you'd see on celebrities posing on the red carpet. They were wildly inappropriate for the dowdy shirtwaist dress that looked as if it had come straight from a television sit-com from fifty years ago.

Still, the dress was her size, and it had deep pockets in the side seams. She took the stash of laxatives and fiber from her pant pockets and slid them into the dress pockets then smoothed down the skirt. Thankfully, her skirt was so full, nothing in her pockets created a bulge.

In the bathroom, the makeup reminded her of the kind they applied for her appearance on the Dawn Williams show. It was heavy, garish. By the time she finished, she looked nothing like herself. Rachel Maxey, ordinary schoolteacher and mother of two, had vanished.

"Hello, Elizabeth," she muttered to her reflection, reminding herself of the role she had to play.

She turned to go and then remembered the perfume. She didn't want to do anything to set the Collector off. It would be impossible to predict what such a madman would do.

When she picked up the bottle, she knew immediately it belonged to Dawn Williams. As if it were yesterday, she remembered the television interview, recalled Dawn naming her signature fragrance the Collector had taken.

Was everything in this house stolen?

Rachel almost gagged when she sprayed on the perfume. Touted for its floral notes, it smelled more like strong chemicals than the perfectly scented oils Delilah always brought back from her favorite perfumery on St. Anne's in New Orleans.

Rachel checked herself in the mirror again then straightened her shoulders and girded herself to put on another big performance.

Her life, and that of two innocent children held somewhere inside this house of horrors, depended on it.

FORTY-TWO

When Rachel walked back into the kitchen, the Collector was standing beside the coffee pot. The aroma of rich coffee almost overpowered her perfume.

"Darling! You look sensational! And you smell wonderful!" He nuzzled her throat. "*Mmm...*"

"Thank you, sweetheart."

He was going to kiss her. She could see it in his face. When he lifted himself on tiptoes, she braced for it, even made herself pretend to kiss him back.

Stop. Stop.

She was going to be sick. She was going to stomp down on his arch with her stilettos and do him maximum harm.

Finally, he pulled back, flushed and proud of himself, and she could breathe again. But he still held a tight grip on her arm.

"My, my," he said. "A little preview of things to come."

Over my dead body. Rachel filled herself with ice. She was an unfeeling glacier, capable of wrecking large ships—and the evil man who hovered over her, watching her with his sickening, predatory gaze.

"I have to get breakfast, sweetheart. You don't want to be late for work on our first day as a family."

Her ploy worked. He released his hold and smiled at her. "That's what I love to hear from a wife."

She swished off to fetch her apron from the pantry before he could get any more ideas about romance in the kitchen. The tawdry stilettos turned her march into an X-rated move he watched with avid interest.

"What do you want me to cook for breakfast, Charlie?"

His eyes slid away from her hips and back to her face. "Bacon, scrambled eggs, toast with butter and strawberry jelly. Mikey will have the same. He's a chip off the old block."

Mikey?

Obviously, he'd renamed Eddie, just as he had her.

"Of course he is."

Rachel set about assembling the ingredients. Why hadn't he mentioned Lulu? She didn't dare bring up the subject herself. He was truly one of the most frightening human beings she'd ever known, his evil so well hidden he'd been in plain sight of the entire community for years and no one had ever guessed what he was.

When he came up behind her and wrapped his arms around her, she steeled herself.

"If only the children weren't here," he murmured. "I know what we'd be doing in the kitchen now."

The only good thing she could say about all this was that he'd mentioned the *children*.

"No need for impatience, sweetheart." She put a seductive purr into her voice. "We'll have all of tonight just for ourselves."

"That's my girl!"

"Will all our children be joining us for breakfast?"

"No. Just Mikey. Star's misbehaving. She's in timeout."

For how long? Did she have food? Water? She couldn't risk

stirring the madman up with questions. Instead, she nodded her approval.

"That usually works," she said.

"If it doesn't, we'll just get rid of her."

Rachel almost dropped the bowl of eggs. He wanted her to help to kill a child? She beat the eggs as if they were his blackened, shriveled-up heart. She didn't stop until she was no longer shaking and she could pour them into the skillet without spilling egg yolk all over the floor.

"Do I need to help Mikey get dressed?"

"No. I'm teaching our children to be independent. He'll be here soon enough." He poured a cup of coffee and handed it to her. "Here, darling. You look like you could use this."

"Thank you."

The coffee might have been the only thing that saved her. She managed to finish cooking and set breakfast on the table. She even managed a straight face and a decent job of hiding her dismay when little Eddie Greene walked into the room.

He looked nothing like the healthy, cheerful little kid who'd been taken weeks earlier. He was thin, pale, and obviously scared to say anything to cross the man who introduced her as *your new mommy*.

"Her name is Elizabeth, and you are to call her Mommy. Do you understand, Mikey?"

The boy looked at his feet and nodded. The mailman ruffled his hair in a show of affection.

"That's a good boy. While Daddy's gone today, you be a good boy and do everything I've taught you. Okay?"

"'K."

"If you mind your mommy and follow all the rules, I'll bring the dogs in again this evening and you'll get to keep them in your room. Fair enough?"

"Yes, Daddy."

The Collector winked at Rachel. "We've got one smart kid, here. With many more soon to come."

Terror washed over her. Was he planning to kidnap more or was he talking about the children he wanted to have with *her*? Both were equally horrifying. She had to find a way to stop him.

Breakfast was a quiet, unnatural affair. Charles Blankenship did most of the talking while Rachel wondered what her own children were doing. She imagined Susan taking the entire responsibility for the kidnapping on herself while she held her pain inside. Joey would be more demonstrative. He'd cry and scream questions and storm around looking for answers.

Jen would come and she'd know what to do. Right now, she'd hold on to that thought plus the knowledge that Hank was searching for her. She'd be strong, for all of them—Joey, Susan, Eddie, and Lulu. Even the stolen dogs she heard barking in the yard beneath the kitchen window.

"Elizabeth."

She almost jumped when the mailman called her name. He was out of his chair and staring at her as if he could see straight through to her mind.

"I'll be back at six. There are sandwich makings for lunch and a roast beef in the refrigerator. Cook that for dinner and whatever side dishes you wish. Make chocolate cake for dessert. I want our first dinner together to be memorable. Understood?"

"Yes." After he'd mentioned killing Lulu, she couldn't even force herself to use an endearment. If she did, her tongue might burst into flames.

"Mikey is allowed to bring certain games from his room into the living room. The two of you can enjoy getting to know each other. He takes a nap at two, and he knows when that is. Make sure he does not shirk."

"Of course. You've trained him well." She flashed him a wide smile that felt stiff and unnatural but seemed to please him. Hoping it wasn't a mistake, she left her chair and sidled close enough to caress his chest. "I suppose you have cameras to ensure our son obeys the rules?"

"Certainly not! Only the weak need crutches. A perfect household has no need for cameras. It's built on trust. Do you *trust* me, Elizabeth?"

"Of course I do, Charlie."

Her little purr of admiration had him preening.

"That's good enough for now. The rest will come in time." He visibly threw back his shoulders and assumed an authoritative posture. "Star is in her room and that's off-limits to you. Do not talk to her or attempt to open her door and take her food. She is not allowed any communication until she learns her lesson. Is that clear?"

"Perfectly."

The thought of Lulu locked away without food made her sick at heart. What other horrors had the innocent child endured?

"Don't look so upset, Elizabeth. She has the cats."

She made herself smile.

"Of course. You know best, sweetheart." The endearment almost choked her.

"All right then. Everybody, come and give Daddy a hug. It's off to work I go."

As Rachel walked into the maniac's outstretched arms, the only good thing she could say about it was that, apparently, he had certain rules about not kissing and carrying on in front of the children. Little Eddie was standing nearby, displaying no emotion whatsoever, not even a child's natural curiosity.

Rachel kept up her cheerful, wifely façade until the Collector undid all the locks and walked out the door. As soon as it closed behind him, she collapsed to the floor. His evil hovered over everything, like the endless Colorado sky. With it removed, she was tempted to lie there and just breathe normally again.

Her eyelids began to droop, and she found herself drifting into nothingness. Suddenly, the scent of magnolias was so overpowering she jumped up, batting at the air to keep from smothering in danger.

Rachel pulled herself together. She couldn't afford to let down her guard for an hour, not even for one second.

She did a quick sweep of the large kitchen and den for hidden cameras. Finding none, she kicked off her ridiculous shoes then wiped the makeup off her face with a tissue from the box on the kitchen counter.

When she turned to find Eddie, he had slid away like a little ghost. She found him in his room, on the floor playing with a set of Legos.

Rachel stood a moment outside his door, watching to make sure he was okay. Then she eased his door shut and slipped across the hall to stand in front of the other door. There was the faint scurrying of movement, then silence. Was it Lulu on the other side of the door listening?

As much as Rachel longed to call through the door and assure the scared little girl that she would do everything in her power to help her, she couldn't risk Eddie hearing then repeating what she'd said to the depraved man who held all their fates in his evil hands.

I'll be back, Lulu.

She made the promise to herself that she'd return when Eddie napped. It would be the only safe time to talk to the little girl.

Filled with regret, she left the closed door and went into the room across the hall to sit on the floor beside Eddie Greene.

"I like to build Lego houses," she said.

He cocked his head to one side. "Do mommies play?"

"This mommy does."

"'K."

How much did he remember? And how much would he

tell? Rachel had to be very careful. It was sometimes easy to get an innocent child to reveal things, but it would be just as easy for the Collector to get him to repeat what she'd said.

It was an hour before Eddie began to lose the haunted look on his face. She finally got him to laugh by telling the story of a little boy she knew who built frog houses and then tried to coax all the frogs inside. Her heart hurt just thinking about Joey.

"I can't go outside."

"Why don't we take the Legos into the kitchen and sit in front of the big window so we can feel the sun? Would you like that?"

He nodded, and off they went. She was relieved to see how the child perked up in the sunshine.

"How about we make it a picnic, too? Do you like s'mores?"

"What's mores?"

"Marshmallows and graham crackers with chocolate."

"Yummy!" Suddenly his face fell. "No snacks. Just lunch. One piece of ham and two pieces of bread. One bottle of water. He knows. He counts."

Rachel wanted to cry, but she knew if she started, she might never stop.

"You are a smart little boy to remember all that, and to make your lunch all by yourself."

"Sometimes Uncle makes it."

Uncle?

All her senses went on alert.

"Uncles are a lot of fun. I know somebody called Uncle Benjamin who keeps lollipops in his pockets." Jen's husband. Always kind, always smiling and ready to lend a hand.

"No treats unless Daddy says so, no running in the house, no TV without Daddy, no crying." The child was solemn as he ticked off the rules on his fingers.

It broke her heart to see all the spontaneity and joy of childhood drained out of this small, solemn captive. She hugged him close.

"You are such a good little boy. Your mommy loves you."

A flicker of comprehension crossed his face. A memory of his own mother? His real home?

"Daddy loves me," he whispered. "He tells me."

"I'm sure he does. And your uncle, too."

The child shrugged. "Uncle comes and he goes. Fast."

She didn't want to further confuse him or damage him in any way. How far could she push trying to discover the identity of this unexpected uncle?

She unconsciously reached toward her pocket for her phone to ask Jen then crashed back to harsh reality. He'd taken her only connection to the outside world. She was on her own.

"He's very busy, then, this Uncle John."

Eddie shook his head. *No.*

"Uncle George, who looks like this?" Rachel squinted her eyes and stretched her mouth with her hands, trying to make the boy laugh.

He giggled. "No, silly. Just Uncle. He wears a Halloween mask!"

Rachel was flabbergasted.

The Collector had a partner.

FORTY-THREE
COLORADO SPRINGS

Charles Blankenship clocked into work as usual, his genius and cunning invisible to the public who viewed him as Nobody. He trudged to the mailroom, holding his delicious secret inside. It was almost too much for him to bear.

Nobody in the mailroom paid him the least attention as he loaded the bags into the mail delivery truck. Nobody called out *Hey, Charlie. How's the wife and kids?* Nobody gave him knowing glances because he would soon be having a night to remember with the most beautiful bride in the world. Nobody asked him how his Spanish lessons were going or when he'd be moving the entire Blankenship family to Mexico.

The compound was already waiting for them, an isolated villa with plenty of space to handle a growing family.

Oh, the planning that had gone into it. The thought for the future, the attention to every small detail.

He salivated at the large number of children who would be born in the compound, a powerful Blankenship dynasty that would achieve such great things they'd surpass the fame of the Manson family. The children would even surpass the fame of their own father.

The Collector's future had never looked brighter.

He waited until he was behind the wheel of the mail truck before he started whistling. He hadn't whistled in years, not since the old bag died and he could draw a free breath. He didn't even know the name of the song. It was one of those zippy tunes he'd heard on the rerun of an old Western during a rare outing to another little boy's house when he was eight years old. He didn't even recall the boy's name.

He didn't have friends growing up. His only relief from the repression at home was an occasional outing to the home of a schoolmate whose mother felt sorry for Charles Blankenship, the little boy with the weird mother and the hand-me-down clothes.

Thinking of his past thrust him into a dark mood. It got even darker as he moved from mailbox to mailbox, dispensing letters and newspapers and grocery store flyers to people who lived their selfish lives, while women like Leona Blankenship dished out wisdom from the cards to her clients and cruelty and hatred to her own son.

The Collector would never be cruel to his children. He was a good father who only punished when it was necessary. He was a wise father who would only terminate a child for just cause.

When his cell phone screen lit up, his mood got even darker. It was the Other.

"The heat's on," the Other said. "We need to step up our move and leave tonight."

"No." He wasn't about to be deprived of his honeymoon with Elizabeth. Besides, she'd be far more mellow and excited about their future in another week. "We stick to the plan. *Next* weekend. That's when we'll leave."

"What's the holdup? The little girl?"

"Partially."

"I told you to get rid of her, didn't I? If you can't, I will."

The Collector couldn't risk the consequences of murdering Star. Elizabeth might turn from him, and he'd have to win her back, or else take her by force.

"No. I'm going to wait. I think the girl will come around."

"We don't need her. We can have plenty of our own."

The Collector's hands gripped the steering wheel so hard he thought it might crack into pieces. There was only one way to handle this situation.

"I won't change my mind or my plans. Calling the gas and electric companies to shut off power and utilities because I'm leaving now would be a giant red flag."

"A red flag is nothing compared to the manhunt that's going on now."

"Are you forgetting who's the boss?" Charles spat. "I made the Collector famous long before you came along."

"Are you forgetting our *agreement*? We build this dynasty together. We take turns with the woman."

"How dare you call Elizabeth *the woman!* She's my wife, and mine alone. There will be no taking turns."

"That's not fair, Charlie. We agreed. Equal partners in everything, including... *Elizabeth*."

The Other sounded whiny and weak. Maybe the Collector had made a mistake in letting him in on the plans.

Too bad, too sad.

He was correcting that mistake now. He wasn't about to let sentiment get in the way of achieving everything he'd worked for.

"There is nothing you can do about it," he told the Other. "This is *my* plan. I call the shots. You're only part of it because I let you in."

The Collector pulled onto the shoulder and shoved mail into the box. Who cared whether it was for that address? Who cared if he botched every delivery on his route today? With the suddenness typical of genius, he knew he'd be walking off the job at the end of the day. No wimpy handing in a resignation and filling out endless forms. No kowtowing to bosses who barely even knew his name.

He'd take his pleasure tonight and enjoy a week of bliss, free of the expectations of everybody, including the Other.

"You *promised*." The Other wheedled and begged. "I risked everything for this, and you assured me I'd be part of it all. It was a gentlemen's agreement."

"I'm no gentleman and neither are you." The Collector tossed mail, willy-nilly, into the next box then roared away.

A sense of power filled him.

"It's too late to back out now." Suddenly the Other sounded more authoritative and impressive, much as he'd been when the Collector first met him.

"What do you mean?"

"Why should you be the only victor to enjoy the spoils? I know everything. I can blow the whistle on you, and still keep my nose out of it."

Ah, a worthy foe. An adversary whose cunning matched his own.

The Collector mulled over the Other's threat while he stuffed junk flyers into the next box and threw the first-class mail onto the ground.

"All right. You can help create the dynasty, but there's a new deal. A much better one, now that I think of it. She's mine until my child is born, then she's yours until your child is born. That way, we can observe exactly how the gene pool plays out in each individual child. We'll still be sharing and sharing alike, as we originally agreed."

It would also assure the Collector that Elizabeth would love only him. She'd view the Other as a mere duty, something she had to endure with good grace until her beloved husband came back to her.

It was brilliant, actually. Having to service the Other would teach Elizabeth her place and let her know who was the head of the household. He couldn't risk his wife feeling so elevated and loved by him that she could get the upper hand.

He loved her. Yes, he did. And she was already head over heels for him. Her soft-spoken endearments and little sideways glances. Even the perfume she'd put behind her ear, knowing that's where he liked to nuzzle, announced her feelings for him.

Still, she had to know he was boss over everything, even her.

"Fair enough," the Other said. "But if you back out the next time, I won't issue a warning. I'll go straight to the authorities and claim I was your victim, too."

His admiration for the Other inched up another notch.

"It's a deal. Stick to your guns. If you keep up this kind of bold thinking, you're going to end up just like me."

"That's the plan. I couldn't have a better role model."

The Other, amiable now and chatty, talked on about his plans for the day while the Collector gleefully scattered mail that went flying into ditches and cow pastures and the wrong boxes. His reward would be thinking of the consternation he'd sowed among every upstanding citizen in Manitou Springs and beyond. They would blow up the phone system at the post office with their complaints.

FORTY-FOUR

THE HIDEAWAY

Sitting with Eddie on his bedroom floor, Rachel reeled over his revelation that he had an *uncle* who dropped by for periodic visits. Trying to outwit the Collector was bad enough. How would she ever have the strength and the fortitude to save herself and the children from *two* madmen?

She hid her fear from Eddie and continued sitting with him while she listened for clues from across the hall. She grew more uncertain over Lulu's fate with each passing minute. There had been nothing but soft scurrying noises all morning long. With little Eddie watching and listening, the best she could do was pause briefly in the hallway and strain to hear.

"Lunchtime," Eddie announced, then solemnly left his toys and went to the kitchen.

Lunch was a heartbreaking affair with the little boy the Collector had turned almost robotic. He ate exactly what he had been told, no complaining, no sneaking an extra bite, just total obedience. What if someone had done that to Joey?

She paid the child extra attention and lavished hugs on him, but she studiously refrained from calling him by his new name.

How much did he even remember about his life before the kidnapping?

Promptly at two, Eddie announced it was time for his nap.

"I'll tuck you in and read you a story." Rachel put all the cheer she could manage into her voice.

"No stories till bedtime. Daddy reads to me."

It was frightening how easily the child had been brainwashed in less than seven weeks. For a horrible moment, Rachel wondered how long it would take for the madman to brainwash her. How long before she became compliant and dependent, living for the rare moment when he would show his approval of her?

Every fiber in her body rebelled against the idea. She would find a way out. She had to.

Rachel tucked Eddie in then stood just inside his room making sure he was sound asleep before she eased his door shut and crossed the hall to tap on Lulu's door. There was no answer.

She tapped again. "Lulu. It's Susan's mother."

"Ms Maxey!" The sound of running footsteps filtered into the hallway then there was a soft thump and swish as the child's body hit the door and slid to the floor. "Help me. Please help me."

"Lulu, listen to me, honey. You have to stop crying and be very quiet. Eddie Greene is here too, but he's napping and we don't want to wake him. Everything we say has to be a secret. Can you do that?"

There was a sniffle followed by a soft, "Yes."

"That's a good girl. Do you have food and water?"

"Just some peanut butter and a few crackers and two bottles of water."

Rage filled her. No child should have to endure what the Collector had done to Lulu.

"Has he hurt you in any way?"

"No. But he scared me. A lot. I think he wants to kill me."

Rachel was chilled to the bone. *This could be Susan.*

Was the mailman out there even now trying to kidnap Rachel's daughter or some other child to take the place of the one who refused to buckle to his demands?

"I'm sorry, Lulu. He scared me, too."

"Ms. Maxey, why are you here?"

"The mailman kidnapped me from the festival. This is a sick man with a twisted idea that he has created the perfect family. The way to stay safe from him is to pretend you are who he wants you to be. If you pretend to be Star and act as if he's your father, I can convince him to let me into your room and help you bathe and dress for dinner."

"I'm hungry. Really, really hungry. And he told me the rats in here would eat me." Lulu choked on another sob.

The rage storming in Rachel became a tornado, capable of destroying everything in its path. Her plans to switch from chocolate cake to cupcakes and lace his with another dose that would keep him busy all night changed to a massive dose big enough to fell an entire herd of elephants. If she was successful, he'd be too weak to get out of bed all day tomorrow, too.

"Lulu, listen to me. There are no rats in this apartment. It's very clean. If you'll act sweet and loving to him this evening, I think we might all make it out of here. Hank Carson is searching for us with his helicopter, and I know the El Paso County authorities will all be looking for us."

"I can do that, Ms. Maxey. It'll be like playing dress-up with Susan and Wendy and pretending we're rock stars."

"Great. I have to go now. There's a lot I have to do before he gets back. Be brave, Lulu. I'm here with you, and I'll do the best I can to get us out of here."

She hoped her best was good enough. Rachel glanced at her watch. How much time did she have before Eddie woke up? She wished she'd asked how long his naps were.

First, she inspected the door leading from the apartment. It was metal-clad, and the Collector had installed three deadbolts that required keys from her side. There was no way she would ever get through that door.

Hurrying now, Rachel combed through every inch of the master bedroom and the adjoining bathroom, searching drawers, corners of the closets, and the cabinets under the double sinks for keys and weapons—anything that would give her a clue about the Collector's partner or his plans.

It would be far too risky to keep her and the children in this house forever. Not with the massive manhunt and search for her and the children that was surely taking place.

Rachel didn't know the location of Charles Blankenship's cabin, but based on the time between her kidnapping at the festival and her waking up in a strange bed, she calculated they were somewhere on the outskirts of Manitou Springs.

The view surrounding the cabin gave her no clues about the location, either. All they told her was that it was secluded deep in the woods. He would likely have chosen a spot with hundreds of acres of woods in all directions, making it seem impossible to escape.

He didn't know the Logan women. Victoria and her granddaughters never gave up about anything, ever.

She shook her fist at the bed he envisioned as theirs.

"You will never win!"

She doubled her efforts, but her search turned up nothing of use. Time raced away from her like a stampede of wild horses, and fear constantly threatened to be her undoing.

She went into the kitchen where the lingering fragrance of magnolias reminded her that she was doing far more than putting a roast in the oven, whipping up some side dishes and baking cupcakes. She was fighting for survival.

She found sugar sprinkles in the pantry that would be

perfect for writing names on the cupcakes so their craven jailer would get his just desserts.

Her family and Hank would love that pun. If she lived long enough to tell them.

"I will live. I *will*!"

On second thoughts, she dug a bottle of aspirin from her teacher's tote and crushed up a heavy dose to add to the Collector's already toxic cupcake. Life would be so much simpler with him asleep.

With a flourish she wrote *Daddy* on the top with sugar sprinkles. His icing also contained most of the laxatives in her pocket. If they couldn't escape soon, she'd run out of ways to spoil his grandiose plans.

With the cupcakes lined up in a dazzling array on a silver tray and the roast in the oven smelling delicious, she repaired her makeup and doused herself with so much of Dawn Williams' perfume she figured Charles would smell it when he came through the downstairs door. Would it be enough to distract him from her real purpose?

Still sore from her fall, she favored her leg on the way to retrieve the ridiculous stilettos from underneath the sofa where she had kicked them off. When she got out of this nightmare, she swore she would never wear a pair of high-heeled shoes again.

Hating the absurd shoes and Charles Blankenship with every step, Rachel crossed to the sliding doors that overlooked the rooftop patio and began her inspection.

The Collector had wedged a big stick into the channel to prevent the doors from sliding open. Even when she removed it and flicked the lock open, the doors still refused to budge.

A closer inspection with her flashlight showed that he had screwed the doors into the wall. Frustrated, she banged on the glass. Then she set out to locate the toolbox. If she could take him down far enough with a near-fatal cupcake, she could unscrew the door and at least get the kids out onto the patio where Hank could get to them.

If he could find them.

Please. Please.

She was on her hands and knees in the pantry, searching behind the bags of dog food, when Eddie walked up behind her.

"Mommy."

There. In the corner. The toolbox. If it contained a screwdriver and a role of duct tape, she'd be in luck.

"Hey, sweetie." She turned to smile at the little boy. "Did you have a nice nap?"

He nodded, solemn. "Did you make a cupcake for me?"

"I did. It even has your name on it. I'll show you."

When she lifted him up to show him the cupcake with Mikey written in sugar sprinkles, she felt a huge twinge of guilt that she was participating in the brainwashing process that would eventually make him forget who he was.

She pointed out the names as she read them off: Daddy, Mommy, Mikey and Star.

He pointed to the one decorated with pink sugar sprinkles. "Daddy said I have a sister. Is that her?"

"It is. And she's very nice. I think you're going to love her as much as I do." She kissed the top of his head and set him on his feet. "Let's get you a bath and changed into something nice for Daddy. Okay?"

"Okay, Mommy."

Another little piece broke off Rachel's heart. She pictured Eddie's mom slowly losing hope of ever seeing her son again. Her pain must be almost unbearable.

I'm going to get him home to you.

Hanging on to affirmative thoughts helped her endure the pretense of being the mother of a little boy who never laughed once during his bath, not even when Rachel created a bathtub race between Eddie and a rubber duck to see who could be the first to get clean.

By the time the Collector got home, Rachel was waiting beyond the door with Eddie at her side, freshly scrubbed and dressed in a clean pair of blue jeans and a blue striped tee shirt. She'd even managed to smooth down most of his hair, which tended to stand up in tufts like the feathers of a startled baby bird.

He beamed when he saw them.

"Surprise, sweetheart!" Rachel smiled at him, playing her role to the hilt. "We wanted to look nice for you."

"Well, you certainly did just that, Elizabeth." He sniffed the air as if he couldn't get enough of the aroma. "Is that roast beef I smell?"

"It is. With all the trimmings and a very special dessert to celebrate." She made herself glance toward the floor as if she were entirely too demure to even hint at events to come.

"Splendid. Let Daddy wash up first and we can get started."

She sent Eddie into his room to play then followed Daddy Dearest into the bedroom. The puffed-up peacock misunderstood her intentions. When he grabbed her and started nuzzling her neck, she hoped he choked on the odious perfume.

"You smell good enough to eat."

"Charlie!" She made herself sound coy and slightly embarrassed. "Not with the children awake."

"You're right, darling. But, oh, who can resist those ruby-red lips?"

What passed with Charlie for kissing was a punishing intensity that made her want to bash him over the head with her stilettos. Unfortunately, she was neither fast enough nor strong enough to take him out with a blow from her high-heels.

She endured while he stretched high on his tiptoes kissing her until his legs gave out. When he let go, she felt as if she'd been released from the jaws of death.

Three cheers for four-inch stilettos.

Finally, he pulled away and his heels plopped back on the floor. But still he stood there, gazing up at her with adoration. She hoped he mistook her hot flush of outrage for the blush of modesty.

"Mrs. Blankenship, you are the most amazing woman I've ever met. We are going to make remarkable children who will be the envy of parents around the world. Yes, indeed, we are!"

"Oh, Charlie. I hope so."

She had never been a good liar, and was relieved when nothing in his face showed suspicion.

"Starting tonight."

"I can hardly wait."

"My darling, that's exactly what I wanted to hear." The maniac smiled knowingly as if he were only moments away from living out his sick fantasies. "It will be an unforgettable evening."

Rachel tamped down her fear.

"Charlie, there's something very important I want to talk to you about before you wash up."

"Of course. I'm here for you any time."

"I substituted chocolate cupcakes instead of a full cake because they are so much easier for children to handle, and I was certain you'd want our Mikey to feel a part of this celebration."

"Is that all? Naturally, I want our son there, darling. You made a smart decision."

"Thank you. I want to please you in all things."

"That's my beautiful girl!"

"Actually, that's not all. I wanted to ask you if Star can join us for dinner?"

"No. You know she's being punished for bad behavior."

"I do, Charlie. And I'm happy to report that it worked! You are so clever. Star has been good all day."

"How do you know?" In an instant, he went from beaming, smiling approval to fierce scowling. "I specifically told you not to talk to her." He caught her upper arms hard enough to hurt. "Did you disobey me, Elizabeth?"

"Oh, Charlie. No. I would never do that."

The tears that sprang to her eyes were real. The bruises he was bound to leave on her arms were the least of her worries. The evil inside him turned his eyes hard and almost yellow. If she didn't know better, she'd think she was looking into the eyes of a wild animal, a wolf or a cougar, or one of the horrible, fierce birds that swooped around the mountains eating the flesh of dead animals.

The man standing before her was capable of anything. Including murder.

"Are you *sure* about that, Elizabeth?"

He dug his fingers into her arm until he broke skin. The minute he drew blood, his face took on such a sharpness she would swear she was looking into the eyes of a horrible black crow.

"I'm positive, Charlie."

"I do not tolerate liars in this house. Oh no, I do not."

"I didn't lie, sweetheart. I didn't go near Star's door all day. You can ask Mikey."

"Do you think I'm an idiot? Mikey takes naps!"

"Of course he does. He did today." Fresh tears sprang to her eyes. There was a real possibility she wouldn't live long enough to save the children. "But I was so busy cooking a special meal for our special night, I didn't have time, Charlie."

His glare never wavered, and he seemed to be growing bigger right before her eyes. Evil was a terrible thing to see. Looking at him was like staring into the depths of a burning volcano. Any minute now she was going to be consumed, treated to the most horrible death the depraved man in front of her could think of.

"ELIZABETH, DO YOU KNOW WHAT HAPPENS TO LIARS IN THIS HOUSE!"

She was afraid to answer, terrified that the least little thing would unchain the beast standing in front of her. All the lipstick and perfume and feminine wiles in the world could not get through to the demon who had taken over Charles Blankenship's soul.

Rachel couldn't bear to think about her children, waiting at home, and the children she wanted to save. She bowed her head, a posture of complete submission, and waited for what would happen next.

The room filled with fog and the overpowering scent of magnolias. Rachel felt herself vanishing into the mist, piece by piece, while time ground to a halt. She was suspended in this unspeakable horror, paralyzed, helpless.

Suddenly Annie's warning came to her. *Don't go near the woods. Danger... Danger... Danger.*

Remembering, Rachel cried silent tears.

The only sound was that of the monster's breathing. Harsh gulps of air. Slobbering intakes of breath that foretold a future too terrible to contemplate.

An eternity later, Charlie stormed from the room. Trapped in her fog, Rachel heard the apartment door slam, heard his horrible roar as he tore through the downstairs, and then a sound that sent chills through her.

The blast of a gun.

He was coming back to kill her.

FORTY-FIVE
DENVER, COLORADO

Hank watched as Jen rolled off the plane like a tornado, her wild black curly hair flying in every direction, her black eyes flashing, and the slash of bright red lipstick making the set of her mouth look even fiercer. She stormed through baggage claim and straight to him.

"Have they found my sister?"

"No."

"Then the search team had better be working through the night, because I won't stand for anything less "

"Neither will I. And they are."

"I'll judge that for myself."

He grabbed her bags, and they boarded the shuttle that would drop them off where his turbo-prop waited.

Hank had just received a phone call from Sheriff Jeremiah Johnson that they had chased so many false leads because of Bruce Wyler's reward money the whole department had been hampered in their search. Hank would love to find the guy and strangle him.

But he wasn't there to prove a point with Jen. He was just

glad to have the support of someone of her fierce intelligence and tenacity helping in the search.

Without fanfare she climbed aboard his plane. "How fast can you get to the house?"

"Hang on to your hat."

"Talk while you drive."

"Fly."

"Whatever." She grabbed the earphones and put them on. "I want to know everything."

She interrupted with so many questions that they were landing on his airstrip in Colorado Springs by the time he'd brought her up to speed.

Another twenty minutes, and they were walking through Rachel's door and into a melee of hugs, laughter, and tears. Even the dog got into the act by licking at the musky perfume on Jen's wrists.

Susan and Joey clung to their aunt, and she sent a glance at Hank over their heads that said, *they come first.*

He went into the kitchen to pour a cup of coffee and give the family some privacy. Soon they all poured in, including the dog. The kitchen became the center of swirling activity. Victoria made hot chocolate, Jen grabbed coffee, the children ate cookies, and everybody talked at once.

Under normal circumstances, the family whirlwind would have been something to savor. With Rachel's loss eating a hole in his heart and the need to be doing something tearing up his stomach, Hank wondered how they would ever accomplish anything useful in this manner.

"It's okay," Jen said. "The children need to know everything that's happening with their mother."

Rachel had always said her sister had an uncanny ability to read minds.

Just thinking Rachel's name conjured up images of the woman who had shared her family with him the last three years, bared her soul to him, and made his life richer in ways he hadn't fully appreciated until she was gone. An old adage he'd always dismissed came to his mind: you never know what you love until you're in danger of losing it.

Jen reached over to squeeze his hand. "It's okay. I'm fixing to get this show on the road."

Fixing. A Southern colloquialism. Rarely heard since he left Texas.

Jen crossed to the kitchen counter where Victoria was putting on another pot of coffee and tenderly slung an arm over her grandmother's shoulders.

"Gran, I need to talk to you."

"Judging by the stubborn set of your jaw, I'd say it's more like quiz me." She wiped her hands on a tea towel then headed to the kitchen table. "I think I'd better sit down."

"Probably so. This is serious." Jen pulled out a chair beside her. "Mom consulted a mystic before I was born. Who was she?"

"I don't know anything about Delilah's doings."

"Yes, you do. You knew everything Mom ever did, and you disapproved of most of it."

"I did not." Victoria sniffed. "That was your granddaddy."

"He adored Mom. You're the one who calls her the Bohemian."

Victoria got the look Rachel always called cagey. Hank had seen it many times. She was thinking how to get out of answering something she didn't want to.

"Lots of artistic people are Bohemian," she said. "Acknowledging that is not disapproval. It's just the truth."

"You never call Annie that, and if you did, she'd get spitting mad."

"Does Annie know about Rachel? I never could get through to her."

"I talked to her this morning before I left Pensacola. She's doing an art show in Venice and has them scheduled all over Italy through the Christmas holidays. She wanted to cancel everything and fly to Colorado, but I told her to stay put."

"You should have let her come. I need Annie here."

"You've got me, Gran. And you might as well quit trying to change the subject. I'm onto you." Jen's armful of gold bracelets glowed against her dark skin and rattled as she set down her coffee cup and reached for a cookie off the platter. "I know you know the fortune teller I'm talking about. Mom said the woman had a little boy, and you were upset about him."

"The Bohemian always did exaggerate." Victoria's frown vanished and she quickly added. "I guess all artistic types do..."

"Mom's exact words were, 'Victoria was so upset about the kid she threatened to turn the woman into child services.' Think, Gran. I know good and well you remember her."

"You don't know the first thing about growing old!"

Hank's impatience to get any bit of information that led him to Rachel must have showed. Jen exchanged a look with him that said *I've got this*.

"I'm not trying to upset you. But you have to understand how important this information could be in finding Rachel."

Victoria sagged, a sign she was giving over to her strong-willed granddaughter. "It's Leona. That's all I know. Leona somebody or other."

Jen grabbed her laptop out of her tote bag, powered it up, and began typing. In a moment, she glanced up at her grandmother.

"And the little boy?"

"I don't remember his name but he was just a toddler, Delilah said. Pitiful. Painfully shy. Nothing but skin and bones. Didn't look like he'd ever seen a day in the sun."

Victoria paused as if the memories were too painful to talk about while Jen's fingers flew over the keyboard.

Finally, Victoria sighed and started talking again. "The only reason I didn't turn the fortune teller in is that she told Delilah he was just a little boy she was keeping for her neighbor, a sorry you-know-what who didn't know how to take care of a toad frog, let alone a little boy." She paused to glare at her granddaughter. "Thinking about him made me sick to my stomach, and I put him out of my mind all these years until *you* stirred things up."

"I know I'm maddening, worse than my mom but totally lacking in her charm." She stared Victoria down. "But you have to understand that everything I do is an effort to help find Rachel. You know that, don't you, Gran?"

Victoria turned away from them to look out the window where there was nothing to be seen except a pale moon sending feeble light through the darkness. She stared at the darkness for a long time, ignoring them all.

Suddenly, she sighed. "She died in a fire."

Jen's head shot up. "Who?"

"The fortune teller. Leona."

"A Tarot card reader?" Hank asked as Jen furiously typed on her keyboard.

"Yes." Victoria rubbed her hands over her exhausted-looking face.

"And the boy?" Jen briefly looked up from her computer.

"I don't know. I guess he was nearly grown by then. Seems like he lived. I hope he did. Such a tragedy." Victoria shook herself as if she couldn't quite get rid of a nightmare. "I've always wondered what would have happened to him if I'd turned that heifer in."

"Listen to this." Jen started reading from her computer screen. "'Leona Blankenship, local Tarot card mystic, died tragically in a house fire. She is survived by one son, Charles.'"

"*Blankenship.*" Hank grabbed his phone. "The mailman."

All the pieces fell into place. The car Wyler heard on the road the day of Rachel's robbery had belonged to the mailman. The timing fit. If the mailman took her, she would never have suspected him until it was too late. Hank would be willing to bet that a map of the Collector's victims would place them all along the mailman's route. He'd also know about the children who lived in the houses where he delivered mail.

The clincher was his calling card—his mother's stained and yellowing Tarot cards.

When the sheriff came on the line, Hank told him everything they'd discovered and what he suspected.

"I'm already on it," Sheriff Johnson told him "We already know Blankenship bought tires that fit the description of our tracks in Soda Springs Park. And he seems to have gone off the rails. He quit today after scattering the mail all over the canyon. The post office had to close early because of irate customers storming the building."

"They'll have his address."

"I'm tracking that down now."

"What can I do?"

"Sit tight, Hank. We don't have enough yet to make a move."

When he pocketed his phone, Jen looked up from her computer and began to tick off facts on her fingers, a habit he'd seen Rachel use.

"Charles Blankenship was suspected of setting the fire that killed his mother, but he was finally exonerated. He was expelled from high school for setting a fire in the baseball boys' dressing room, starting food wars in the cafeteria, and stealing teachers' supplies. He spent two years at a reform school then finally got his act together, graduated from college *with honors,* went to work for the postal service in Denver, and finally ended up here in good old Manitou Springs where he apparently fell off the good citizen wagon. Again. After leaving behind the bones of two children in Denver."

Victoria gave her oldest granddaughter a suspicious look. "How do you know all that?"

"I'm a psychologist. I have access to lots of helpful resources." She winked at the children. "And I inherited a great big independent streak from the Bohemian. So did your mom. She's going to be all right. Okay?"

They nodded, then moved in to hug her.

"Read us a bedtime story, Aunt Jen," Joey said, and even Susan echoed the request.

"That sounds like a wonderful idea." She linked hands with both the children then turned back to Hank and Victoria. "All right, you guys, when I come back down here, you'd better have that low-life's address."

"Yes, ma'am." Hank saluted and Jen gave them a thumbs-up sign before she led the children upstairs.

Sam dutifully got up to follow. He knew his routine as well as anybody in the house.

It was a pity Hank didn't feel as confident about his next move. Every instinct told him Rachel was in grave danger. With every fiber of his being, he wanted to be doing something, anything, to find her.

Common sense and a massive effort at control kept him from racing off and blundering through the night. The only thing he could do now was meticulously check every window and door in the house then settle in to keep watch through the night over Rachel's children.

FORTY-SIX

THE HIDEAWAY

Rage was a hot, living, writhing thing inside the Collector. Everywhere he looked was red: red walls, red furniture, red floors, red ceilings—all dripping with the rich, red blood of Elizabeth. His love. His bride. His betrayer. Yes, she was.

No, she was not.

He tore at the yellow wig on his head, tore at his scalp. His fingernails came away coated with blood.

He felt his power rising within him. His lust.

He had to get out, get away from her, her luscious body and seductive ways. Her lips capable of speaking both love and lies. Elizabeth was a witch. She had bewitched him. Yes, she had.

And he was lost in a red haze of uncertainty. That's what she had done to him, Charles Blankenship, King of Crows, the almighty Collector who had left a trail of mayhem and fear all over the canyon.

His beauties were landing in the tree, the rustling of their black wings and the secrets they told in their language singing through the crow's blood coursing through his body. He could hear their magical song through the walls, the ceiling, the closed doors. He could have heard it from the other side of the ocean. Yes, he could.

He spread his wings and flew through the door.

"There you are, my fiendish friends! My diabolical brothers!"

The Collector took aim, and the first shot found its mark right over the heart of the largest crow on the branch. The dark bird floated downward, his dying song still on his beak, words of eternal gratitude that he had been chosen by the famous man with the gun.

Three more shots in quick succession, and he had his daily quota of four, his feathered pile of power. He scooped them up and made quick work of plucking feathers from the still-warm bodies. Excitement burned through him, and he felt his rage receding.

He was electrified with power and fame. His name would blaze across billboards all over Colorado. America. The world.

He beat the dead bodies against his chest and cawed his triumph. Blood, beautiful ruby red, dotted his scalp, his face, and his white shirt. Glorious, delicious blood.

A hunger unlike any he had known—except for Elizabeth, always Elizabeth—overtook him. Cups and table manners were not for the likes of him. No, they were not. He was a god, and the manna was his.

He slid his pocketknife out of his pocket, slit the first body, and drank straight from the source. Glorious blood pouring from the crows who offered themselves each evening into the legend towering in the last light of evening, head and shoulders above the trees.

Another crow, and yet another until all four were nothing but drained carcasses. He waited, waited, while the red elixir worked its magic. He was so tall, so powerful he could touch the stars. The hot, bright stars that arranged themselves in configurations reflected in the Tarot cards. His future written in the sky.

A murder of crows still sat in the trees, watching him, admiring him, hoping they would be selected next. He cawed his triumph to them, screamed out his destiny in a language they knew.

Everything was his. It had been written in the stars long ago. The approval from the murder of crows confirmed it. All his dreams were still alive. He could still have it all. Yes, he could.

Ever their gracious king, he bowed to the crows.

"Fly away, my beauties. Fly away. You've done your work, and I have much left to do."

They beat their wings against the sky, black on gathering blackness, darkness upon approaching darkness, and then he smoothed his hand over his scalp and went inside where everything waited for him.

Everything.

FORTY-SEVEN

When he was back in the cabin, Charles locked his gun in the stainless-steel gun cabinet downstairs. The door to his upstairs apartment was locked, just as he had left it.

The Collector congratulated himself. No matter what kind of mood other people put him in, he could always count on his own brilliance and meticulous nature to make sure his private life was private.

He flipped open the deadbolts then put his hands in his pockets to make sure the keys were still there. They were sticky with blood, but that didn't matter. Nothing mattered now except knowing he had the only means of escape in his pocket, moving forward with his plans.

When he pushed open the door, he left behind a palm print of blood. Badge of courage. Symbol of power.

"Daddy's home!"

Little Mikey stood on the other side of the door, waiting for him, still dressed in his sweet little jeans and shirt.

"Hi, Daddy."

The son he was molding into his own image was unfazed by the sight of blood decorating him.

"Did Daddy's gun scare you?"

"No, Daddy. I hear it every day."

"Good boy. When we get to Mexico, I'm going to get you a gun of your own and teach you how to shoot it. You're old enough to learn, aren't you?"

"Yes, Daddy."

"Has my Mikey been a good boy while I was gone?"

"Yes, Daddy."

"Has Mommy been good, too?"

"Yes, Daddy."

"Did she talk to your new sister?"

"No, Daddy. She made chocolate cupcakes. With our names on the top."

"Good boy." He patted his son's hair, leaving behind a smear of blood. It was never too early to start teaching the children how to be tough and clever and take exactly what they wanted. "Go to your room, shut the door, and don't come out until Daddy calls you. Do you understand?"

"Yes, Daddy."

He watched until Mikey was down the hall then he went into the master bedroom to join his bride. She wasn't there. Panicked, he searched inside the closet, behind the chest of drawers, and even under the bed.

"Elizabeth? Come out. Daddy's home..."

No answer. Not a peep.

Panic started rising, followed by red rage. What had Elizabeth done now? She would soon learn that if she tried to spoil his plans, she would suffer the consequences.

He flew into the bathroom. It smelled like her, the powdery feminine scent of makeup and the intoxicating floral bouquet of her perfume. His rage tamped down a notch, giving way to erotic fantasies and wild imaginings.

"*Dar-ling*? Where are you?"

He flung open the shower curtain, but there was nothing

except cold porcelain emptiness. The same emptiness that started filling him up. A cold void. A nothingness unlike anything he'd ever felt.

He glanced in the bathroom mirror to see if he was disappearing. A splendid specimen decorated with blood-red courage stared back at him. He puffed out his chest with pride. He was still there. Whole and perfect in every way, the perfect father, the perfect husband. Oh yes, he was.

He smiled at his reflection and was rewarded with a sight so breathtaking Elizabeth would fall at his feet with adoration. With one last look, he turned to the door, calling his wife's name.

"Oh, *Eliz-a-beth*! Where are you?"

She couldn't be far. She had nowhere to go.

He slid down the hallway, past the closed doors of his children, and into the den and kitchen area where the aroma of roast beef took his breath away. He was ravenous for meat. Ravenous for all things.

He rounded the corner of the bar, then reached toward the platter of roast beef, grabbed a chunk, and stuffed it into his mouth. Juices ran down his chin. He licked them off with satisfaction. Elizabeth got a star for being a great cook.

He stood at the bar in the dark, contemplating whether to grab the whole platter of meat and scarf it down, or find Elizabeth first then turn on the lights and have a proper dinner with Mikey.

He had to think a long while before the key word came to him. Family. He was building the perfect *family*.

Satisfied, the Collector went into the kitchen, and there she was. Elizabeth. Piled in a heap on the floor in front of the patio doors. Lit by starlight and gilded by moonlight, she looked so impossibly beautiful that he felt his excitement rising.

"Elizabeth. Daddy's home."

She didn't stir. Didn't respond.

Was she dead? Had he killed her?

He couldn't remember. He didn't have any idea how she got from the bedroom into the kitchen, or why.

He tiptoed around her and stowed his keys in a secret compartment he had created under a floorboard underneath the rug in the panty. No one would ever find them, even if they searched from now until Kingdom Come. Then he knelt beside her and caressed her face. The blood looked like roses against her dusky skin. Smiling, he made a circle of crimson on each cheek. Yes, he did. Now his bride wore the crow's courage. He beat his chest with pleasure.

"Elizabeth." He leaned close, whispering in her ear. "Wake up, darling. Tonight is our honeymoon."

Did her eyelids flicker? He put his hand on her pulse. Was that Elizabeth's pulse pounding, or was it the fresh crow's blood pounding through his own system?

The Collector went to the sink and wet a dishcloth. He was not about to let her deprive him of anything he wanted. Especially tonight.

He sank beside her and dragged her onto his lap. Sweet, delicious weight. Irresistible. He leaned down and licked her lips. Blood blended with her lipstick. The rusty smell, mingling with her perfume, created such a heady aroma he threw back his head and cawed.

Her hair spread over his lap drew his attention. It was a mass as black as a crow's wing, the curls as sleek and shiny as feathers. He ran his fingers though Elizabeth's feathers, marveling. Why hadn't he noticed before? She was all crow, the Queen of Crows. Yes, she was. And she was all his.

He rocked her a while, crooning in crow, and then he leaned down and pressed the cold cloth to her forehead.

Her moan sounded like the death rattle of a crow. She couldn't be dead. Not until he said so.

"Elizabeth! Speak to me."

Her eyelids fluttered open and she stared at him. Still, unmoving.

"Darling! You're awake. How are you feeling?"

She lay as still as a carving. Had her mind snapped? Had he taken his lessons too far? He waited, holding his breath. Finally, her lips began to move.

"Good, Charlie. I'm good. What happened?"

How should he know? When he was King of Crows, the rest of the world vanished. Nothing mattered except the golden future spinning through his head. Feeling his wings expand, he sat up taller.

"Nothing that Daddy can't fix, darling. Don't you fret about it. Leave all the worry to your doting husband."

"Oh, Charlie. You don't know how relieved I am to hear that."

"Give us a kiss, then."

She sat up like the obedient wife she was becoming and gave him such a kiss he knew she would conceive his first child that very night. When she drew back, her face was flushed with crow's blood and modesty.

"There now, darling. That's what Daddy comes home for every evening. Don't you forget that."

"I won't, Charlie."

"Did you make everything for dinner like I asked?"

"Yes, I did."

"Good girl. Can you stand up now?"

"I think so. I must have fainted..."

"That's all right, darling. I love a wife who is not afraid to show that she's weaker than I am. Let me help you."

She dutifully clung to him. Yes, she did. A sign that boded well for their future. He steadied her, reveling in her new compliance.

See. That was all it took to turn a woman into a true wife. A show of power and force. A little talk that let her know who was boss.

"I think I'll be all right now, sweetheart." Elizabeth gave him a gentle smile, then patted his cheek. He loved that she didn't cringe at the sight of blood she smeared on her fingers.

"Are you sure?"

"Yes, Charlie. I want this to be a very special night. For all of us."

"That's what I like to hear from my girl. Shall we get Mikey and go into dinner?"

"Sweetheart, there's something I need to ask you first, if that's all right?"

"Anything you want, darling. Daddy is all ears."

He wanted to hop around the room and sing the crow's song of triumph. Elizabeth was truly glorious in her new-found obedience. Yes, she was.

He rewarded her with a smile that showed his love and promised remarkable things to come.

Yes, he did.

FORTY-EIGHT

The Collector's smile was a gruesome, blood-covered baring of teeth that made Rachel's heart pound so hard she thought she might faint again. Once was more than enough. The thought of what he might do next while she was out cold kept her upright and determined.

She never should have raced from the bedroom to look out the patio doors when she heard the shot. She never should have watched the horror of bird slaughter and the nightmare of the bloody ritual she saw in the moonlight under the trees. It had chilled her to the bone, terrified her so much she lost all oxygen and keeled over. Her head still hurt where she had knocked herself out against the metal door frame.

But a headache was the least of her worries. She had to bite the inside of her cheek to keep from cowering at the sight of her blood-spattered, mad-as-a-hatter captor.

Cringing inside, she put her palms on either side of his garish face and crooned to him. "I'm so glad you said that, sweetheart. You're the best husband in the world, in the whole *universe.*"

"Yes, I am."

"Very smart, too. Star has been good all day. I haven't heard a peep from her room." She caressed his shoulders and let her fingers trail inside his bloody shirt and down his bare chest. "You were brilliant to keep her in timeout all day so I could properly take care of Mikey and our home and prepare us a good meal. I wanted everything to be perfect for the first night of our real honeymoon."

"Bravo, Elizabeth. You've learned so quickly. A wife who appreciates her husband's genius is worth her weight in gold. Yes, she is."

"I do, Charlie! You're amazing, and so powerful." She squeezed his biceps, alarmed at the size of his muscles. Had she used enough sedatives to fell a man of his physical condition? "Could we please have our daughter join us for dinner?"

"Hmmm." He covered her hand and squeezed. "That might work out extremely well. Yes, it might..."

"Does that mean she *can* join us?"

"Let me go in and talk to her first, and if I think she's ready, she can eat with the rest of the family."

"Wonderful, sweetheart!" She kissed him on the cheek, careful not to get the crow's blood in her mouth.

"You can come and wait in the hall," he said. "If she's ready, I'll wash up while you help her dress for dinner."

As he went into Lulu's room, Rachel heard little Eddie playing quietly across the hall behind a closed door. She moved closer to Lulu's room without fear of detection.

"Hey, Daddy."

Bravo, Lulu!

"Well, hello, Star. Does this mean you've changed your mind about being part of the family?"

"Yes, Daddy. I love the kitty cats, and you said you'd give me some nice furniture and toys if I behave."

She'd used a child's greed as the bigger part of her motive.

Even better, she was showing no signs of fear at the sight of this bloody apparition calling himself Daddy.

"Smart girl. Daddy always does everything he promises. *Everything*. Do you understand that, Star?"

The wretch was threatening her with rats. If Rachel had time, she'd add more laxatives to his chocolate.

"I *do* understand."

"Good girl. Mommy's going to come in now and get you cleaned up while I dress for dinner."

Rachel stepped back from the door then stood there wringing her hands as if she didn't already know the outcome of the conversation.

"How did it go?"

"Splendid. Get her ready for dinner. I'll see you shortly, darling."

He was whistling when he went down the hall, and she felt a small rush of relief. Her tension was so high she wondered her whole body was not shaking.

She slipped inside Lulu's room and cringed. There was no bed, no chair, no furniture of any kind. Not even a blanket. The child had slept on the floor with nothing but the cats to keep her company.

Their litter box was in the corner along with the cats' food and water dispensers. He had cared for the cats better than he had a little girl.

Rachel hugged her close. "Smart girl, Lulu," she whispered in her ear.

"What was all that blood? Did he kill the dogs?"

"No. They're still outside. That was crow's blood."

"*Eww...*" Lulu wrinkled her nose, a response so like the carefree child she had been before her kidnapping that Rachel hoped it wouldn't take her long to adjust to normal if they got out of the nightmare.

"He is allowing you to join us for dinner."

"I'm so hungry! Thank you for everything, Ms. Maxey."

"We're not done yet, Lulu."

As Rachel helped her into the ensuite bathroom to wash her face and hands, untangle her hair, and put on one of the dresses hanging in her closet, she outlined what would happen at dinner.

"Don't show any emotion except sympathy for him," she cautioned. "Just follow my lead."

"It will be almost like playing games of pretend with Susan and Wendy."

"Hang on to that thought. We're playing a game."

With life-or-death consequences.

When Rachel and Lulu went into the combined den and kitchen, the Collector was already at the table beside the patio wearing fresh clothes and smelling of soap from the shower. Thankfully, there was not a speck of blood showing.

Rachel felt a quiver of alarm. "Where's Mikey?" She hadn't thought to check when she and Lulu came out of her room.

"I brought the dogs in so he could play with them while I inspect our daughter. Turn around, Star." She did as she was told. "You look presentable. Have you learned your lesson?"

"Yes."

"Yes, what?"

"Yes, *Daddy*."

"All right. Go get your little brother then take your seat on Mommy's right. If you behave throughout the meal, I'll consider letting you remain part of the family."

Chills went through Rachel. "Thank you, sweetheart," she said then glanced at Lulu.

"Thank you, Daddy."

She was one of the savviest children in Tanya Beasley's class. She proved it once more when she left to do his bidding. Rachel folded her hands in her lap and waited.

The Collector was now studying the table setting, looking

for flaws, searching for a reason to punish her. She knew this from her sister, Jen, who was always dispensing advice whether you wanted to hear it or not.

Rachel, avoid an abuser. The thing about abusive people is that you can never satisfy them, no matter how hard you try to please them. If you learn to avoid the traps they set for you, they will simply set other traps then wait for their chance to pounce.

Rachel said a silent prayer that she could please him long enough to get the children free.

As Lulu and Eddie slid silently into their chairs, he said, "Elizabeth, this table shows exactly the kind of class I want our family to have. Well done, darling."

Rachel was profuse in her thanks, peppering it with endearments.

She had learned how to give dinner parties from her own mother. Delilah had enjoyed nothing better than entertaining her friends as well as her husband's business associates with sit-down dinners complete with the best china, silver, and crystal perfectly placed on a linen tablecloth. The centerpiece always featured lots of candles and whatever fresh seasonal flowers the florist had to offer.

Delilah didn't have the green thumb of her mother-in-law, Victoria, nor did she ever aspire to have one. She was a Bohemian artist, through and through. She'd hated the dust and muss of the ranch almost as much as Victoria loved it.

The hateful gargoyle smiled at Rachel, crashing her back to reality. "This is certainly an auspicious beginning for our soon-to-be ever-growing family."

Picturing that horror almost unraveled her carefully constructed composure.

"Thank you, Charlie."

"Sit, sit!" He pulled out her chair with a flourish. The perfectly carved roast beef was missing a chunk, but he didn't seem to notice as he served their plates and held forth about the wonderful future that lay ahead.

For the rest of the meal, all Rachel had to do was smile encouragement at the children and pepper the Collector's nonstop talk with *thank you* and *that's wonderful, sweetheart* while she bided her time for the big finale.

Finally, she cleared the table and got the silver serving tray of cupcakes. "Drum roll, please."

"TA-DA!" the Collector shouted, grinning as if he'd won the lottery.

He ate his cupcake with great relish. "Marvelous, darling!"

As Rachel watched for the first signs her toxic concoction was working, the deviant put on a stern face and glanced around the table, making eye contact with them, one by one.

"Nobody leaves the table until Daddy finishes his after-dinner coffee."

Eddie nodded and Lulu said, "I know, Daddy. It's good manners."

"Exact..." The rumble of distress cut him off. He glanced at Rachel, sudden comprehension dawning.

Oh no. Two times in a row was too much. What now?

"Charlie. Are you okay?" She jumped up from the table then clutched her stomach. "Oh my goodness. It must be a stomach virus going around."

Suddenly Lulu bent double. "Daddy, my tummy hurts!"

"Did you catch it from somebody at the post office, sweetheart?" Rachel glanced anxiously at him, but he didn't reply. He was already out of his chair and racing down the hall.

"Star, run to your bathroom!" She all but shouted so the monster could hear. "Mikey, let's get you to your room. Quick!"

Her hands shook as she grabbed another cupcake for the little boy. This fight was far from over. The Collector was capable of such unspeakable acts, she couldn't even think beyond this moment, or she might faint again and wake up with Charlie's gun at her head.

"Are you all right, Mommy?"

"I soon will be." She spoke quietly to the little boy in case, by some miracle, the Collector could hear over his emergency bathroom activities. "I want you to stay in your room and play till I come back to tuck you in. You can have a picnic with your teddy bears."

She gave him the cupcake and two paper napkins.

"For real?"

"For real. And don't worry about making a mess. If you do, I'll just clean it up. Is that a deal?"

"Deal."

Rachel grabbed a throw blanket off his bed, spread it onto the floor, then arranged two teddy bears exactly like the one the monster had left for Joey. She closed the door behind her and went back into the kitchen where Lulu was already eating her second cupcake.

"You did great, kiddo."

"Thanks," Lulu whispered, then licked her fingers and ran her tongue over the chocolate that rimmed her mouth. "But I'm still scared of him."

"I know you are, but I'm going to do my best to keep you safe. Okay?"

"Okay."

"Good girl. Now, I want you to go to your bathroom and act as if your stomach is really hurting. Be loud about it, and every now and then, flush the toilet."

"Got it." She clutched her stomach and moaned. "I'm *soooo* sick."

Rachel gave her a thumbs-up. "I'll come and get you before bedtime. You can sleep in here with me tonight."

For one thing, there was no bed in Lulu's room. For another, the Collector had already mentioned doing away with the child. Rachel would take no chances.

When she was finally alone, she went into the hall bathroom and put on a show of being sick, just in case Charles could hear anything through the walls over his own distress. Afterward, she headed toward the pantry, but the sights and sounds outside the patio door stopped her cold.

The air was black with wings, and filled with the awful cawing of crows. They were flying into treetops, perching on the porch railing, and teetering on top of the support poles. Some were even bashing themselves against the glass doors. Repeatedly.

Terror paralyzed her. Were the black crows going to crash through the glass and into the cabin to peck her and the children to death?

The crow's blood smeared on the glass spurred her to action. She jerked a large pot out of the cabinet and banged it with a metal soup spoon until the birds flew off in such large numbers they were a black cloud, covering the moon.

Rachel was shaking when she stowed the pot and the soup spoon. Wrapping her arms around herself for comfort, she went into the pantry to retrieve the toolbox then just stood there, deep breathing, until she could function again.

The toolbox contained screwdrivers with every size head she would possibly need as well as a plentiful supply of duct tape. How her sisters and Gran would laugh if she ever got to tell them this story.

When. Not if.

She stowed her toolbox within easy reach then changed into her comfortable clothes and sat down on the sofa to wait. Her turn was coming. She had much to do. If the Collector thought the laxatives were bad, he hadn't seen anything yet.

FORTY-NINE

Rachel catapulted off the red sofa. How long had she been asleep? When she had finally gone to bed last night, she had only shut her eyes for a moment's respite.

With her heart pounding too hard, terror sliced through her and held her frozen in place, a disheveled woman dressed in the same cargo pants and shirt she'd worn when the world was halfway sane, and her family waited for her at the picnic tables at the festival.

It was still dark outside with not even a hint of dawn coming through the sliding glass doors. The clock on the mantle told her it was only four-thirty, the wee hours of the morning.

That was good. She still had far too much to do, and she had no time to waste.

She listened for sounds, anything to tell her the whereabouts of the killer in the house. Nothing came to her except scratching on Eddie's door.

The dogs. She'd forgotten about them.

"I'm sorry. You'll have to hold on a bit while I make sure *he* is secure."

She spoke aloud, the sound of her own voice reminding

her that she wasn't Elizabeth, obedient and subservient captive. She was Rachel Maxey, single mom, and she had a plan.

She donned her boots then gave a satisfied nod. A woman always felt more powerful in boots.

She headed into the kitchen to get her weapon of choice, then paused on her way to Charles' bedroom to check on the children. Last night, Lulu had opted to sleep in Eddie's room, which worked to Rachel's advantage. The little girl had been through far too much. She didn't need to know everything Rachel had done while everybody slept, including the Collector.

It had taken longer than she'd expected for the massive dose of aspirin she'd ground into his cupcakes to knock him out, but after his lengthy affair with the toilet the tablets had finally done their job.

Considering everything she had been through, Rachel was amazingly calm and confident. Still, she approached Charles' door with caution. Who knew what a man this evil could do?

He was awake, writhing and straining against the duct tape she'd used to bind his wrists and ankles to the bedpost. To ensure he wouldn't get loose she'd strapped his forehead down with duct tape that ran all the way across the mattress then under the bed and across again three times.

The memory of being under the bed in the witching hours of last night while he was passed out above her sent chills through Rachel. Still, keeping one hand behind her back, she marched to his bedside with the confidence of a woman who has the upper hand. She even smiled at him.

"Oh, we're awake are we, *sweetheart?*" She put every ounce of contempt she felt into her question.

"I know why you're doing this, Elizabeth." Amazingly, there was still hope in his voice. "It's because I tied you up. I get that. I admire spunk. I can even forgive you."

"I don't know. Since I met you, I've discovered I'm a vengeful woman."

"Come on now. Cut me loose and quit playing around. I've quit my job and we can have a *real* honeymoon before we move to Mexico. You'd love that, wouldn't you? You could even be pregnant by then and we could have a real family."

Rachel covered her horror by taking a step back and pretending to think about his proposal. She found herself face to face with a trio of watercolors whose trademark style suddenly leaped out at her. That she'd been so long recognizing them was not surprising, considering she'd been kidnapped by a raging maniac who intended to turn her into a brood mare.

"Does this move to Mexico include Bruce Wyler?"

"How did you guess?"

He'd just confirmed her worst nightmare. Suddenly her renter's strangely obsessive behavior and the things she'd found in his apartment made sense to her.

"The watercolors." She nodded toward the wall. "They're everywhere. Unless you've stolen them or have a fortune to spend on his art, then you've made some kind of deal with him. And it probably includes me. "

"You can put your mind at ease, darling. You're *my wife.* Until I say the time is right for him to have his turn, he will not touch you. I want to make that very clear to both of you. This is *my* perfect family, and *I* call all the shots! Got that?"

"Got it," she said, mocking him.

If looks could kill, Charles Blankenship would have been dead on the spot. She wanted one thing from him, and one only.

"Where are the keys?" Last night after he passed out and she trussed him up, she'd searched every inch of the apartment.

"You'll never find them, and I'll never tell you."

He strained against his bonds so hard his face turned red. His expression, defiant and slightly triumphant, told its own story. He would never reveal the hiding place of the keys, and somewhere in his twisted mind he still believed he had the upper hand.

For a moment, she wished she were the kind of woman who could beat the information out of him.

"The dogs need to go outside," she said.

"Shoot them and put them out of their misery."

Horror coiled in a tight knot in her stomach. He would do exactly that. Was that how he had planned to get rid of Star? Was that what he had planned to do to her when her usefulness was over?

She brought her emotions under control so not a hint of fear showed. She refused to be intimidated by him.

"Okay," she said, deadpan. "Where's the gun?"

"Downstairs where you'll never go. The machete, too, but then I don't think you have the stomach for blood." His struggle against the tape was so fierce the bed shook. "Enough of this! Let me go!"

"Oh, I don't know." She moved closed enough to lean over as if she might be going to kiss him. "Maybe I'll leave you here a few days so the rats in Star's room can have a go at you. I might even leave you a bottle of water, but then, you'd have a hard time reaching that, wouldn't you, *sweetheart?*"

"You *witch*! You're as bad as my evil mother. Worse, because you're smarter."

"Thank you. I'm smart enough to know that if you're going to be doing all you proposed in such a short period of time, you need more beauty rest."

She swung the heavy cast iron skillet she'd been holding behind her back and landed a knock-out blow to his head. The reverberation shook her arm all the way up to the socket of her shoulder.

"There now. Wasn't that better than the thermos I used on the goofball in the park? Shouldn't you have seen that coming before you decided to steal me and these children from our real families?"

He was out cold. She leaned closer and pinched him hard to make sure. He didn't even flinch.

There was no use wasting another minute in a futile search for the keys. Rachel ran back to the den, grabbed the toolbox, and set to work removing the long screws the Collector had used to bolt the sliding patio doors shut. Without a power drill, the work was slow and tedious.

The scent of magnolias added an edge of terror to the process. The Collector was out for now, but he seemed to have superhuman powers. Who knew what he was truly capable of?

FIFTY

The Collector was awake, and he had a plan.

If Elizabeth thought she could get the best of him with some duct tape and a frying pan, she was sadly mistaken. She would curse the day she ever tried to ruin his plans.

She was as dispensable as those two useless children in Denver. And her bones would bleach just the same as theirs.

He hadn't decided yet what he would do with Star and Mikey. Should he keep them or kill them?

Thinking of all his delicious choices, he felt his power rising. He was made of steel and feathers, indestructible and cunning.

He moved his hands against the tape. Slow and steady. That was the trick.

The human body produces enough oil and sweat that eventually the adhesive on the tape would start to break down. Combine that with the pressure of movement, especially from a man of his strength, and his hands would soon be loose.

He would be free.

It was only a matter of time.

FIFTY-ONE

By the time Rachel removed the final screw and lifted the doors out of the tracks, the first rays of sunrise were painting the sky. She stepped onto the small deck and sucked in the fresh air as if it were the first breath she'd ever taken. She wanted to jump up and embrace the overhanging branches. She wanted to shout and dance. She wanted to scream and cry with relief and joy.

But it was too soon to celebrate.

Suddenly the dogs raced onto the deck, their joyful barking a clear signal they'd take relief wherever they could get it.

Eddie, in his pajamas, and Lulu, already in one of the dresses the mailman had hung in her closet, stood in the kitchen, staring at the spectacle.

"Where's Daddy?" Eddie rubbed his eyes.

Now was not the time to start trying to undo his brainwashing.

"He's still asleep." She held out her arms. "Come out here. It's okay."

Lulu hurried to join her, but Eddie tiptoed out as if he might be apprehended at any minute. Her heart broke for him, and she prayed she would be equal to the task ahead.

The children shivered from the chilly morning air and the excitement of being outside again, free from tyrannical rules and cruel imprisonment at last. She held them close for a moment then hurried them back into the kitchen and fixed two bowls of cereal.

"After you've finished eating, get dressed in your warmest clothes, and come straight back here. We're going on a grand adventure. Okay?" She gave Eddie a reassuring hug.

"'K."

"Good boy." Rachel turned to Lulu. "Help him dress as fast as you can. Then strip all the sheets and bring them onto the deck. There are extra ones in the drawer under the coffee table. We're making a rope."

Would there be enough to make a rope that would reach the ground? Could she trust it to hold the children, and the children to hold on if they needed to climb down?

"Mrs. Maxey." Lulu gave a look far wiser than her years, as if the kidnapping had turned the seven-year-old into a grownup overnight. "It's going to be okay."

"Yes, it will. We'll make sure of that."

While they finished their cereal, she retrieved the shirt Eddie had worn when he was kidnapped and the gown Lulu had been wearing. Then she detoured by the hated master bedroom. The Collector's eyes were shut.

Was he still passed out or was he pretending? She considered checking his pulse, but rejected the idea as both useless and foolhardy. If he was playing possum, he might grab her. She couldn't take that chance, and she couldn't afford to waste time dealing with him.

When she got back to the kitchen, she smiled her encouragement at the children, who were still eating breakfast. Then she went outside to study the deck. It was surrounded by trees, but the overhanging branches were not sturdy enough to support her weight. If she were young and agile, she might climb the railing and make an acrobatic leap that would land her in a tree, but she was no Tarzan. She wasn't even a Jane.

Defeat threatened to swamp her when she suddenly spotted her own butterfly art. It was in a far corner of the yard, lit by the morning sun, every bit as whimsical and uplifting as it had been in her own yard.

Rachel approached her task with renewed vigor. The deck had four support poles as if the Collector had intended to put on a roof but then changed his mind. She stuffed the kids' clothes into her huge pockets then sucked up her courage and began to shinny up the pole where she would have the most unobstructed view of the sky.

As she inched upward splinters dug into her palms. and her legs trembled with the effort of hugging the pole. If she ever got high enough, it would take a miracle to hang on to the pole and tie the makeshift flags. It would take another miracle for Hank to fly over this house, spot them, and recognize them as distress signals.

A wave of vertigo hit Rachel. She'd had very little sleep, and the constant stress had weakened her. She closed her eyes, ignored the pain in her hands and legs, and continued her tedious climb.

Don't let go. Don't fall.

She pictured her own children asleep in their beds. She pictured her grandmother, already up, surely, brewing coffee, staring out the window and praying. She pictured her sisters, waiting for her.

Hank would be with her children. He would have his rescue helicopter in the air as soon as there was enough light for a search.

Her sister Jen would probably be at the ranch, too. But she wouldn't be sleeping. She'd be making plans and issuing orders and running the show.

By now, Annie might even be there, too.

Her family was waiting for her. They needed her.

But for the moment, she had to get to safety with Lulu and Eddie. They had no one except her to rescue them.

I can do this. I can!

Rachel felt the top of the pole and opened her eyes. There was nothing as far as the eye could see except trees, spread out for miles like a red and gold patchwork quilt. How would she ever lead the children through that wilderness and find their way home?

Don't quit now!

Rachel eased her left hand toward her pocket and pulled out Eddie's tee shirt. Then she got a death grip on the pole and tied on the first distress flag.

FIFTY-TWO
LOGAN RANCH

Hank gave up on whatever paltry amount of fitful sleep he'd had and untangled himself from the blanket wadded around his legs. No need to dress as he'd never removed his clothes.

He washed up, put on his boots and headed to the kitchen. The smell of coffee told him that he'd find Victoria there. Jen was with her, both of them fully dressed, clinging to their coffee cups and looking as bleary-eyed and anxious as he felt.

"Any word from the sheriff yet on that pervert's address?" Jen said.

"No. But it's early yet."

"If I haven't heard from him in the next hour, I'm going to march into his office and rattle a few cages."

There was no use trying to talk Rachel's sister out of anything. He'd learned that from Rachel a long time ago. But in spite of the trust Hank placed in the sheriff's department, he still saw cases where the old adage proved true: the squeaky wheel gets the grease.

He was just pouring his own cup of coffee when his cell phone rang.

"The sheriff?" Jen asked.

"No. I hired a PI." Hank put his phone on speaker. "Dustin, what's up?"

"I've hit the jackpot on that Bruce Wyler character."

Victoria sank into a kitchen chair and Jen moved to stand beside her with a hand on her shoulder.

"What have you got?"

"Wyler has a long history of cruelty to animals, starting when he was twelve. He's drowned most of the neighborhood cats and puppies in the family pool. Only his daddy's influence kept him out of a juvenile facility."

Jen banged her cup down on the kitchen table. "Let me at that fool!"

Hank shook his head. Cruelty to animals was terrible, but it proved no connection to theft and kidnapping.

"Good work, Dustin," he said. "Anything else?"

"The Wylers are not his birth parents. He's adopted."

Hank's intuition told him this was significant. He just didn't know how or why. And adoption records were sealed.

"That's not all," Dustin added. "His mother's death from a fall down the stairs triggered a murder investigation."

The women gasped and Hank felt the familiar chill in his bones that had always preceded a military maneuver that took him and his comrades into the jaws of death.

"Both Wyler and his father were at home when she died," Dustin added.

"They were questioned?"

"Yes, but ultimately her death was ruled accidental."

"Anything else?"

"That's all I have for now, Hank."

It was more than enough.

"Thanks, Dustin." By the time he got his phone back into his pocket, Jen was already storming toward the basement door.

"*Jen!*" He caught up to her. "What are you doing?"

"I'm going to clean that rattlesnake out of my sister's basement."

"No." He grabbed the doorknob and held the door shut.

"What? You want me to sit by with my hands folded while we wait for the sheriff, and that snake slithers off into some mountain hideaway?"

"No. I want you to take Victoria upstairs and keep her and the children there until I get back. I don't want witnesses."

"Oh yeah?" She lifted one eyebrow. "You know how to break and enter?"

"Yes."

The glint in her eyes was so like her sister's, Hank had to rein in his emotions.

"Okay. Go get him, cowboy." She raised both hands and made her expression innocent. "I didn't see or hear a thing."

As Jen made her way up the stairs with Victoria, Hank fetched his flashlight. Then he opened the door to the basement.

Wyler's apartment was dark. Not even a night light illuminated the gloom.

Hank waited until his eyes adjusted. Using the stealth he'd honed in the battlefield of jungles and deserts and twisted streets of foreign cities, he crossed the room until he towered over the sleeping man. Turning the flashlight on high, he aimed the beam into Wyler's eyes.

"Sit up!" Hank ordered. The man startled and squinted up at him. His head was bald as an egg. A quick glance showed the blond toupee on his nightstand. "Raise your hands above your head." Wyler lay among the covers, probably trying to decide what to do. "If you make a stupid move, it will be your last."

Finally, Wyler sat up with his hands lifted high and squinted into the bright light. "I should have known. Rachel's watchdog."

"Where is she?"

"How should I know?"

"Wrong answer. Try again."

"Listen, Hank. Carson, isn't it? I don't..."

In one swift movement, Hank pinned the man to the headboard and thrust two fingers into his windpipe. Hard.

"No, you listen! I advise you not to move. I know your sordid history with animals and *accidental* killing."

Wyler got the terrified look of a rabbit caught stealing cabbages. He even squeaked a few times, not unlike a trapped hare.

His reaction was enough for Hank to take a calculated gamble.

"I know your birth family, so start talking."

Wyler lifted his hands higher. "Please!" His voice was squeaky and terrified. "I'm a victim, too."

Hank eased the pressure on Wyler's windpipe. "So, talk."

"When I started doing those things, my mother, my adopted mother, started treating me like an outsider. She even taunted me. Told me she'd give me back to the crazy witch who gave me away."

Hank thought he knew the identity of the woman, but he merely nodded his approval. "Go on."

"See. She knew my birth mother. She had influence. I begged her to tell me so I could understand why I had these... dark fantasies. But she wouldn't tell me. I grew to hate her. I guess I was just taking my rage out on those animals. It gave me a feeling of power, of being in control."

Wyler stopped to suck in air. He looked winded, weak, and vulnerable, exactly the way Hank wanted him to be. Knowing that strength comes from silence that keeps people guessing, he waited for Wyler to speak.

Wyler licked at the nervous sweat beading his upper lip.

"Finally, I... got the truth out of her. We were both so upset when she told me that Leona Blankenship is my real mother, we struggled. She... fell down the stairs. It was an accident. The investigation cleared me of any wrongdoing." He looked briefly at Hank and then his gaze slid away. "I swear, that's all I know."

"No, it isn't. I've seen you sneaking out at night to meet your brother. Your *famous brother*, Charles Blankenship, the Collector."

The comprehension and sudden fear in Wyler's face said he clearly didn't know the sheriff had already discovered the identity of the Collector.

"I have nothing to do with him. We grew up in different households. I'm nothing like him..."

"Wrong again, Wyler. I know you're studying Tarot cards and the habits of serial killers. I know about your secret notebook filled with drawings of Rachel."

The thought of Wyler watching the video feed in the dead of night, studying the woman who had become Hank's world, dreaming sick fantasies as he created image after image of her, made Hank want to grab the man by the throat and choke the truth out of him.

He brought himself under control and rammed his fingers into Wyler's throat again.

"Evidence doesn't lie. You're up to your neck in the abduction of Rachel and the two minors. Unless you want to spend the rest of your life behind bars, start talking. Where are Rachel and the children?"

"He made me do it! When I came out West looking for him, I just wanted to find my brother and maybe find out why I had this... penchant... for destruction. I had nothing to do with the thefts and the kidnappings. All I did was help him feed the children. I swear!"

A sheen of sweat coated Wyler's face and his pupils were dilated.

"He forced me not to tell! He said he'd kill me and destroy my adopted dad if I didn't play along."

Fear and rage boiled through Hank. This evil man in Rachel's basement had known the whereabouts of the children all along. He dug his fingers deeper into Wyler's throat.

"Where is the Collector holding them?" The deceitful look that came into the scumbag's face told Hank he was planning to lie. "If they aren't where you say they are, I will make it my mission to find and destroy you. There is nowhere on this earth you can hide. I'll hunt you down to your grave. DO YOU UNDERSTAND?"

When you're facing the enemy, there is always a telling moment when you know he has given up the fight. Hank's moment came when Wyler sagged against the headboard and heaved a long sigh of resignation.

All the swagger was gone from the renter as he told Hank the address of the hideaway where the Collector was holding Rachel and the children hostage. He sat meekly by while Hank pulled out his cell phone.

"Sheriff, Charles Blankenship is holding Rachel and the children in a wilderness hideaway on a trail off Deer Canyon Road. It's one of the cabins I marked on the map the day of my air search." Hank added the address.

"How do you know?"

"Let's just say I took a shortcut to getting the information."

Hank gave a brief rundown of everything else he knew, and then they made a plan. While he waited for Sheriff Johnson to arrive, he sent a text to Jen.

> *Wyler told me where Rachel and the children are being held. I'll be leaving to get them as soon as Sheriff Johnson gets here and snaps the cuffs on Wyler. He's the Collector's brother and knows more than he's telling. The sheriff will use the outside basement door and be as unobtrusive as possible. I trust you to take care of Victoria and the children in whatever way you think is best.*

Her response came flying back.

I'll handle the home front. Bring my sister and the children back alive. That's an order, cowboy!

It was also Hank's intent and his fervent hope. A lot could have happened since Wyler was last at the Collector's hideout and Hank got back to Colorado Springs to take off in his chopper with a S.W.A.T. team.

As he waited for the sheriff, Hank's mind whirled. In the military, the only helicopter he'd flown that featured hover hold was the Apache, a gunship designed so the pilot could fire without having to worry about the controls. Even the Black Hawk, a two-pilot ship, didn't have the ability to hover unless one of the pilots was at the controls.

Hank's fleet included a two-pilot rescue helicopter, which was large enough to hold everybody on the rescue team and the medical personnel Sheriff Johnson would have waiting at Hank's hangers in Colorado Springs.

Pulling out his cell phone, he notified his best pilot, CW_4, David G. Wesson, retired from the Mississippi Air National Guard, to have the rescue chopper ready and prepare to copilot.

By the time Hank finished making his preparations, Sheriff Johnson had arrived outside the door of the renter's apartment with minimum fanfare. Rachel's ranch was suddenly filled with purposeful activity.

Still, Hank couldn't tamp down his sense of unease. Even when the Collector's partner was led off in handcuffs for further grilling at the sheriff's department, Hank knew the Collector might be communicating with other sources in Manitou Springs about the latest developments.

By the time the sheriff arrived at the hideout by car and

Hank by helicopter, Charles Blankenship could be miles away with his captives. Or worse...

Hank wouldn't let himself go down that trail. The mere thought of a world without Rachel was unbearable.

One thing was certain: Bruce Wyler had lied when he said he was a victim. Everything in his body language and his facial expressions told Hank so.

Charles Blankenship had not evaded the law for such a long time by happenstance. He had not taken a bizarre range of household items, one woman and two children by chance. He had a partner, and he had a masterplan.

Nobody except Bruce Wyler knew what it was.

And Bruce was no longer talking.

With the precision of men experienced in organizing and carrying out manhunts, the massive team separated into groups. A long line of cars snaked down Rachel's driveway then spread out in different directions, forming a net to catch the slippery criminal who had become a household name.

As Hank clipped off the miles to his charter company, he sent out a silent plea.

Hang on, Rachel. I'm coming.

FIFTY-THREE

THE HIDEAWAY

Rachel was shaking when she climbed down from the pole, but the makeshift flags were in place.

"Mrs. Maxey," Lulu said, "your hands are bleeding."

"I'm okay."

The children had gathered on the deck, dressed in their warmest clothes. Eddie was warm enough in his jeans and sweatshirt and down jacket with a hood. But in spite of the jacket the Collector had bought for her, Lulu shivered in one of the ridiculous dresses he'd chosen.

Was he still unconscious?

Rachel hurriedly knotted the last sheet to the string of bedding she'd already turned into a makeshift rope. Even without hanging it over the edge of the railing, she could tell it wasn't long enough to reach the ground. She wasn't sure the knots would hold, either.

She glanced upward at the flags she'd made with the children's clothing. They flapped in the breeze that had come along with the cold front, but would anybody see them? She'd heard no signs of a helicopter, and she'd certainly not seen any neighboring houses from her earlier vantage point at the top of her flagpole.

Taking her flashlight from her tote bag, she flashed the SOS signal. Still, there was no sign of a rescue. How much longer should she wait before attempting to get the children down a flimsy so-called rope?

"What's this game called?" Eddie asked.

"Operation escape." She told him.

"We're stranded on a mountaintop," Lulu told him, flinging her arms wide. "See? There are fierce animals and scary monsters all around us, and we have to get away before they can catch us."

"Goodie!" Eddie clapped his hand. "Can the dogs come, too?"

"I hope so." Rachel wasn't going to lie to him.

She'd seen the inside of some of Hank's helicopters. Though they were big enough for small tour groups, she had no idea how many people he'd have to bring with him.

If he comes.

She had to think positive. *When he comes.*

She handed her flashlight to Lulu with instructions to keep flashing the SOS signal, then she went back inside. Grabbing her skillet, she hurried down the hall.

There were no sounds coming from the direction of the bedroom. That could be good or bad.

Rachel slowed her steps, peered around the bedroom doorframe and let out a shriek. The Collector had maneuvered his head out of the duct tape and was flailing around on the bed.

"How *dare* you coming sneaking back with that frying pan!" He actually snarled at her. "If you set foot in this room, I'll make you wish you were never born."

Was he bluffing? His hands and feet appeared to still be bound, but was it true? He might have worked them loose and just be lying in wait for her.

She decided to call his bluff.

"You've already tried that, Charlie *dearest.* It didn't work."

She marched into the bedroom.

"You stop right there!" he yelled.

"Or what?" Rachel stationed herself out of his reach.

"I don't know what you think you've got up your sleeve, but it won't work. You can't do whatever you're doing and watch me at the same time. You're going to get what you deserve. It's just a matter of time."

"I beg to differ." She took a step closer and raised the skillet.

The Collector laughed. "Fire away. Reinforcements will be here any minute."

Shock ricocheted through her. "Bruce?"

"Exactly!" His smirk was a little crooked where she'd whacked his head earlier and caused facial swelling. "I've changed my mind about keeping you all to myself. The only way you're going to learn who's the boss is for both of us to have a go at you."

"*Never!*" She swung the skillet as hard as she could.

He sagged onto the bed, and for a horrible moment she thought she'd killed him. That would make her no better than him. She checked his pulse and, despite everything, was relieved to feel the steady thump of his heart. She didn't want to be a murderer.

Now she could leave him without a backward glance or one shred of remorse. The heft of the skillet felt just right in her hand. If he magically escaped his bonds or his cohort in crime surprised her, she'd be ready for them.

Rachel kept up the pep talk to herself as she detoured by the pantry and retrieved the hammer from the toolbox. If she was going to have to deal with two madmen, she wanted two weapons.

When she finally joined the children on the deck, Eddie was playing with the dogs and Lulu still flashed the SOS signal, a stark reminder that every action Rachel took could either save or doom the children.

She searched the skies. There was still no sign of rescue. Her tension went up another notch. Charlie's henchman was on the way. What now?

Should she wait behind the door and try to knock Bruce Wyler out as he came through? Or should she try to get the children out before he came? Both options had their risks.

Lulu pulled on her sleeve. "What do you want us to do now?"

Looking into the trusting face of the kidnapped child, who might have been her own daughter, Rachel sucked up her courage. She was done playing defense to whatever horror the Collector had in mind. She *had* to be.

"Now, who's ready for an adventure?" she said.

Both children raised their hands. Acting with more confidence than she felt, Rachel tied the sheet rope onto a corner support post opposite the flags and lowered it through the overhanging branches of a tree. It lacked about five feet touching the ground.

Lulu peered over the railing. "Awesome!"

"Do you think you can climb down first and help me get Mikey down? You'll have to use the tree branches."

"Sure, I can."

Rachel held on to Lulu while she climbed over the railing and got a firm grip on the sheets. With the natural ability of a kid who had been climbing trees all her life, the little girl twisted her legs into the sheet rope and inched downward.

Rachel hardly breathed. Lulu was suspended in thin air with nothing to prevent a fall except a fragile rope of sheets. Would the knots hold? Would the sheets bear her weight?

Lulu briefly disappeared among the leaves. When Rachel saw her again, the little girl was using the larger branches of the tree as footholds.

"Good girl!" Rachel called out her encouragement. "Keep going!"

Once she was on the ground, Lulu would be able to instruct Eddie how to climb down.

Rachel dared not look back to see if Bruce Wyler had come storming into the hideout. Her neck and chest felt hot in spite of the chill. It had to be the burning flush of adrenaline. She'd been in both fight and flight mode since before sunrise. And she was a long, long way from freedom.

"Mrs. Maxey, I made it!"

Lulu's shout and proud smile gave Rachel a fresh burst of energy.

"Great. Stay right by the rope. I'm going to help your brother start and you can help me talk him down."

"I bet he can climb better than me."

"I'll bet he can."

Still worry gnawed at the back of Rachel's mind. While she'd been pre-occupied had the Collector come to, escaped his bonds, and sneaked out of the apartment?

"Lulu, I want you to look and listen for anybody who might come up behind you. At the first hint of trouble, you grab this rope and climb as hard as you can. Okay?"

"Got it."

Should Rachel run back to check on their captor or press forward? She was exhausted and so very tired of making life-and-death decisions. She needed a safe place to lie down where she didn't feel as if any minute her sleep would be interrupted by the Collector with some fresh horror. Every muscle in her body was tightened and ready for fight or flight.

As she mulled over the pros and cons, she heard sounds. Jerking into fight mode, she grabbed her hammer and her frying pan.

"Look! A helicopter!" Eddie was in the corner of the deck, shielded by the overhanging branches of the huge tree, while the dogs pranced around him and Lulu stood on the ground at the base of the tree.

"I know." Relief flooded Rachel. "Both of you stay right where you are."

Hank had come. In her heart, she'd known he would, all this time. The million things she'd left unsaid through the years tumbled through her mind. She wasn't going to waste another second keeping her feelings locked away in some misbegotten tribute to Max. He'd want her to be happy. Maybe on some level, he'd been trying to engineer that when he asked Hank to watch over her and the children.

As the bird dipped lower, she moved to the center of the deck and strained to see the first sign that Hank was the pilot. She saw the unmistakable lettering of his logo on the side of the helicopter.

Yes, yes, yes! Thank you, thank you, thank you!

The mantra coursed through her mind, equal parts prayer, gratitude, and hope.

"Hank!" she shouted. "Oh, Hank, I knew you would come!"

Did he hear her? Did he see? She waved her arms frantically.

Suddenly, the unmistakable fragrance of magnolias shivered Rachel's soul, and arms closed around her from behind.

"Do you think I'm going to let him have you?" The Collector pinned her arms to her side and tightened his hold. She lost her grip on her skillet and her hammer. Her hopes plummeted as they clattered to the floor. "You're mine," he hissed in her ear. "I'll never let you go."

Terror seized Rachel. Even as she turned her face upward to see a S.W.A.T. team lifting their weapons, she knew Charles Blankenship would use her as a shield.

"*Suckers!*" the Collector shouted, and then she felt his hot breath against her cheek. "Elizabeth. Listen to me. They can't help you. Nobody can. Before I kill you and the children, you're going to wish you were dead..."

FIFTY-FOUR

"Don't shoot!" Hank shouted, "He's got Rachel!"

Every man suited up in S.W.A.T. gear would hold back until he had a clear shot. Hank knew this, but his whole world stood below his helicopter, in the line of fire.

He watched the scene on the deck with growing horror. In an instant, the rescue mission had turned deadly. Charles Blankenship was not only hiding behind Rachel, but he was screaming taunts toward them.

Hank turned to big Jim Shumpert, leader of the S.W.A.T. team and also a lip-reader, who viewed the scene through binoculars. "What's he saying?"

"Go ahead. Shoot. Kill her." Shumpert put a megaphone to his lips. "You're surrounded, Blankenship! Surrender!"

"Never!" As the Collector inched Rachel toward the edge of the deck, she looked up at the helicopter, her dark eyes pleading.

Hank had never felt as helpless in all his life.

One of the team shouted, "He's moving for the cover of the trees!"

Another yelled, "He's got a gun!"

While another shouted, "He's putting Eddie Greene in the line of fire!"

"Can you get us a better position?" Big Jim Shumpert moved closer to the cockpit.

As Hank maneuvered the helicopter, he steeled himself against his emotions. The lives of the innocent on the deck as well as everybody in the helicopter depended on his judgment. Get too close to the massive tree, and the chopper would go down. Fail to get a clear view of the Collector, and the team had no hope of taking him out before he could harm Rachel and the children again.

Or he might vanish entirely. He'd done it when he left behind the children's bones in Denver. With Hank and his team in the air and the cars bringing the sheriff and his team not yet there, Charles Blankenship could disappear into the wilderness.

What was the Collector's plan? Would he manage to escape using the cover of the trees and the makeshift rope Hank saw hanging off the side of the balcony? If he had a gun, would he shoot the pilots so the chopper would crash, and escape before Sheriff Johnson could arrive?

Hank found the best spot as close to the tree as he could manage and hovered his bird.

One of the team of sharpshooters shifted position, his finger poised over the trigger. "I think I have a head shot."

Hank wanted to roar, *Thinking is not good enough,* but big Jim beat him to the punch.

"Hold your fire! Rachel is too close and Lulu's behind her, on the ground!"

The entire team was helpless, and so was Rachel. Everything Hank had dreamed for three years could end on the Collector's deck. Memories spun through his mind, small things, laughing over a children's video with Susan and Joey, making s'mores in the kitchen, quiet moments with Rachel in front of the fire, listening to her heartaches, her triumphs, her fierce determination.

The karate lessons he'd given her.

Hope seized Hank. He dipped a wing of the chopper in her direction.

Remember, Rachel. Remember!

"Carson?" Big Jim thundered out. "What are you doing?"

"Sending Rachel a sign." Hank leveled out the bird, then hovered to watch.

Did she notice?

He strained to see Rachel's every move.

There! The Collector held her arms straight down at her side... and she was inching them around so they would be behind her back. Her hands would soon be on a perfect level with the Collector's private parts.

Hank held his breath. Could she do it?

He saw the flash of excitement on her face, and then the moment of pure triumph. One mighty twist of Rachel's hands, and the Collector was on his knees. Screaming in agony.

Everybody in the helicopter cheered. Rachel grabbed the skillet and flipped him backward with a blow to the head, and the S.W.A.T. team went wild.

The Collector was out cold, and they hadn't fired a single shot.

FIFTY-FIVE

The sight of Rachel standing on the deck, her beautiful face lifted upward, her dark hair blowing in the wind, her arms wrapped protectively around little Eddie Greene, brought tears to Hank's eyes. He didn't try to hide them as he maneuvered the helicopter so he could hover over the deck and lower the basket with the rescue team inside, led by Jim Shumpert.

After they secured the Collector, the children would be brought up first, and then the woman he could no longer pretend was only his friend.

In the distance he spotted the long line of official cars with flashing blue lights as the sheriff and his men converged on the Collector's hideaway. It was over. The residents of Manitou Springs and the surrounding area could breathe again. They could go back to their normal routine.

As the delicate operation began of rescuing the children and putting them in the hands of the medical staff waiting in the chopper, Hank drew a deep breath he felt as if he'd been holding for three years. There would be no going back to normal for him. These last incredible hours without knowing whether Rachel was dead or alive had taught him the folly of keeping his love private. The minute he'd seen those makeshift flags flying and Rachel standing beside them, proud and elegant in spite of her ordeal, he knew he was going to declare his love the minute she set foot on his helicopter. And he didn't care who heard him.

He wanted the whole world to know. He'd shout it from the top of Pikes Peak if she asked. He'd fly banners all over the twin cities of Manitou and Colorado Springs.

A radio crackled somewhere in the helicopter behind Hank, and he heard the voice of big Jim Shumpert come over the air waves.

"You don't see this every day."

"What?" The answering voice belonged to Sgt. Rankin, a burly deputy law enforcement veteran of twenty years.

"Rachel Maxey has a cast iron skillet in one hand and a hammer in the other. She said she duct-taped the Collector to the bed like a whining schoolgirl and then cold-cocked him with the frying pan. She thought Bruce Wyler was coming, and she was planning to take him out with the hammer. She deserves a medal and her own parade tonight for the finale of the Emma Crawford Festival."

The Collector was now being led from the house in shackles by the entire S.W.A.T. team and secured in the sheriff's vehicle. A round of applause went up in the helicopter.

"She deserves Citizen of the Year, too," Rankin said. "Soon as we get back, I'm going to put her name in the hat."

The woman of the day was now suspended in the basket below Hank, a glorious sight swinging in a clear blue sky that seemed to go on forever. The once-in-a-lifetime vision burned into his memory. The women in his office would have called such a rare sight a good omen, a promise. And so did he.

He angled his neck so he could see behind him. "Hey, guys. Do you mind if I kiss the lady first? I'm going to declare my honorable intentions, and I wouldn't mind having an audience."

Amidst the applause and cheers, Hank turned to his co-pilot. "David, take the controls."

David winked. "Got it. Go get your girl."

Hank got out of the pilot's seat and stretched his long legs, then moved to the door so his would be the hands that caught Rachel and brought her through the final leg of her journey to safety.

The wind had whipped her hair into her face, and she reached blindly for him.

"Thank you," she said. "I can never thank you enough."

Without a word, he closed his hands over hers, and she gasped.

"Hank?"

"It's me." He brushed her hair back from her face then studied her as if he could condense years of longing into one moment.

"Don't let go..." she whispered.

"I don't plan to. Not for the rest of our lives."

Warmed by her sudden smile and cheered on by their small audience, he kissed her then, right there in the tight confines of the helicopter. He'd been rescued as surely as he'd rescued Rachel and the lost children.

The kiss was filled with all the tenderness a love should hold, and with the exquisite promise of passion. It was filled with gratitude and loyalty and friendship that had endured much and would become the firm foundation for their future.

The kiss was an ending, but most of all, it was a beginning.

EPILOGUE

LOGAN RANCH

One week after the rescue

Evening dropped its curtain over the Rockies, turning the backyard at Logan Ranch into a wonderland of starlight and sparkles of red, yellow, and blue from the colored spotlights Hank had installed to illuminate a wide area around the tree house Joey claimed as his own. But he was only too happy to share with his sister, especially after dark when she climbed the ladder to their treetop paradise carrying a sack-full of cookies fresh from Victoria Logan's oven.

Rachel stood at the kitchen window, watching her children at play. Though the Collector and his partner, Bruce Wyler, were both in jail awaiting trial, she had not forgotten their reign of terror, nor how close it had come to destroying her family.

"I should call them inside," Rachel said, and Jen came up behind to put a hand on her shoulder.

"Be happy they bounced back so fast, Rachel. Let them be children again."

"That's what Hank said."

"He's right." Jen lifted Rachel's hand to admire her new

engagement ring. "Lucky for me, I'm getting a brother-in-law I don't have to train. Especially since I'm leaving tomorrow."

Rachel's sister was only half-kidding. She didn't know if Jen was bossy because of her training as a psychologist, or because she was the oldest of the three sisters, or because she was just being a stubborn Logan. The reason didn't matter. Jen was family, and that counted most.

Victoria marched into the kitchen in her cowboy boots and best Western shirt, tied on her apron, and took charge, as usual.

"Hank's going to be back from the airport in Denver any minute with that big Texas family of his," she announced. "I've got chicken and dumplings to tend to."

"I'll help," Jen said. "Unless you want me to kill the chicken?"

"It died right in the freezer at the grocery store," Gran said, deadpan. Then she got the chicken out the refrigerator and spread the pieces on her cutting board. "Take Rachel outside to watch Susan and Joey before she breaks her neck trying to watch them out the window. She's going to hover like a helicopter till Hank gets here to calm her down."

"I am not," Rachel said, but, of course, Gran was right. Hank did calm her down. Still, she might hover for a few weeks or even months. How long did it take a mother to forget the most awful thing she'd ever experienced and live normally again?

"Yes, you are." Gran switched on the small TV. "Go on. I want to watch that heifer on *Sunday Night Special*."

That heifer was Dawn Williams, on set in Colorado Springs with the parents of Eddie Greene and Lulu Vargas. Both sets of parents expressed gratitude to law enforcement for rescuing their children, but their most effusive praise went to Rachel. They called her a hero.

Dawn had asked Rachel for another interview, but she had declined. Her fifteen minutes of fame was over. She had no intention of reliving the worst days of her life for a TV audience or otherwise. And she certainly didn't want the label *hero*. *Survivor* was more like it. Or *the mother who wouldn't give up*.

"Come on." Jen slung an arm over Rachel's shoulder and led her out the back door. "Soon it will all be a memory."

"How did you know what I was thinking?"

"Because we're sisters, and because I know you have the strength of character to overcome the past and embrace your wonderful future."

They sat on a bench beneath the tree house, side by side, while the children poured onto the deck and called down to them.

"Mommy! Aunt Jen! Come on up!" Joey's red hair glowed like fire as he bounced up and down under the lights.

"In a little while, Joey." Rachel waved at her children, her heart full of gratitude and love.

Susan plopped onto the deck with her bag of cookies and swung her pink tennis shoes over the side. "That means *probably not*, Joey. Mom's too old to climb."

"That's okay," he said. "Hank can climb." He grabbed a cookie from the bag and went back inside with Susan racing behind him, yelling, "Hey, you took the last chocolate chip one!"

"They love him, don't they?" Jen said.

"Yes. And so do I." In the distance, she saw headlights turn onto the long winding driveway, Hank in the lead followed by the rental cars carrying his brothers and their families, all coming to Logan Ranch to meet the woman and children he had chosen to be his own.

Rachel felt a jolt, as if the sun had burst through her, wiping out shadows and burning away nightmares until there was nothing left except the golden glow of a future filled with love and promise.

Her sister stiffened, and suddenly Rachel smelled the

faintest fragrance of the dreaded white flower. "Jen, what's wrong?"

"I caught a whiff of the ocean."

"That's impossible. It's more than a thousand miles away."

"I know." Jen went very still, a posture she always adopted when her visions warned her of terrible things to come.

Alarm skittered through Rachel. "I smell magnolias. But the scent is faint, as if it's very far away."

"As far as the ocean." Jen shook off her somber mood, then stood up and pulled Rachel with her. "None of this is about you."

"How do you know?"

"Because *I know,* Rachel. Forget it. Okay?"

"Okay."

Did that mean the warnings were for Jen? Rachel couldn't bear the thought of more trouble on the way... for any of her family.

As the headlights came closer, she could make out Hank behind the wheel, and all her problems seemed to vanish. The tall man sitting in the passenger seat must be one of his brothers. Hank parked in front of the ranch house and began to stride in her direction.

"I promise the warning is not for you." Jen squeezed her hand. "Smile! The man of your dreams is headed your way. And if you don't kiss him, I might have to do it myself."

Trust Jen to make her laugh. Rachel closed the distance to Hank and found herself in an embrace that suddenly included her two children, who had scurried from the treehouse and launched themselves at him. Their happiness was contagious.

As long as Rachel had this—a family built on the foundation of love remembered and love newly born—she could face anything. Even the unknown that hovered beyond her reach, cloaked in the scent of magnolias.

A LETTER FROM PEGGY

Dear reader,

Thank you so much for reading *Black Crow Cabin*. If you want to keep up to date with all my latest releases, just sign up at the following link. Your email address will never be shared and you can unsubscribe at any time.

www.bookouture.com/peggy-webb

One of my greatest joys is creating lead characters who could be your best friend and stories that lure you into another world. Rachel is as down-to-earth as your next-door neighbor. And, oh my! The villain in *Black Crow Cabin* sprang onto the page, so fully formed and horrifying he knocked my socks off!

I hope you loved the chilling and yet mystical world of the Logan sisters as much as I enjoyed creating it. If you did, I would be very grateful if you could write a review. I'd love to hear what you think, and your feedback helps new readers to discover one of my books for the first time.

To loyal fans who have been with me through the years and to new fans who have joined me on this thrilling writing journey with Bookouture—my heartfelt thanks!

I love hearing from you! Do stay in touch on my social media pages and my website. My regular FB page is chock full of fun posts, including my music videos. Though I've been writing for many years, my author FB page is new, so bear with me while I populate it with good stuff and good friends. You'll find my blog with insider info on my website, and some surprises, too!

Thank you so much for being such amazing, supportive readers!

Peggy Webb

www.peggywebb.com

facebook.com/peggywebbauthor
instagram.com/peggy.webb.92
youtube.com/@PeggyWebbOnPageAndPiano

ACKNOWLEDGMENTS

Black Crow Cabin would not have been possible without the encouragement and support of these amazing people: Debra Webb and Vicki Hinze, best friends and fellow authors who are *always* my cheerleading team; Laura Deacon, who first loved the book then acquired it; Jess Whitlum-Cooper, whose sure eye and deft hand made the editorial process a dream; and Ruth Tross, Imogen Allport, and the entire, wonderful Bookouture team whose brilliant concepts for cover, title, and marketing brought my thriller to life and to your bookshelves.

A special thank you to my cousin, CW4 (ret), Roger A. Hussey, Mississippi Army National Guard, who answered all my questions about flying helicopters. *It's complicated!* Any mistakes I made in all the flying scenes are entirely my own!

Also, a big thank you to the Chamber of Commerce and the good people in Manitou Springs, Colorado, for the wealth of insider information that made it possible for me to bring the setting alive for you. Dustin, as promised, one of the characters is named for you.

I owe a special debt of gratitude to my parents, Clarence and Marie Hussey, deceased, who made sacrifices so I could take piano lessons, beginning when I was eight years old. Those lessons fostered an enduring love and knowledge of music that made it possible for me to compose the lyrics to the blues songs credited to my character, Delilah Broussard Logan. In the novel, Delilah wrote the lyrics as Li'l Rosie. *I* am Li'l Rosie. All the lyrics—and a few of the melodies—to those blues songs are in my music composition notebook, handwritten in blue ink.

As always, my wonderful children and grandchildren in Florida and New Hampshire have loved me and cheered for me through the entire process of writing *Black Crow Cabin*.

Hugs to all!

Peggy

PUBLISHING TEAM

Turning a manuscript into a book requires the efforts of many people. The publishing team at Bookouture would like to acknowledge everyone who contributed to this publication.

Audio
Alba Proko
Sinead O'Connor
Melissa Tran

Commercial
Lauren Morrissette
Hannah Richmond
Imogen Allport

Cover design
Eileen Carey

Data and analysis
Mark Alder
Mohamed Bussuri

Editorial
Jess Whitlum-Cooper
Imogen Allport

Copyeditor
Dushi Horti

Proofreader
John Romans

Marketing
Alex Crow
Melanie Price
Occy Carr
Cíara Rosney

Operations and distribution
Marina Valles
Stephanie Straub

Production
Hannah Snetsinger
Mandy Kullar
Jen Shannon

Publicity
Kim Nash
Noelle Holten
Myrto Kalavrezou
Jess Readett
Sarah Hardy

Rights and contracts
Peta Nightingale
Richard King
Saidah Graham

www.ingramcontent.com/pod-product-compliance
Lightning Source LLC
LaVergne TN
LVHW041620060526
838200LV00040B/1368